The Lioness
and Her
Knight

The Lioness and Her Knight

BY GERALD MORRIS

sandpiper

Houghton Mifflin Harcourt
Boston

With gratitude to Rebecca,
And also to the wonderful Georgette Heyer

The text of this book is set in 12.5 point Horley Old Style.

Library of Congress Cataloging-in-Publication Data

Morris, Gerald, 1963–
The lioness and her knight / Gerald Morris.
p. cm.
Summary: Headstrong sixteen-year-old Lady Luneta and her distant
cousin, Sir Ywain, travel to Camelot and beyond finding more
adventure than they hoped for until, with the help of a fool,
Luneta discovers what she really wants from life.
HC ISBN-13: 978-0-618-50772-6
PA ISBN-13: 978-0-547-01485-2
[1. Knights and knighthood—Fiction. 2. Adventure and adventurers—
Fiction. 3. Self-actualization (Psychology)—Fiction. 4. Middle
Ages—Fiction. 5. Great Britain—History—To 1066—
Fiction. 6. Humorous stories.] I. Title.
PZ7.M82785Kn 2005
[Fic]—dc22   2004015782

Manufactured in the United States of America

RRD 10 9 8 7 6 5 4 3

4500376601

Contents

I   Luneta   1

II   The Storm Stone   28

III   The Faery Ring   50

IV   The Wooing of Lady Laudine   83

V   Laudine the Laughless   114

VI   The Madness of Ywain   146

VII   In the Other World   174

VIII   The Knight of the Lion   202

IX   Questing   228

X   The Land of Diradvent   250

XI   The Mightiest Battle Ever   282

XII   The Lioness and Her Knight   313

Author's Note   341

I

LUNETA

As soon as Luneta heard her father come in the side door from the fields, she hurried to the upstairs sitting room. She had discovered just recently that if she closed her eyes and listened very intently at the chimney in this room, she could hear everything that was said in her mother's parlor, which was directly below. Today not having gone well, she suspected that her mother would have some things to say.

Sure enough, seconds after directing her ears toward the fireplace, Luneta heard her mother say sharply, "It's going to be either her or me, Gary. I don't know if I can take it any longer. You're going to come back some evening and find yourself childless."

"Wait a moment," Luneta's father drawled in his

calm voice. "I'm sensing something. An aura of some sort. I see . . . I see . . . wait, it's coming . . . you and Luneta have been having a row."

"Shut up, Gary," Luneta's mother replied, but her voice was less strident. Luneta grinned to herself. It was hard for anyone, even her mother, to maintain a snit in the face of her father's unruffled good humor. "Your daughter is willful, stubborn, disrespectful of her elders, and rebellious."

"Very disturbing," Luneta's father replied placidly. "I can't imagine where children pick these things up."

"Gary," Luneta's mother said in a silken voice, "if you're implying something about your beloved wife—"

"Oh, no, not that one. I was thinking of you."

There was a brief pause. Then Luneta's mother sighed loudly and said, "You are very annoying and not at all funny, but thank you anyway. I'm over the worst of it now. But I still don't know what I'm going to do with her. I know that I never spoke to *my* mother as she speaks to me."

"My dear Lynet, the cases are hardly the same. Luneta's sixteen years old. Your mother died when you were tiny and never had the pleasure of encountering you at that age."

"Perhaps, but I wouldn't have—"

"Less of it, my love! Remember that I met you when you were exactly Luneta's age, and I remember nothing

2

demure about you. As I recall, you took my sword away from me and stole my supper."

"It was burned anyway, and at least I never called you names. Gary, what does *porcella* mean?"

There was a slight pause. Luneta hunched her shoulders slightly, waiting for her father's response. "Did Luneta call you *porcella?*"

"Yes."

"How . . . how gratifying that she's keeping up her Latin studies. I thought that she had abandoned them."

"Don't change the subject. What does *porcella* mean?"

"I believe it means 'woman with shining eyes.'"

"Gary, you are the worst liar I have ever heard."

"Well, it's better than being a good liar, isn't it?" Luneta's father continued, a bit hurriedly. "Look, Lynet, I don't know a whole lot about mothers and their nearly grown-up daughters. My only sister died when she was thirteen, and my own mother wasn't all that typical anyway—"

"You might say that," Luneta's mother interjected dryly. "And while you're at it, you might include your grandmother and your aunt. You don't have a normal female in your family."

"Yes, I've often thought that," Luneta's father agreed. "But as I was about to say, I have sometimes noticed in other families that a certain amount of friction is to be expected between mothers and daughters."

"I might expect it, but that doesn't mean I have to accept it," she said sharply. "And I won't. Gary, if you could hear the way she speaks to me . . ." She trailed off with an angry sigh.

"I believe you, Lynet. And I even agree that it's unacceptable. I'll go talk to her, but I can't imagine that it will help for me just to tell her that she ought to be a good girl. We need to have a plan."

"What do you mean?"

"It's your own idea, actually. Your very first words to me this evening were 'It's her or me.' By the way, that wasn't strictly correct. What you should have said was 'It is *she* or *I*,' since one uses the nominative case following the verb of existence."

"What?"

"You learn these things when you study Latin."

Luneta's mother's voice was dangerously calm. "What plan, Gary?"

"Send Luneta away."

There was a long pause from downstairs, and upstairs Luneta sank slowly to her knees before the fireplace. She could hardly believe her father's words. Neither could her mother.

"You can't mean that, Gary. She may be the most irritating little wench alive, but—"

"I don't mean drop her off at the foundling hospital, Lynet. I just wonder if she needs to get away from you, ah, from her parents for a while. Go for a visit. I've already been wondering about sending her to visit family, but I couldn't think of any suitable family members. All of my brothers live bachelors' lives, except for Gareth, who's married to your sister—"

"And my sister's an idiot."

"Yes. There's Morgan, but I can't really think she's suitable."

"She isn't."

"And that's as far as I've gotten. I believe it would do our lovely daughter good to get away and see the rest of the world a bit, but I can't think where. Do you have any friends who might be interested in having a young houseguest? Not someone too old, but someone we could trust?"

Luneta was hardly able to believe what she was hearing, as her initial feelings of dismay changed to a growing excitement. For more than a year she had been yearning to get away from her family's estate, which—as noble and honorable as it was—was at the far northern edge of civilized society. Actually, her dream had been to go to King Arthur's court at Camelot, but any court where there were ladies-in-waiting and courtiers and balls and banquets would be better than Orkney Hall, where her father rode over the estate wearing a plain leather jerkin just like the field hands and where her mother drove out nearly every day in a shabby cart pulled by a fat pony to visit one or another of their tenants. You would never guess, looking at the simple life that her parents led, that they were both of noble blood. Indeed, her father was himself a knight of King Arthur's Round Table—Sir Gaheris of Orkney—and brother to the famous Sir Gawain, but neither her father or mother had ever shown the slightest interest in court life. They had visited Camelot rarely and never stayed long. Luneta held her breath, waiting for her mother's reply.

"Maybe," Luneta's mother said at last. Her voice was not encouraging, though. "Don't think I'm convinced. She's very young to be off on her own, yet . . ." There was a brief pause. "Don't say it."

"I didn't say anything," Luneta's father replied mildly.

"You were about to say that I left my home at the same age, but that was different. And, anyway, it's just because I've done it myself that I know how dangerous it is."

"My love, I wasn't suggesting that she go off alone. We would escort her with all due decorum, of course."

Luneta wasn't sure she liked the sound of that. The thought of being escorted by her parents "with all due decorum" seemed very tame and stifling, but she felt that she could put up with anything that would get her away from Orkney Hall. She fell into deep thought, imagining life at a real castle, and ceased listening to her parents' conversation, with the result that she didn't

6

notice when their voices stopped, and barely had time to leap up from the fireplace to a chair when her father rapped twice on the door and entered.

"Oh, hello, Father," Luneta said, smiling innocently.

Her father's lips twitched. "Good evening, Luneta. How very guilty you look, to be sure."

"Guilty?" Luneta repeated, smiling even more brightly.

Her father lowered himself into a chair opposite Luneta and said, "I hope you haven't been trying to listen to our conversation downstairs."

"What do you mean, Father?"

"Because it won't work. Remember that I grew up in this castle, too. My brothers and I used to listen at that fireplace, trying to hear what my parents were fighting about, but we could never hear more than a few choice phrases. So you're wasting your time. By the way, you should dust the soot from your knees."

Luneta had heard her parents' every word as clearly as if she were in the room with them, but she decided not to mention that. She brushed off her dress.

Her father plunged in at once. "How would you like to go away?"

"Away?" Luneta asked, feigning surprise. Luneta's father nodded, and Luneta said, "I'd like it. I want to see the rest of the world. Do you think I could go to

7

King Arthur's court? The last time you took me, I was only twelve."

"Has it really been that long?" her father asked ruefully.

Luneta nodded. "I was too young to go to the ball, but I sneaked into the minstrel's gallery and watched."

"You did what?"

"Sir Dinadan helped me. Then, when you and Mother started to leave the ball, he stopped you at the door and held you up long enough for me to get back to bed and pretend to be asleep."

"He did, did he? And, may I ask, was this my friend Dinadan's idea?"

"Oh no, it was my own plan."

"And how did you compel poor Dinadan to follow your instructions, I wonder." Luneta only smiled, and her father's eyes grew slightly wary. "I begin to think that in sending you away, we may be letting a lioness loose among the cattle."

"So can I go to Camelot?"

"Not for the whole visit, but we can certainly stop there on the way. Your mother is writing a letter to a friend of hers, a lady only a few years older than you who has recently married the lord of a great castle in Salisbury. She thinks that Lady Laudine might like to have a noble young guest."

"Then Mother has agreed to this?" Luneta hadn't heard that part.

"She has agreed to write to Lady Laudine, anyway."

"But that's wonderful! I didn't think she would ever let me go off on my own! Oh, I have so many plans to make!"

Her father raised one eyebrow. "It is when you make plans that I fear you the most, my child."

Luneta smiled again. "When do we leave?"

"Ah," he replied. "There's the sticking point, I'm afraid. It's just about time for the planting, and Murdock and I are trying some new crops this year. I won't be free for at least six weeks, maybe two months."

"Two months!" Luneta's heart sank. "Can't Murdock do this himself? He's your steward, after all."

"Normally, yes, but this year I need to be here. I'm afraid you'll have to wait."

"I hate waiting!"

Her father's good humor disappeared. "Then I suggest you learn to hate it quietly, and learn quickly, too. I perhaps should have mentioned at the start that this visit we have planned depends entirely on whether you can get along with your mother between now and then."

Luneta looked at her feet. "Yes, Father."

Her father sighed. "You also frighten me when you're demure." The smile was back in his voice. He rose to his feet and walked back to the door. At the threshold, though, he stopped and looked over his shoulder. "But I'm quite serious. This means, my dear,

9

that for the next few weeks you will oblige me very much if you will refrain from calling your mother 'little piggy,' even in Latin."

Luneta dimpled. "Can I tell her that she's a woman with shining eyes?"

Her father raised one eyebrow and gazed at her for a moment. Then he said, "Certainly not," and left.

Luneta had no intention of waiting longer in Orkney than she had to, and she immediately began making plans to speed her departure. She had found that when she put her mind to it, she could almost always get people to do what she wanted, and she began at once to work on Murdock, her father's steward, to convince him that he could manage the spring planting without her father this year. The dour highlander was unusually resistant to persuasion, though, and while she didn't doubt she could sway him, it looked as though it would take a long time. Weaving plans kept her mind busy, however, and Luneta managed to brush through three whole weeks without having a row with her mother. Luneta's mother even commented on the change in her daughter's attitude. "If you keep this up," she said, her eyes wrinkling at the corners with wry humor, "I'll almost be sorry to see you go."

Luneta's mother got a reply from her friend, the Lady Laudine, inviting Luneta to come for a visit as soon as she was able and to stay as long as she wished, so all was set, but still Luneta was stuck at Orkney Hall. At the end of the third week, though, something happened that changed their plans. Her father returned from the fields early one day, and with him rode a young knight. Luneta, who had been crossing the castle courtyard when they arrived, could only stop and stare, because this knight was unquestionably the most handsome young man she had ever seen. He had long reddish-blond hair tied behind his head, and a firm, smooth chin. His eyes were a piercing blue, and he wore his armor with assurance and grace. He was smiling at something that Luneta's father had said as they approached, and his smile only improved his looks. Luneta's mouth opened, but she caught herself and closed it again before the two men looked at her.

"Ah, Luneta," her father said. "Allow me to present to you your cousin."

"My cousin?" Luneta said, with surprise and a trace of disappointment.

"Isn't that a bit vague, Cousin Gaheris?" the young knight said, still smiling. "I mean, shouldn't we specify second or third cousin, twice removed, or something?"

Luneta's father grinned. "Maybe, but I've forgotten how to do it. Let's see now, your grandfather Uriens was my father's first cousin, which makes you my . . ."

They looked at each other for a moment, frowning.

Then the young knight said, "Cousin. Good enough."
He turned to Luneta and said, "My name is Ywain."

"Oh, I've heard of you!" Luneta exclaimed. Then
she frowned. "But I thought you were older."

"Older than what?" Luneta's father asked, dismounting.

"Older than he is," Luneta said.

Luneta's father said, "But you see he isn't. In fact, he
is exactly as old as he is."

"You know what I mean. Wasn't Sir Ywain one of
King Arthur's earliest knights?"

"That was my father," Ywain said, lowering himself
from his horse. "I have the same name, which is no fun
at all, let me tell you."

"I know just what you mean," Luneta said. "It's a
sad trial to be named for a parent."

"How would you know?" Luneta's father said.
"Why don't you run inside and tell your mother that
we have a guest for the evening?"

"I do too know," Luneta snapped. "You named me
for my mother, even if you did change a few letters."
Luneta looked at Ywain and explained, "My mother is
named Lynet, and I'm Luneta."

"Don't be ridiculous, child," Luneta's father said, a
lofty expression on his face. "The similarity of your
names is a mere coincidence. In fact, I named you for a

12

dog I had when I was a child." He smiled reminiscently. "Sweetest little brachet I ever owned."

"You named me for a dog?" Luneta gasped.

"Yes, but it didn't work," her father replied with a sigh. "The dog used to do what I told her to."

Luneta caught the slight tremor in his voice and knew that he was teasing her, and she scowled at him. She didn't mind teasing—much—but not in front of strangers. With a toss of her head, she stalked inside to tell her mother about their guest.

Ywain, Luneta discovered at dinner that night, had only dropped by for a short visit before leaving for Camelot. His father had retired from court life some years before and taken up residence at the family estate in Scotland. Young Ywain had grown up there, nearly as far away from the center of civilization as Luneta herself, and his feelings about his childhood in exile were exactly like Luneta's. "I couldn't take it anymore," he admitted. "Trotting around the fields on great chargers that ought to be leading the way in battle, polishing armor that never gets used."

"Don't you have any tournaments in Scotland now?" Luneta's father asked.

Ywain shrugged. "Oh, a few. But they're so far away from court that no one famous ever competes in them, and after you've won them all three years in a row, they don't seem like much anymore." He broke off abruptly, and his face turned scarlet. "Oh, dear," he said. "I sounded like a terrible coxcomb just then, didn't I? I really didn't mean to."

"Ay, you did, that," Luneta's father drawled pleasantly, "but I don't doubt you. I'm not much for the knightly arts myself, but I've spent enough time around great warriors to know when someone has the gift. I'd say you do."

Ywain flushed again, but he looked gratified. "Well, that's what Cousin Gawain said. He stopped by to visit last time he came up to see you, and we sparred a bit. He said . . . he said I wasn't so bad. Anyway, that's why I'm off to Camelot. I want to find out just how good I really am, to measure myself against real knights."

Luneta's mother rolled her eyes very, very slightly, but her father only smiled tolerantly and said, "Well, I hope you find what you're looking for at court."

"But that's it!" Luneta said suddenly.

"What's what?" Luneta's mother asked.

"Ywain can escort me to Camelot!" Luneta said quickly. "Then you won't have to leave during the planting—"

"I wasn't planning to," Luneta's father reminded her.

"—or even after the planting's done! Ywain can take me as far as Camelot, and you can write a letter to send along with me to Uncle Gawain, and he can take me to

Salisbury to your friend's home when he's able to get away." Part of Luneta's mind was already weaving plans for extending her time at Camelot once she arrived, but with the rest of her attention she was watching her parents' faces.

Before either could speak, Ywain said, "But that sounds delightful! Were you already planning a trip to court? I would be honored to take you with me!"

Luneta's mother looked grim, but Luneta could tell that her father was turning the idea over in his mind, and her hopes rose.

"I don't like it, Gary," Luneta's mother said. "It isn't seemly for a girl that young to travel so far alone with a young man."

"He's my cousin, Mother," Luneta said. "How could that be unseemly?"

"A very distant cousin, my dear."

Luneta changed her tactics. Allowing her face to fall, she said, "I see. You don't trust Cousin Ywain."

"Now, Luneta, that's not what I meant!" her mother said hastily.

"Then what do you mean, Mother?" Luneta asked, making her eyes as wide and innocent as she could.

Luneta's mother stared at her for a moment, but then the little wrinkles at the corners of her eyes appeared, and she looked at Luneta's father. "She's good, isn't she?"

"Best I've seen," her father admitted.

"And if I say that I don't think it's safe for her to travel with only one knight . . ."

"She'll remind us of all those tournaments that Ywain has won," her father said. Luneta kept her eyes wide, forcing herself not to smile. In fact, that was exactly the reply that she had planned to use.

Her father said, "She might even manage to remind us that I'm not so handy with a sword myself and hint that she would be safer traveling with Ywain than with us. And, in truth, she would be right. In the unlikely event of danger on the road, I feel sure that Ywain would be much more protection than I would be."

At this point, Ywain spoke up. "I would take the very best care of my cousin. That I promise you both."

"And you don't think she would be a nuisance?" Luneta's mother asked.

Ywain grinned impishly. "To be honest, I would very much like to have her along. I'm sure it's childish, but I can't help thinking that with a lady at my side I'll look like a knight on a quest and not like any other untried knight going off to try his mettle."

Luneta's mother chuckled suddenly and said to her husband, "I' faith, Gary, I like this cousin of yours." She looked back at Ywain. "Your frankness does you credit, Ywain. All right. Take her along with you, but even if she makes you feel like a questing knight, no questing along the way, do you hear?"

"You have my word," Ywain said, and Luneta gave him her brightest, most dazzling smile.

All in all, Luneta had gotten her way much more easily than she had expected. She was especially surprised at how easily her mother had agreed. Knowing that her mother was a dictatorial, controlling woman who never liked any idea that Luneta had, her acquiescence seemed strangely out of character. All Luneta could imagine was that her mother hadn't wanted to show her real self before a guest. Whatever the reason, though, it had all worked beautifully, and Luneta could not help congratulating herself on how well she had managed everyone.

That evening was spent packing, which was a horrible experience, since her mother's notions of what colors and styles were acceptable for a young girl at court were positively antiquated. Several times Luneta had to bite back angry comments. Only the reflection that her mother could very easily withdraw her permission for this journey enabled Luneta to endure in silence the sight of all her most insipid clothes being folded and packed. She could always get rid of those whites and pale blues once she was there. Maybe Lady Laudine's dressmaker could make her a bright red silk dress.

Luneta and Ywain set off the next morning. The parting was awkward. Luneta was angry to discover a lump in her throat and to feel the ominous presence of tears just out of sight. She set her face in a severe expression so as to maintain control of her emotions and mounted her horse beside Ywain. "Well?" she asked gruffly. "Are we leaving today or not?"

"Let your escort get mounted, my dear," Luneta's mother said in an abrupt voice. Luneta allowed herself to glance at her mother, whose face was austere. Ywain mounted and took courteous leave of his host and hostess while Luneta tightened her jaw and looked at her parents.

Luneta's father glanced from mother to daughter, then sighed and said, "I'll miss you, lass. Try not to turn Lady Laudine's castle upside down. Perhaps we'll drop by for a visit someday soon."

Then they rode off—a knight, a lady, and a packhorse for Luneta's gear. Ywain didn't speak for nearly half an hour, for which Luneta was grateful, because by the time he made his first comment—a polite gambit about the scenery—she was fully in control of herself. They made good time, riding at an easy pace but stopping seldom. Ywain was a courteous and thoughtful companion, and if his conversation was rather heavily concerned with tournaments and feats of arms, he was not self-absorbed. Twice he broke off and, laughing ruefully at himself, apologized for prattling about arms and armor. They camped that night nearly forty miles from Orkney Hall, and Ywain told Luneta before they went to sleep that now that he'd seen that she was a fine horsewoman, they could go a bit faster the next day.

On the second day, just as Luneta's stiffness from riding all the day before was easing, she and Ywain came upon a large pavilion set up in a field. There were horses tied at one side, marking this as a knight's encampment, and servants hurried about on evidently urgent errands. At the center of the bustle, under the main tent, a knight lay on a pile of pillows, surrounded by attendants. At his left was a sniffling lady, wearing a dress of the most dashing shade of pink and holding a handkerchief in one hand and a vinaigrette in the other. On the knight's right, a tall man in multicolored clothes was tossing a small ball up in the air and catching it in one hand.

"Of course it's juggling," the man in motley was saying as Ywain and Luneta approached. "You know what your problem is, Sir Grenall? You've been seduced by the lure of spectacle. Sure, I could juggle three or four balls and use two hands, and that would be very impressive, but then what would I do after that? Five balls? Three hands? You see how it goes? Now me, I'm an artist, trying to recapture the original purity of the art form. This"—the man nodded at the ball he was tossing up and down—"this is the essence of juggling."

"Yes, yes," the knight said absently, his attention focused on the approach of Ywain and Luneta. "Good morrow, Sir Knight," he called.

"Is it morrow already?" the man in motley exclaimed. "I wasn't even done with yesterd!"

"With what?" the knight asked, his brow creased. Luneta suppressed a smile.

"Good day, Sir Knight," Ywain said, inclining his head courteously.

"Forgive me for not rising to meet you," the knight said from his pillows, turning away from the juggler. "You see, I have been grievously wounded."

At these words, the lady at the man's right burst into gusty sobs and buried her face in her handkerchief.

The man in motley glanced at her, then tossed his ball up and caught it in his other hand. "There," he said. "See what I did, my lady? To cheer you up I juggled with two hands. I just compromised my artistic principles for your sake. I hope you will applaud now. I couldn't bear to have made such a sacrifice for nothing."

The lady ignored him. "Oh, *poor* Sir Grenall."

"No, no, my lady," the man said earnestly. "You've gotten them confused. It was Sir Lorigan who was poor. Sir Grenall is very rich."

"Silence, fool," said Sir Grenall from his pillows. Now that they were near, Luneta could see the knight and the lady more clearly. The lady was very young,

20

perhaps only a year or two older than Luneta herself, and the knight was at least forty. The fool—who looked to be in his early twenties—caught the ball and stowed it in a pouch at his side.

"I know when I'm not appreciated. I'll have you know that when I performed in York, I had them all in tears of laughter, even the old men." He smiled pleasantly at the lady, who was still weeping quietly into her handkerchief. "You'd have liked it, my lady—all those old men, I mean."

"Silence, fool," Sir Grenall said, an edge to his voice.

Ywain finally spoke. "I am sorry that you have been injured, Sir . . . Grenall, is it?"

"Sir Grenall of the Firth," the knight said jovially, settling himself more comfortably on the cushions. He didn't sound like someone who had been grievously injured, Luneta thought.

Ywain must have been thinking the same thing, because he said, "Er . . . how exactly are you injured, Sir Grenall?"

"Ah," said the fool, "you've been misled by my master's courage. You were wondering how someone who seemed so comfortable could be injured, but I tell you that it is all an act. Sir Grenall is so brave that he will not let his pain show."

Sir Grenall smiled modestly and murmured, "Yes, well, code of honor and all that."

"You are too modest, sir!" the fool cried. He looked back at Ywain and Luneta, his face solemn and inspired. "Does Sir Grenall *want* to lie on pillows all day? Of course he doesn't! Only the need to hide his injury forces him to do something so repugnant! Does he want to drink wine and eat sweetmeats through the morning? Don't be silly! It's all an act! Sir Grenall is bravely trying to hide his pain!"

Sir Grenall smiled again, but with less pleasure.

"Indeed, his courage goes beyond even this," the fool added. "Sir Grenall is so brave that even the doctors themselves can't find his wound!"

"There, there, that's enough, fool," Sir Grenall interposed hastily, but not before Luneta, taken by surprise, had allowed a giggle to escape. The knight glanced at her, but she quickly assumed an expression of sympathy, and he looked away. Her eyes met those of the fool, who winked at her, then turned toward Sir Grenall again. Luneta blinked with surprise at the fool's effrontery, but decided not to be offended. She was enjoying him too much.

"If I must speak of it," Sir Grenall was saying, "then I must. I am Sir Grenall of the Firth—but I've told you that, haven't I?"

"Most excellently well, Sir Grenall," the fool said, applauding politely.

22

"And this is my lady, the Lady Golina. Not three days ago, a villainous recreant knight struck me down in this very field, seeking to steal my lady from me. Naturally, I should have defeated him, but Sir Lorigan fought like a villain and struck me from behind. I was left lying senseless on the field."

"Then why is your lady still here?" Luneta asked. It seemed a reasonable question, but it appeared to annoy the knight, and even the lady shot her a nasty look over the handkerchief.

The fool stepped into the awkward silence, saying, "Perhaps Sir Lorigan, having seen the fury of Sir Grenall's sword, knew that he could never defeat him a second time and so chose not to steal the fair lady, after all."

"Yes, that might be," Sir Grenall said, his face brightening.

"I wouldn't bet on it, myself," the fool added thoughtfully, "but it's at least—"

Sir Grenall continued, "I lie here until I am restored, but someone must stop this knight before he attempts to steal another fair lady."

"Oh, I doubt he will try that," the fool said. The light tone had left his voice. "Remember the fury of your sword."

"He must be stopped and slain," Sir Grenall said,

"before he ravages more fair damsels! If only . . . but I cannot ask. I do not even know your name."

"I am Ywain, son of Ywain, grandson of King Uriens," Ywain said grandly, "and I would consider it an honor to take on this quest. I shall leave at once!"

"Bravo!" Sir Grenall cried.

"Ywain?" Luneta said.

"Yes, Luneta?"

"Er, didn't you promise not to start any quests until after we'd gotten to Camelot?"

Ywain's face froze, then fell. "I did, didn't I?" He looked apologetically at Sir Grenall. "I'm sorry, Sir Grenall, but I've a prior promise to keep. Perhaps after I've taken my cousin to court, I could come back and—"

"That sounds like a coward's excuse!" Sir Grenall said with a sneer.

Ywain stiffened, but before he could speak, the fool said, "Don't try to argue with him, Sir Ywain. If any man in England knows cowards' excuses, it's Sir Grenall."

Sir Grenall turned and glared at the fool. "And what do you mean by that, fool?"

The fool replied, "It means that I'll be leaving you now, Sir Grenall. I'm afraid that I no longer find you amusing."

"*You* find *me* amusing!" Sir Grenall said. "*I'm* not the fool."

24

The fool shook his head, then glanced at Ywain and Luneta. "See what I mean? Far too obvious to be funny. Did I hear you say that you were going to court?"

"Yes, we are," Luneta said.

"Would you mind having another companion? I've my own horse."

"Yes, of course," said Ywain, who was still looking back and forth between the fool and the knight, a bemused expression on his face.

"I'll be with you shortly," the fool said, disappearing behind the tent.

Ywain looked back at Sir Grenall, whose brow was stormy and who had raised himself up on his elbows. "I will bid you good day, then," Sir Ywain said.

"Or good morrow," Luneta murmured.

"Are you indeed stealing my fool?" Sir Grenall said, his eyes blazing.

Ywain blushed and looked uncomfortable, but Luneta answered, "Actually, it feels more as if your fool is stealing us." She smiled brightly at the knight. "It's a pity you can't stop us, what with your injury and all."

"Good . . . good day," Ywain said again, and then they were trotting away, leaving Sir Grenall sputtering impotently behind them. They rode toward the horse enclosure, where the fool was saddling a large, strong-looking white stallion.

"That's your horse, fool?" Ywain said.

"My name's Rhience," the fool said over his shoulder. "And yes, this is my horse."

"What a fine animal!" Ywain said admiringly. "He looks like a knight's charger!"

Rhience sighed. "Yes, he does. Pity that he's so stupid." He tightened the girth with a sure hand.

"Stupid?" Ywain asked.

Rhience swung into the saddle. "He lets a fool ride him, doesn't he? How could any proud warhorse allow such a thing unless he was a bit of an ass?" He settled into the saddle, then turned to Luneta. "I heard Sir Ywain's name, but I'm afraid I missed yours, my lady."

"I'm Lune—ah, the Lady Luneta," Luneta said.

"I'm charmed, my lady," Rhience said. He smiled and nodded to Ywain. "Shall we go, before Sir Grenall forgets that he's grievously wounded?"

"I'm not afraid of him," Ywain said, but he kicked his mount into a trot anyway.

"Nobody's afraid of Sir Grenall," Rhience said. "At least not in that way. His only strength is the power of too much money. I doubt he could hurt you with a sword if he came on you asleep, but if you're an impoverished knight betrothed to a young lady who dreams of riches, he's very dangerous indeed."

The light dawned for Luneta. "Sir Lorigan?" she asked.

Rhience nodded approvingly. "Very good, my lady. Yes, Sir Grenall stole Lady Golina from young Lorigan with promises of fine clothes and jewels. Lorigan found them in the fields on a hunting excursion, bashed Grenall about for a bit, then left Golina with him. Bad luck for both of them."

Luneta giggled. "And you were their fool?"

"Fool, yes, my lady, but not theirs. I'm a wandering fool, and I'd already decided that I'd been with those two for long enough. When he tried to use Sir Ywain here to get revenge on Lorigan, that was enough." He glanced at Ywain. "It's none of my business, of course, but if I were you I'd be a little less quick to volunteer."

Ywain nodded thoughtfully, and they pressed on to the south.

II
THE STORM STONE

The journey to Camelot took more than a week, but despite the monotony of constant riding Luneta had never enjoyed herself so much. Her two companions, each in his own way, made this journey the most pleasant she had ever known. Ywain, for his part, was very solicitous for her comfort and protection, at least when he wasn't lost in a dream of winning knightly glory. Whenever they met someone on the road, Ywain immediately moved between Luneta and the stranger. Luneta privately considered this a bit excessive, inasmuch as most of the people they met were farmers and tradesmen who really didn't pose a threat, but it was nice to be thought of. As for Rhience the Fool, he did nothing for her physical comfort, but talking with him made the time pass amazingly quickly.

One could never tell what Rhience would say next. One day, after Ywain had protected Luneta from a farmer driving a flock of geese, Rhience nodded approvingly and commented to Luneta, "A very good guardian you have, Lady Luneta."

"He promised my mother he would care for me, you see," Luneta replied, a bit apologetically.

"You don't have to explain it to me," Rhience said. "I understand perfectly. He is doing what a man should, on account of your being defective."

Luneta blinked, not sure that she had heard correctly. "I beg your pardon?"

"'Defective and misbegotten' I believe is the full translation."

"Translation of what?"

"Of Latin, of course. Why would I translate something from English?"

Luneta took a slow breath. "I meant, what writing were you translating?"

"Oh, that was a bit from a theological book I once read."

"Don't be ridiculous. There are no theological books about me."

"Not about you specifically, Lady Luneta—about women in general."

Luneta frowned as an incongruity occurred to her. "Why would a fool read theology?"

"I can't tell you how often I've wondered that," Rhience replied, shaking his head sympathetically. "But they seem to do it anyway. For my part, I read that book because I was studying for the church. That was before I rose to my current profession, of course. Now, let's see if I remember the argument exactly . . . Yes, I think I have it. Now listen closely: for a child to be born requires a male and a female—stop me if I'm getting too complicated."

"Thank you," Luneta said coldly, "I think I'm able to keep up so far."

Rhience whistled softly. "Impressive, what with your being defective and all."

Luneta wasn't sure whether to be angry or amused. She itched to slap the fool for his impertinence, but curiosity restrained her. She glanced ahead at Ywain, to see what he thought of Rhience's foolishness, but his face was dreamy and distant, and she knew he was off winning a tournament or slaying a dragon in his imagination. "Go on," she said to Rhience.

"Now, when that child is born, it is either male or female. Are you still with me?"

"Yes, idiot. I'm still with you. Go on."

Rhience clucked his tongue chidingly. "Is that how you speak to someone who's trying to improve your theological education?" He sniffed expressively, then continued, "Now, the way it works is this: the male parent transmits masculine perfection to the child, but that perfection is always marred a bit, on account of the female parent's involvement. If the baby's really badly marred, it turns out a girl."

"You made that up," Luneta said scornfully.

"Not at all. It's from one of the theologians at the University of Paris, a holy monk and doctor of theology."

"How does he know which parent gives what to the child?"

Rhience frowned. "I admit, I wondered that myself when I read it. You wouldn't expect a pious monk to know much about the matter, but when I asked my tutor, he said only that it was not for us to question things that were written by our betters in Latin."

Luneta blinked. "What does its being in Latin have to do with anything?"

"My tutor thought that anything in Latin had to be true. It's God's language. You wouldn't understand, though, on account of your being def—"

Luneta didn't let him finish. Pulling a long pin from her hair, she reached across to where Rhience rode beside her and jabbed him in the fleshy part just above the saddle. Rhience yelped and lurched away from her, losing his grip on the reins and tumbling into the dust on the other side of his horse. Ywain whirled around in his saddle, his hand on his sword, a fierce battle-light in his eyes, but there was no danger for him to face—only

Rhience lifting himself from the dirt and gingerly rubbing his backside. Luneta met his surprised gaze and said austerely, "*Es asinus*. And that's in Latin, so you know it's true."

Rhience began to laugh, and Ywain said, "What's true?"

"She says I'm an ass," Rhience explained.

"In truth, I think she's right," Ywain said. "Whatever made you fall off your horse like that?"

"I'm defective," Rhience said, climbing back into his saddle. "I think it's my father's fault." He grinned at Luneta and said, "*Pax?*"

It was impossible to be angry with the fool for long. Luneta returned his smile and said, "*Pax.*"

Rhience turned back to Ywain. "Listen, Ywain old chap. Next time that we meet a fishwife or tinker, why don't you protect me instead of Luneta? She can take care of herself."

Camelot was everything that Luneta remembered, but seeing it without her parents' comforting presence was unexpectedly intimidating. Riding through the great courtyard ringed with the banners of the Round Table knights, she felt very alone and uncharacteristically shy. Ywain, however, could barely sit still in his saddle for excitement. As they crossed the courtyard toward the stables, he began identifying all the coats of arms. "There's Sir Bedivere's escutcheon! And Cousin Gareth's! There's Sir Griflet Fise de Dieu's! And Cousin Agrivain's!" Luneta began to feel somewhat re-assured; she had forgotten how many of the knights of the court were related to her.

The last trace of nervousness disappeared a moment later when, stepping together out of the royal stables, they nearly ran into Luneta's famous uncle Sir Gawain. Seeing her and Ywain, Gawain shouted with delight and immediately swept them away to show them around the court. It was a very strange and exalted feel-ing for Luneta, being introduced as an equal to people whom she knew primarily as the heroes of minstrels' stories: Sir Kai, Sir Lancelot, Sir Bedivere, and—last of all, King Arthur himself. Of course, she had seen many of these famous people before, on earlier visits with her parents, but it was different this time. She wasn't a child holding her mother's hand, but a lady in her own right. Gawain was careful to include Ywain and Rhience in all his introductions, but it was clear that his greatest pleasure was in presenting the daughter of his favorite brother. As a crowning honor, King Arthur in-vited the three travelers to join him at his own table at dinner that evening.

Dinner was glorious. Each course was followed by one more splendid than the last. Luneta noticed that the king himself ate sparingly, and then only the simplest dishes, but for her part she tried everything that passed by. So did Ywain, seated on her right, but Rhience, on her other side, spent most of his time watching Luneta.

Noticing the fool's grin, she asked suspiciously, "What's so funny? Do I have food on my chin?"

"Remember, I'm a fool. We're permitted to smile at odd times."

"Not at me."

"*Pax*, my lady. I'm not laughing at you," Rhience said. "I just enjoy watching people have fun. And you are, aren't you?"

Luneta dimpled, then nodded quickly. "Ever so much! I think it's the most splendid evening of my life. It's just what I always imagined court life to be! If only there were a ball after dinner!"

Gawain, seated on Rhience's other side, heard this remark and turned sharply. "Good Gog, Luneta! Why on earth would you wish for that?"

"Don't you like going to balls?"

"Horrible things!" Gawain said decisively. Then he added, "Not that I've ever found a lady, besides your worthy mother, who shares my view of the matter. I'm afraid, Luneta, that there are no balls scheduled at court for some time, but if you're still awake after the meal you're putting away, why don't you come to my chambers? I'll invite the rest of the family, and we'll have a private party." He looked over his shoulder at his squire. "Terence? Can you arrange it? Invite all the family that's at court to my chambers this evening to welcome Luneta and Ywain." The squire bowed wordlessly, and Gawain glanced at Rhience. "And you, too, if you like, friend."

"I'm honored, Sir Gawain," Rhience said. "But is it proper for a fool to mingle with knights and ladies? I shouldn't even be sitting at this table, but for the king's invitation."

"Oh, don't worry about that," Gawain said, smiling. He glanced at his squire again. "You don't mind having a fool in our chambers, do you, Terence?"

The squire bowed again. "I never have before, milord."

Rhience looked startled at Squire Terence's words, and even more at Gawain's answering chuckle, but Luneta only grinned. Throughout her childhood, Gawain and Terence had been frequent guests at Orkney Hall, and she knew that they regarded each other as equals. Terence had been Gawain's squire for nearly twenty years now and had shared his every adventure. When they were at Orkney Hall, Luneta's parents treated Terence with a regard that was equal to or (Luneta had sometimes thought) even greater than the respect they showed Gawain.

Sure enough, that evening in Gawain's chambers, once it was just family—or very nearly so—Terence abandoned his proper squirely attitude and stretched

35

out comfortably on the floor beside a lady that Luneta didn't know. Except for this one lady, Lady Eileen, though, Luneta recognized everyone there. Besides Gawain and Terence, there was Gawain's brother Agrivain and three cousins named Florence, Lovel, and Aalardin. With Luneta, Ywain, and Rhience, Gawain's chambers were quite full, and when Sir Kai and Queen Guinevere stopped in on some pretext and joined the party, Luneta began to feel as if she were a part of an exclusive society.

Sir Gawain greeted the queen when she entered, then turned at once to present her to Luneta. "Your Highness," he said, "we missed you this afternoon, and I had no chance at dinner, but allow me to introduce to you Lady Luneta of Orkney, my favorite niece."

Luneta dipped her lowest curtsy, blushing slightly. The queen's lips parted, but before she could speak, a loud guffaw came from across the room. "That's not saying much, Gawain," said his brother Agrivain. "After all, she's your *only* niece."

In a gravelly voice, Sir Kai said, "Thank you, Agrivain, for enlightening us."

Agrivain shrugged and picked up a flagon of wine. Queen Guinevere, ignoring both Agrivain and Sir Kai, smiled at Luneta and said, "I am delighted, Lady Luneta. Do you make a long stay at Camelot?"

It was the first time since arriving at court that

36

Luneta had thought about her plans. "Oh, no. I mean, I don't think so. I'm on my way to visit a friend of my mother's, Your Highness. I'm supposed to ask Uncle Gawain if he'll escort me."

The queen smiled impishly, and a chuckle spread through the room.

"Uncle Gawain," Terence repeated, his eyes glinting with laughter. "Dear old uncle."

"I'm sure Uncle Gawain will be glad to oblige you," Sir Kai said, "provided his rheumatism allows him to travel."

Gawain grunted. "Laugh all you want, Kai. There's no fear of anyone addressing you with a title of respect."

Luneta blushed, but she looked up into Gawain's eyes and said, "But you *are* my uncle. What else am I to call you?"

" 'Gawain' will do nicely, my child."

"All right," Luneta said at once, "provided you don't call me 'my child' again."

Everyone laughed (except for Agrivain), and Gawain bowed his head in mock surrender.

For several minutes, the family and friends chatted about ordinary things. Luneta heard Ywain asking Agrivain and the cousins about upcoming tournaments, while Gawain and Sir Kai discussed some matter of court business. Terence and Lady Eileen were talking with Rhience, and Luneta was content to sit beside the queen and feel amazed at being at her very first grown-up party. Then the door swung open and a tall, amazingly beautiful woman swept into the room. Conversation stopped briefly, but then Gawain said, "Morgan. I had no idea you were back at court. It's good to see you."

The woman's icily beautiful face seemed to warm somewhat, and she replied, "I heard that you had a visitor."

Gawain nodded and gestured to Luneta. "Lady Morgan, allow me to present your, ah, your niece, the Lady Luneta."

Luneta could almost feel the force of the woman's gaze on her face. So this was Morgan Le Fay. Luneta had known for years that there was an enchantress in the family, but she had never met her—or, indeed, any enchantress. Her heart beat quickly, but she raised her eyes and met Lady Morgan's stare. "How do you do, Lady Morgan?" she said in her best attempt at a casual voice.

Lady Morgan's lips twitched once. "Yes," she said. "You have your father's face, but you got your eyes from your mother." She turned abruptly away and looked at Terence. "What do you think, Terence?"

"I think you should join our little gathering," Terence replied softly. "Then you could come to know your great-niece for yourself."

Lady Morgan's face grew taut at the words "great-niece," and she said, "I've no time for that. Will she do or not?"

"As always, my lady," Terence said, "that will depend on Luneta."

Luneta listened to this exchange with growing indignation, then said, "Do you have a question that you wish to ask me, Lady Morgan? After all, I'm in the room, too."

Luneta knew that it was impertinent for her to address her elders so, and she was prepared for Lady Morgan to be angry, but Luneta's words seemed almost to please the enchantress. She turned back to Luneta and said, "Yes, I do. But I believe I shall wait. At least you don't want for spirit." And then Lady Morgan turned and disappeared through the open door with a flourish of velvet and silk.

The room was silent for a moment; then Terence rose and went to shut the door. "I would think that it would be exhausting," he commented mildly, "to feel that every time I entered or left a room, it had to be an event." His eyes rested briefly on Luneta as he walked back to his spot, and he murmured, "Good girl."

The rest of the party resumed their conversations as if Lady Morgan had not interrupted them, which gave Luneta a chance to catch her breath and wonder why the enchantress had been so interested in her. Ywain's voice rose above the rest. "Look here, this isn't any good," he was saying. "I'm beginning to feel that I've come all this way for nothing. There are no tournaments, no dragons, no giants, no wild beasts, no recreant knights holding ladies prisoner in their castles. How's a fellow supposed to make a name for himself in such a tame country?"

"The same way the rest of us do," growled Agrivain. "Sit on your backside and wait until a chance comes."

Ywain laughed. "I can't do that! I need adventure! Hasn't anyone here heard of a magical beast or rogue knight to overcome? Is there no more magic in England?"

"Is that what you want, Ywain?" a voice asked pleasantly. It was Rhience. "Are you sure?"

"Of course I'm sure! I need a quest. It doesn't have to be magical, I suppose—just something with a bit of fighting."

"Oh, I can give you magic, too, if you really want it," Rhience said.

Everyone turned to look at the fool. "Is this a joke, Rhience?" Ywain asked.

"Nay, Ywain. I'll put aside my cap and bells for a bit. I can tell you about an adventure, if you like."

Agrivain snorted into his wineglass. "He's having you on, Ywain, and you're believing him. What would a fool know about knightly adventures?"

"I could ask you the same thing," Rhience said casually, "but that would hardly be helpful, would it? And of course you're right that my current profession has little to do with adventures. As it happens, though, I met this adventure before I became a fool."

"What were you then?" asked Sir Kai suddenly.

"I was a knight," Rhience said.

Sir Kai broke the startled silence with a chuckle. "I thought I'd seen you before, at your father's place in Sussex. Sir Calogrenant, aren't you?"

Rhience nodded. "Yes, but that wasn't my real name. I took it when my father knighted me because I thought it sounded more knightly. I'm just Rhience."

"But I thought that you had been studying for the church," Luneta said, staring at her companion confusedly.

Rhience grinned. "That was even earlier. I gave it up. I wasn't much good at religion, you see. I kept laughing at the wrong times. So I thought I'd try knighthood, and my father—Sir Navan of Sussex—obliged me with a title. And in time I set off, dreaming of tournaments and of winning glory and the hand of a fair princess."

"Exactly!" Ywain said.

"And as I dreamed, I rode through Salisbury on a fine spring day—it was the first of April, the Fool's New Year, you know—and came to a little shepherd boy. Or perhaps not a boy. He was a boy's size, but he had a little beard."

Terence sat up suddenly. "Go on, Rhience. You've begun to interest me very much."

"Well, this shepherd asked me if I was looking for adventure, and when I said I was, he told me about a great magic to be found in the little copse of trees to my south. At the center of that copse, he said, was a small spring beside a stone basin, and if I took some water from the spring and poured it into the basin, I would soon have all the adventure I wanted."

"He was having you on," Agrivain said. His words were slow, as if he were taking care not to slur them.

"What did you do?" Ywain demanded.

"Just what I can see you would do," Rhience replied. "I went to give it a try."

"What happened?" Ywain asked.

"Let our friend tell his story, Ywain," Gawain said. "You only slow him down with questions."

Rhience nodded to Gawain, then continued. "It took me no time to find it. Not many stands of trees in those plains. There it was, a little spring and an ancient-looking stone basin right beside it. I rode right up to it and dipped water into the basin." Here Rhience paused for a moment. "I don't know if you'll believe this or not, and I'm not sure that I'd believe it myself if I were told, but as soon as the water touched the basin the sky grew dark with thunderclouds. A moment before, it was as pleasant and clear a day as you could ask for, and the next moment it was as black as night and beginning to thunder.

42

"For the next ten minutes I truly feared for my life. I've never been in such a storm. Lightning flashed all around me, shattering trees nearby, and that thunder . . . I covered my ears and still thought they would burst. The rain—it felt more like standing under a waterfall than being in the rain. Then, after a few minutes, it stopped, as quickly as it had begun."

"What a curious tale," Queen Guinevere said.

"Is that all?" asked Ywain.

Rhience shook his head. "No, it isn't, for all I thought so at the time. When the storm stopped, I thanked God I was alive and mounted my horse to leave, but I hadn't gone two steps before I heard a crashing through the trees behind me and turned to see a huge knight in red armor approaching. He called out, 'Are you the fool who disturbed the Storm Stone?'

"I told him that I was no fool but that I had indeed poured the water into the basin. He just lowered his lance, shouted out, 'We'll see if you're a fool!' and attacked."

"Now we're getting somewhere!" Ywain exclaimed. "Did you defeat him?"

Rhience grinned wryly. "Hardly, my friend. I've never taken such a toss in my life, and once he'd unhorsed me, he jumped off and attacked with his sword. I was no match for him, and in minutes he had disarmed me and was holding his sword at my throat."

Luneta stared at Rhience. Though she had heard

stories of knights and battles all her life, it had never occurred to her to wonder what it would be like to be defeated and in danger of death.

"What happened then?" Ywain asked.

"The red knight asked if I still thought I wasn't a fool. I said I still thought so, and he let me feel his blade a bit." Here Rhience pulled back his motley jerkin and showed a long, still livid scar just where his neck met his shoulder. "So I thought about it some more and told him that perhaps I was a fool after all."

"No!" Ywain exclaimed. "You didn't!"

"I did."

"You gave in to him? I would never have done so! Why did you say such a thing?"

"Because it wasn't true, I suppose," Rhience replied.

Ywain looked confused. "What?"

Sir Kai emitted a rumbling laugh. "Don't you see, lad? If he really had been a fool, he would have kept on denying it—and died."

"Oh," Ywain said, frowning slightly.

"I admit, that's what I thought," Rhience said. "So the red knight didn't kill me. Instead, he made me vow to never again disturb the Storm Stone, which was easy since I had no wish to do so anyway, and then he began to laugh. He commented that since it was Fool's Day, he'd just had an idea. He made me vow that for the next full year I would not take up arms against any man, but rather would put on the cap and bells of a fool. That was a month ago."

Agrivain laughed loudly. "And you're still wearing those clothes? You *are* a fool!"

"I gave my word, you see," Rhience replied mildly. "And I must say that the life of a fool hasn't been as unpleasant as I'd expected. You meet such interesting people, and you can say nearly anything to them and they'll think you're joking."

"This knight did not behave honorably toward you!" Ywain exclaimed. "He must be taught a lesson in honor!"

"Wait!" Rhience said, his mouth opening in mock surprise. "Let me guess what you're about to say—"

"I shall go challenge this knight myself!"

"You didn't let me guess," Rhience said plaintively. "And I had the right answer, too."

"You?" demanded Agrivain. "Why should you get this adventure? Some of us have been waiting for years for something to come up, and you've been at court less than a day!"

"But this outrage was committed on the person of *my* friend!" Ywain said.

Rhience looked gratified. "Why, Ywain, I'm touched! I hadn't known until now how close we were."

Several people laughed, and Ywain had the grace to blush. "Well, at any rate, I know you better than Cousin Agrivain does."

45

"You'll wait your turn for adventures like the rest of us," Agrivain declared belligerently.

Sir Kai yawned loudly and said, "Enough of this. I'm not sure, myself, that anything must be done at all. It sounds as if this knight is bound somehow to protect the land from these magical storms, and if so, we would do wrong to stop him."

"But what about his unchivalrous behavior toward Sir Calogrenant?"

"Rhience," the fool said.

"That's between the two of them," Sir Kai said. "If Rhience wants vengeance, he can do something about it himself."

Ywain looked at Rhience, struck by this. "I beg your pardon, my friend. I had not thought. Have you sworn vengeance on this red knight yourself?"

Rhience pursed his lips and said, "I meant to, actually. I really did. But what with one thing or another, I've never gotten around to—"

"There, Sir Kai, you see?" Ywain said.

"We'll take this to Arthur and the other knights at the next gathering of the Round Table."

"And how long will that be?"

"Two weeks," Sir Kai said.

Ywain's eyes widened, and he started to speak but then subsided. "Very well," he said.

46

"Now you know how it feels to wait," Agrivain said with satisfaction.

Ywain said nothing. Luneta, watching him, felt sure that he had something in mind other than waiting, but she couldn't imagine what.

She found out the next morning. She was awakened at least an hour before dawn by a lady-in-waiting who informed her that her escort was waiting for her in the courtyard. From the lady's tone, it was evident that she thought that Luneta had overslept, but searching her memory Luneta could not remember having arranged any escort for this morning. She certainly had not intended to leave Camelot so soon, but if Gawain had risen this early to take her to Lady Laudine, she could hardly keep him waiting. Dressing hurriedly and throwing her gear together, she ran down to the courtyard.

Only it wasn't Gawain but Ywain who waited for her, and behind Ywain was Rhience, mounted on his great white horse. Her own two horses were nearby, saddled and ready. "What is this?" Luneta demanded. "I thought Gawain was taking me."

"Oh, we've worked it out," Ywain said airily. "If I have to wait two weeks for the next Round Table meeting before I can go adventuring, I might as well have something to do. You don't mind, do you? The thing is,

47

you were already asleep when it was decided, and I didn't want to disturb you."

Luneta shook her head. "No, of course not, but why so early?"

Rhience snorted but said nothing. Ywain stammered, "I . . . ah . . . didn't realize that it was so early."

"Unworthy, Ywain," Rhience said. "And what will you say when she asks why I've been brought along?"

Ywain helped Luneta to mount her horse and said, "We can talk while we travel. As long as we're up this early, we shouldn't waste time."

"Yes, why did you bring Rhience? I don't mind, of course, but I thought—"

"All in good time," Ywain said hurriedly, mounting his own horse. "Shall we go?"

Luneta was sure that Ywain had some plan in mind, and she bent her mind to figuring it out. It didn't take long. They were barely half a mile from the castle when she said, "Oh, I understand now. You're off to that Storm Stone, aren't you? The stone is in Salisbury, which is where Lady Laudine lives, too."

"Well," Ywain admitted, "I thought I might drop in as long as I was in the neighborhood."

"And you need Rhience to give you directions to the stone."

"Very good, my lady," Rhience said.

"But it won't work," Luneta said. "If I can figure out

what you're doing, so can everyone else. Uncle Agrivain won't let you get ahead of him."

"Ah, but he won't know I'm going near the Storm Stone, will he?"

"Of course he will. Rhience said last night that the Storm Stone is in Salisbury."

"True, my lady," Rhience said, "but they don't know that that's where your mother's friend lives. You didn't mention that last night. Ywain knew, of course, but no one else will guess that Ywain is really only using you as an excuse to go early to his adventure."

Ywain grinned. "I left a note for Gawain that I was going to escort you myself while I waited for the Round Table meeting, but I may have forgotten to mention where Lady Laudine lives."

Luneta was mildly indignant at having been used as a pawn in Ywain's game, but as someone who prided herself in her ability to weave other people into her own schemes, she had to admit a certain reluctant admiration for Ywain. He had executed his plan very neatly, and there was nothing left to do but settle down and enjoy the journey.

III

THE FAERY RING

When Lady Laudine had sent her invitation for Luneta to visit, she had included directions to her husband's castle, which was a very good thing, as it turned out, because it gave Luneta something in writing to wave in front of Ywain's face so as to remind him where they were going. Her cousin had a tendency to forget who was accompanying whom and to assume that they were all going off together to find the Storm Stone. At one point, lost in his dream of victory in battle, Ywain even warned Luneta that she mustn't get in the way while he was fighting the red knight. Luneta rolled her eyes, and Rhience asked innocently, "Oh, Lady Luneta! Do you mean to visit the Storm Stone as well?"

"No," Luneta said bluntly.

Ywain looked surprised for a second but recovered

quickly. Bowing to Luneta with rare grace, he said, "Forgive me, cousin. My mind is far too busy with my own affairs. Of course you will be at your friend's home before I meet the knight."

Fortunately, given Ywain's tendency to forget where he was supposed to be going, Lady Laudine's castle appeared to be quite near to the magical stone, judging from Luneta's directions and Rhience's memory. As a result, the closer they drew to Lady Laudine's castle, the more excited Ywain grew. Every stand of trees that they passed prompted him to ask if it were the copse he was looking for. At last the three travelers topped a small hill and looked down on a stately castle, just where Lady Laudine's directions had said it would be. Luneta reined in and looked at it silently for a moment.

"Is that it?" Ywain demanded.

Luneta nodded. "If the directions are right," she said. "Yes, that's it. See how the farthest tower is a little higher than the others? Lady Laudine mentions that in her letter."

"Well, let's go, then," Ywain said eagerly.

Luneta didn't move. Until this moment, concerned with finding her way, she had been able to push to the back of her mind any worries related to her visit, but now that she had arrived, she was suddenly assailed with doubts. What if Lady Laudine didn't like her? What if she was as old-fashioned and frumpy as Luneta's mother? What if she was offended by Luneta's showing up earlier than expected? What if—?

"Nay, lass," Rhience said at her elbow. "Don't be bashful now. Remember that the other night, you faced down a sorceress."

Luneta was startled at how accurately the fool had divined her thoughts, and she quickly lifted her chin. "Who's bashful?"

"Come on!" Ywain said. "The sooner we get there, the sooner I can face this knight at the Storm Stone!"

"Will you hush, cloth-head?" Rhience said wearily. "You'll get there in plenty of time. That copse you've been imagining under every rock is just over that hill to the east, not half a mile away."

"So close!" Ywain exclaimed with glee. "Then . . ." He hesitated. "I say, cousin, do you need me anymore? I mean, I've seen you to the castle and everything."

"You're not going to leave her to go in by herself, are you?" Rhience demanded.

"Well, it isn't as if she's in any danger. She's been invited, hasn't she?"

Rhience started to reply angrily, but Luneta interrupted. "No, Ywain, I don't need you. You run along and look for your knight to battle."

Ywain's face lit up. "Wonderful! Come along, Rhience!"

"Not by half," Rhience replied promptly. "If you

won't accompany Lady Luneta, I will. Don't worry. You'll find your adventure soon enough."

Ywain hesitated. Then, glancing over his shoulder at the hill, he said, "Very well. Wish me luck!"

He started to ride away, but Rhience called him back. "Wait, Ywain! Since I won't be with you, I've something to say! You go right ahead to the copse and find the magic spring and wait for the knight there, but whatever you do, don't pour the water into the basin. I'm serious, here. This storm is the most destructive thing I've ever seen."

"I'm not afraid of a storm," Ywain said.

"Listen to me, gapeseed! At the moment, I don't much care if the storm kills you or not, but you aren't the only person who might be hurt by the storm. Is it worth some farmer's death for you to make a name for yourself?"

Ywain frowned, then nodded. "Very well. I'll wait at the spring." Then he was gone.

Rhience watched him go. *"Asinus,"* he murmured.

"It's all right," Luneta said. "He's just excited. And besides, even if he did go with me to the castle, you don't really think he'd be of any use, do you? He'd be so eager to get away and fight this knight, he wouldn't hear a thing said to him."

Rhience grinned. "True," he said. "You can lead an ass to water, but you can't make him think."

53

So the two of them rode down the hill to the great gates of Lady Laudine's castle.

Exactly as had happened at Camelot, Luneta's initial nervousness proved unnecessary. Lady Laudine welcomed her with a delight that was almost overwhelming. One would have thought that Luneta was Lady Laudine's long-lost sister, so effusive was her greeting, and far from being offended at Luneta's early arrival, it appeared that Lady Laudine had been wishing every day since Luneta's mother had first written that Luneta could come sooner. As for Rhience, Lady Laudine's delight at having a real, live fool at her court was almost as great as her pleasure in having Luneta. "Oh, you can't think how often I've wished for a fool to brighten my days and make me laugh!" she exclaimed. "For—you mustn't tell my husband I said this—a life of luxury is horribly dull sometimes."

"Indeed, my lady," Rhience replied solemnly. He glanced around at the richly furnished sitting room where Lady Laudine had received them. "I can't tell you how sympathetic I am. It all seems very dreadful."

Lady Laudine sighed. "Thank you for understanding," she said.

"But I must warn you, my lady," Rhience continued. "You're sadly out of fashion regarding fools. We don't try to make people laugh anymore; that's quite gone out of style. The latest thing from Camelot is for fools to make people solemn and mournful. I wonder: have you considered your sins lately?"

Lady Laudine blinked, but Luneta giggled, and Lady Laudine's face cleared. "Oh," she said. "Is it a joke?"

Rhience bowed. "Even so, my lady."

"I'm sure it's very funny," Lady Laudine replied with a forced smile. "You must stay with us, too. I won't take no for an answer! Malvolus! Malvolus!"

A gaunt, unsmiling man who had been standing unobtrusively in the shadows strode majestically forward. "Yes, my lady?"

"Malvolus, please have a room made up for this fool. He is to stay with us."

The gaunt man bowed, but very slightly. "I will present the matter to the master," he said. Then he turned and began to stalk away.

"Why, my lady!" Rhience said admiringly. "I had no idea you were so accomplished! Pray, what language were you speaking just now?" Lady Laudine looked confused, but Rhience continued. "In English, it sounded to me as if you had given this gentleman a command, but he must have heard it in a different language. How clever of you both!"

The austere servant stopped abruptly, then turned slowly around to look into Rhience's eyes. Hastily,

Lady Laudine said, "Oh, don't worry about him, Malvolus. He's a fool, you see. Please, go and speak to my husband. I should have directed you to do so from the beginning."

Malvolus's bleak eyes held a momentary gleam of triumph, and then he turned again and made his unhurried way to the door.

When the door was closed, Lady Laudine said nervously to Rhience, "Oh dear, I should have warned you. Malvolus does not appreciate jokes."

"No!" Rhience said.

"To be honest, he terrifies me," Lady Laudine confided. "But he's been my husband's steward for years and years. But enough of such things! Let me look at you, my dear!" She held Luneta at arm's length and gazed into her face. "You don't favor your mother very much, do you? But, forgive me, that's not entirely bad, is it? Lynet never cared very much for being a beauty, so it's all right for her, but you, my dear, are a most taking little thing! Why, with a few silks and a bit of primping, we shall turn you out quite a belle!"

Luneta smiled. She had woven several plans for persuading her hostess to dress her in more fashionable clothes than the ones that her mother had packed, but it didn't look as if these schemes would be necessary. Indeed, looking at Lady Laudine, Luneta decided that there probably weren't any dowdy dresses in the whole castle, for never had Luneta seen a more gorgeously clad woman in her life. Lady Laudine was like a princess in a children's story—clothed in the richest of cloth and sparkling with jewels. Most of all, Lady Laudine was a true beauty. Her face was as astonishingly perfect as had been Morgan Le Fay's, but Lady Laudine's bright smile and vivacious good humor made her far more appealing than the sorceress. *I've landed on my feet here,* Luneta thought. *No doubt about it. By dinnertime, I'll be better dressed than I've ever been in my life.*

She was not mistaken. As soon as Lady Laudine conducted her to her room and saw the dresses that her mother had packed for her, she gave a shriek of horror and quickly stuffed them back into Luneta's bags. "Oh, dear!" she moaned. "I've never thought it healthy for Lynet to live such an isolated life in the country, but if this is what she thinks is suitable, then she must have been alone too long! Tell me, dear, is she quite mad?"

Luneta wasn't entirely sure that she liked this last question, but since she agreed completely with the rest of this statement, she was able to ignore the insult to her mother and enter into the spirit of the moment. Within minutes, Lady Laudine had dragged Luneta off to her own enormous bedchamber and had begun turning out all the wardrobes for dresses that could be altered to fit Luneta. Then, once seven or eight sumptuous gowns had been chosen, Lady Laudine opened her jewelry drawer.

At this point even Luneta began to feel uneasy. It wasn't that she didn't admire the ropes of pearls and glowing gem sets in Lady Laudine's collection, but she had a strong suspicion that a sixteen-year-old girl who wore such ornament would look more ridiculous than spectacular. She allowed Lady Laudine to put a few jewels on her, but she felt like a little girl playing dress up and soon removed them. "Don't you have anything less . . . less brilliant?" Luneta asked. "If I wore any of these diamonds, I'd never be able to relax, for fear I should lose them." She dipped her hand into the drawer, moved a brooch aside, and drew out an unjeweled ring, of glowing gold that was curiously carved with the semblance of a serpent. "What is this?"

Lady Laudine's eyes sparkled, and she leaned close to Luneta in a conspiratorial manner. "How interesting that you should have found that ring of all others!" she said in a low but excited voice. "I must tell your mother. Truth be told, that's the most valuable ring of all."

"This? Why should this ring be more valuable than the rubies and diamonds?"

Lady Laudine leaned even closer. "Because it's magic, of course. It's a faery ring!"

Luneta had now spent enough time with her hostess to think it very unlikely that she was making a joke—

Lady Laudine didn't seem the sort, somehow—but she glanced sharply at her all the same. All she saw in Lady Laudine's face was impish excitement. "What's magic about it?"

"Try it on," Lady Laudine said.

Giving her hostess one more suspicious glance, Luneta slipped the ring onto her finger. It fit perfectly. "There," she said. "What's so magical?"

"Don't you see?" Lady Laudine said, suddenly smiling broadly. "Oh, I made a joke! I said, 'Don't you see?' Get it?"

Luneta fought back the urge to step away from her suddenly incomprehensible hostess. "No, I don't."

"Of course you don't see!" Lady Laudine said, her eyes bright. "Look at your hand, Luneta!"

Luneta looked down, and something jolted in her stomach. She knew that she was holding her hand out before her, but it simply wasn't there. She moved her hand from side to side. There was nothing. No hand. No arm. She looked down at her legs and body. Nothing was there. "Where am I?" she managed to whisper.

"Now take the ring off so I can see you again," Lady Laudine said. Luneta felt for her finger and drew off the ring. At once she was visible again.

Luneta looked at the ring in the palm of her hand. "*Per deas!*" she said breathlessly. "A real magic ring."

Lady Laudine nodded quickly. "Isn't it exciting? The

only thing is, it's not very useful. I don't know how many times I've thought that this ring would be just the thing to wear with a certain gown, but of course it wouldn't be, because once you put it on, no one could see how well they went together—or anything else, for that matter."

Luneta, who had no trouble thinking of uses for such a ring, reluctantly put it back in the jewelry drawer. "Yes, of course," she murmured absently. Then she looked up, puzzled. "But Lady Laudine, how came you by such a thing?"

Lady Laudine's mouth opened slightly. "Didn't your mother tell you?"

"Tell me what?"

"Why, that I'm an enchantress!"

Luneta sat alone in her room, staring into the fire, her eyes glowing with excitement. To have arrived for an indefinite stay in this luxurious castle, where she would wear the finest clothes and most of all get to know a real enchantress, was more than she could ever have hoped for. It made her drab and relentlessly humdrum childhood at Orkney Hall seem like a dark and unpleasant dream. Her plain and ordinary mother couldn't have known that Lady Laudine was an enchantress, or she would never have let her come here for a visit. Luneta wondered if she could persuade Lady Laudine to teach her some magic.

A soft tap came from her bedchamber door, and Luneta said, "Come in."

The door opened, and Rhience's face appeared. "There you are!" he said with a sigh, stepping into the room. "What a rabbit warren this castle is!"

"Have you been looking for me?"

Rhience didn't answer for a moment. One eyebrow rose expressively as he surveyed Luneta's clothes. "I thought I was, my lady, but I was mistaken. Please, do you know where I might find the Lady Luneta?"

Luneta giggled and stood so as to show off her gown of rich purple silk. "Isn't it beautiful?"

Rhience frowned. "There's something missing," he said pensively. "Ah, yes, I have it!"

"What? What's missing?"

"An elderly lady to wear it."

"*Asinus*," Luneta replied without rancor. "I think it's gorgeous, but my mother would never let me wear such a thing."

"Ah," Rhience replied. "I gather that your mother is a woman of taste."

Luneta stuck out her tongue at him. "You're not funny, you know."

"That's all right," he replied with a grin. "You're funny enough for both of us. So, aside from your sartorial finery—"

"What's that mean?" Luneta demanded.

"From the Latin, of course. *Sartor*, tailor. Refers to clothes. Apart from that, are you comfortable here?"

"Oh, yes, Rhience. It's beyond everything great! Have you ever seen such a room?"

Rhience glanced around ruefully. "Not recently, I can tell you that."

Luneta's eyes widened as she remembered their different positions. "What about you? Where are you quartered?"

"Quartered is right. I have about a quarter of a room down in the servants' hall. But that's not so bad. It has a bed, after all. No, the bad part's the company down there. In those infernal regions of the castle, we are all ruled by Sir Stiffus Rumpus."

"That steward fellow that Lady Laudine's afraid of?"

Rhience nodded. "And for some reason he's taken a dislike to me. Even after I was so solicitous for his health!"

Luneta was almost afraid to ask. "What did you say to him?"

"I only mentioned that I'd known someone who walked the way he did, but once the boils on his bottom cleared up he was much better and didn't look quite so silly anymore."

"And he took offense at that? Imagine!"

"I even offered a remedy. You sit in a bucket filled

62

with mashed turnips for two days, and the boils go right away. Was he grateful? Not at all!"

"I can't help but think it might have been wise to hold your tongue," Luneta said. "Especially if he's such a tyrant."

Rhience's shoulders began to shake. "Yes, indeed. I should follow your example and be quiet and demure."

"I've never told anyone that he walked as if he had boils on his bottom, anyway," Luneta said tartly.

"No, instead you jabbed me in the bottom with a hairpin. Much more civil!"

"I was lancing a boil," Luneta replied with a sniff. "Seriously, are your quarters that bad?"

Rhience shook his head. "Nay, my lady. I'm comfortable enough, and after all, I'm free to leave when I want. It's your comfort that matters here. How do you think you'll get along with Lady Laudine?"

"Famously!" Luneta said. "Oh, and Rhience, you'll never believe it, but she's an enchantress!"

Rhience looked skeptical. "Are you sure? She doesn't seem to have the look."

"I promise you! She has a magical ring, and I've seen it work! I'll admit that I thought the same as you at first. I mean, the only enchantress I've ever even seen is Morgan Le Fay back at Camelot, but Lady Laudine certainly doesn't seem to be like her."

"Except for their beauty," Rhience commented. "Well, you appear to be pleased with this discovery, and that's what matters. I say, have you met the master of the castle yet?"

Luneta shook her head. "No. Lady Laudine said he spends his time in his own chambers, but it's a bit odd, isn't it? I mean, shouldn't the master of the castle greet a guest?" Rhience nodded. "Have you met him?" Luneta asked.

"Nay, and I've heard the same as you. He spends his time in his rooms mostly. None of the servants dislike him, but they fear him. When his bell rope rings, it's a wonder to see how they run to answer."

Luneta stifled a feeling of disquiet and said practically, "Well, if he stays in his own rooms he can be as fierce as he likes, and it won't make any difference to me."

"Very true," Rhience said, smiling. He stood. "I'd best be off. I'm supposed to perform at dinner tonight. Mayhaps we'll meet the elusive lord of the land then."

Rhience was right. Luneta got her first glimpse of the master of the castle, Sir Esclados, at dinner that night, and all she could do was stare at him with dismay. It wasn't that he was disfigured or ugly. In fact, considering the matter dispassionately, she admitted that Sir Esclados was quite handsome for someone of his age.

But that was the problem. Lady Laudine was not too many years older than Luneta herself—certainly no older than twenty-five—but Sir Esclados was fifty if he was a day. Trying to hide her revulsion, she cast her eyes to the floor and dipped a very proper curtsy to her host, but he barely glanced at her on his way to the great chair at the head of the table. "Yes, love," he growled to his wife. "Malvolus told me your visitor had arrived. Earlier than you said, ain't it?"

Lady Laudine blushed like fire and seemed unable to speak. Out of sympathy for her tongue-tied hostess, Luneta said, "Indeed, sir, I *am* early. I hope that it is not an inconvenience. An opportunity to make the journey sooner arose, and I had no time to send a courier ahead to warn you."

Now Sir Esclados turned his eyes to her, his gaze direct and stern. Luneta had a sense that he was unused to people speaking to him until he had spoken to them first. He looked at her in silence for a moment; then his gaze sharpened. "What's this, my love? Isn't that one of the dresses that I gave you?"

"Y-yes, my dear. I . . . I was sure you wouldn't mind if I let dear Luneta wear some of my . . . my clothes. Her own dresses were not . . . not . . ." Lady Laudine trailed off helplessly.

Sir Esclados scowled. He said, "They're your

65

dresses. You do what you like with them. It has nothing to do with me." From his tone, though, it was clear that he was displeased.

Lady Laudine embarked on a string of inarticulate apologies, but no one was listening. Sir Esclados had turned to his food, and Luneta's attention had been attracted by Rhience. The fool had been standing in a corner of the dining hall, waiting for his call to perform, but he had moved behind Sir Esclados and was clearly trying to convey a message to Luneta. He kept jerking his head at Sir Esclados and then pointing at himself, and his eyes were wide with dismay. Luneta had no idea what he was trying to communicate and was just beginning to wonder if she could excuse herself from the table for a moment to speak with him when dinner came to an abrupt end.

Since it was late spring, there was still light even at seven in the evening, but suddenly the room become almost as dark as night. Luneta barely had time to wonder what had happened when the most ear-splitting crash of thunder that she had ever heard shook the table and overturned some of the crystal goblets. That crash was followed immediately by a second, and rain began to fall in cascades against the roof. Sir Esclados leaped to his feet so sharply that his great chair fell over behind him, and he uttered a shocking oath, called for his steward, and ran from the room, followed by all the servants. Lady Laudine, Rhience, and Luneta were left alone in the great dining hall, but Lady Laudine hardly counted, because she had covered her ears and closed her eyes. Luneta turned her eyes to Rhience, who looked grim. Once he tried to speak, but his words were drowned out by the thunder.

It didn't matter, though. Luneta understood. This was the storm from the Storm Stone. Ywain had put the water into the basin and summoned the storm. Luneta also understood what Rhience had been trying to tell her. When he had pointed at Sir Esclados and then back at himself, he had been pointing at the scar on his neck. Sir Esclados was the red knight, the man who had defeated Rhience and made him vow to be a fool for a year, the man Ywain had come to challenge.

In a few minutes the storm passed, as quickly as it had come, and Luneta assumed what she hoped was an expression of curiosity and said to her hostess, "My goodness, Lady Laudine, do you often get such storms in these parts?"

Lady Laudine hesitated, but only for a moment. "I'm not really supposed to say, but I must tell you. This land is afflicted with a dreadful magic. Not far from here is a magical spring, and if people disturb it somehow or other it causes these storms to come up. They're just awful! And the magic also says that the master of the land is bound to this castle, never to leave so long as the storms might come, and he has to defend the land against these storms. That's where my husband went, you see. Whenever someone disturbs the spring, he has to go out and fight them and make them promise never to do so again. It's dreadful, I tell you." She shuddered. "I've never liked storms at all, and these storms are . . . they're horrible!" She rose shakily to her feet. "Please excuse me, Luneta. I must go and . . . oh, I am always so afraid when the storms come and Sir Esclados goes off to fight!"

Luneta patted Lady Laudine's hand reassuringly. "I understand. You go compose yourself. I'll find my own way back to my room."

Lady Laudine smiled gratefully, her eyes bright with tears, and then hurried away.

"Well," Luneta said, "this is a pretty mess."

Rhience began to smile, then to shake with silent laughter. "Ay, lass. You could say that. I should have known that your cousin wouldn't be able to wait long by the spring before trying it." He frowned with sudden concern. "I hope old Ywain is all right out there."

Luneta stood. "Don't you think we should go down and wait for Sir Esclados to come back? Ywain might get hurt and need our help."

Rhience nodded, and together they went down the long stairs to the main courtyard. There they watched a crowd of well-trained soldiers take positions just inside the front gate. Luneta looked but saw no sign of Lady Laudine. Minutes passed slowly. Some of the soldiers began to look at one another and shuffle their feet nervously.

"How long do fights like this usually last?" she whispered to Rhience.

"The longer it goes, the better for Ywain. It means he's holding his own. I can tell you that my own fight with Sir Esclados didn't take this long."

A lookout on the castle wall shouted something to the servants waiting below, and immediately two of them drew their short swords and climbed up on either side of the open gate.

"They're getting ready to cut the ropes holding up the portcullis," Rhience said. "That's odd. Usually you just lower the gate slowly. It looks as if they need to close it in a hurry."

"What does that mean?" Luneta asked.

"I scarcely dare think it, my lady," Rhience said.

"What? Scarcely dare think what?"

"It almost seems as if Sir Esclados must be running back to the castle and they need to close the gate behind him, because—"

"Because he's being chased?" Luneta demanded. Rhience nodded, and then Luneta heard the pounding of horses' hooves approaching from across the plain.

Everything happened at once. A great horse ridden by a knight in red armor—Sir Esclados, Luneta supposed—burst into the castle with a clatter and then a bang as the red knight fell heavily from the horse's saddle onto the flagstones. Luneta saw blood spattering the stones, but she had no time to look because the servants with the knives had cut the ropes holding up the great iron portcullis and with a shriek it began to fall. Just before it fell, though, a second horse leaped through the gate. Luneta recognized Ywain's armor and horse, and they nearly didn't make it. When the portcullis crashed down, it left a long gash in Ywain's horse's flank. The horse stumbled, and Ywain was thrown violently to one side, bouncing against a wall. The horse scrambled to its feet—which meant it had no broken bones—but it was maddened with pain from its wound, and it joined Sir Esclados's mount in rearing and slashing with its front hooves at anyone who came within range. Servants dodged and screamed and called for help. One of them had managed to pull Sir Esclados's helm from his head, and Luneta's stomach felt sick and empty at the gory sight that was there. Then Rhience plucked her sleeve.

"Come on, my lady, we've got to get Ywain."

Luneta looked blankly at Rhience for a second, then nodded and ran with the fool to where Ywain had been thrown by his falling horse. By the time they arrived, he had already risen to his feet and was holding his sword out before him in readiness.

"Halt!" he called to them, seeing them approach. Then his sword lowered. "Luneta? Rhience? Oh, Lud, you don't mean to tell me that the red knight is . . . of course he is. He's your host! Well," he said, straightening up and sheathing his sword, "that settles it. I won't finish him off, after all."

"From the looks of it, I'd say you already had," Rhience commented.

"Think so? I couldn't be sure with his helm on. But I won't fight him any more now. To be honest, I wasn't sure I was going to, anyway. A bit awkward to attack someone lying in a courtyard surrounded by people tending his wounds, you know."

"Ywain," Luneta said impatiently, "will you please shut up and think for a moment? What are you going to do now?"

"I just told you. I'll not continue the fight."

"And then what? Ywain, what are you going to do if he dies?"

Ywain lifted his chin. "He attacked me first."

Luneta nearly screamed with impatience. "Who cares, Ywain? Do you see all those soldiers gathered around Sir Esclados? They're busy with him right now, but what do you think they'll do to you once they notice you here?"

Ywain lifted the visor on his helm and looked out at

Luneta and Rhience. "You think they'll be angry?" They both nodded. "I see," Ywain said. "Will they attack?" They nodded again. Ywain set his lips and allowed his visor to drop. "I'm not afraid."

"You should be," Rhience said. "I hear that Sir Esclados has more than fifty men here."

Ywain raised his visor again. "You think I should leave?"

Luneta sighed with frustration, and Rhience said, "That would be splendid. Do you mind telling me how you intend to do it?"

At last the full significance of his situation seemed to dawn on Ywain. "Oh, yes. The gate's closed, isn't it? Is there another way out?"

"Probably," Luneta said, "but I don't know it. We've only been here one afternoon."

"What should I do, then?"

"I think you should hide," Luneta said, trying to keep her voice calm.

"Hide?" Ywain repeated distastefully.

"Or you could die," Rhience pointed out.

Ywain hesitated, but as it happened, at that very moment a soldier called out, "Send for the rest of the guard!" and Ywain said, "All right. Where should I go?"

Neither Luneta nor Rhience had any immediate ideas for hiding places, but they dragged Ywain around a wall and into the first door they could find. Out of the courtyard was a good first step. And by the time they had Ywain out of immediate danger, Luneta had thought of exactly where to hide Ywain.

"Shh," Luneta said, leading Ywain by the hand down the dark halls of the castle. "I'm nearly sure that this is the right corridor. We're looking for a great door with two candles in sconces on either side of it."

From behind Ywain, Rhience said, "I still think we should have gone down to the cellars, if we could find them. Maybe we could cover him with stove wood or something."

"That doesn't sound very comfortable," Ywain said pleasantly. For one whose life was in danger he seemed amazingly cheerful.

"No, the cellars won't do," Luneta said. "Think for a minute. Even if no one saw Ywain fall off his horse—"

"I didn't fall; I was thrown."

"Be quiet. Even if they didn't see Ywain, they have his horse and they'll know that he's somewhere in the castle. Before long we'll have search parties, and the cellar is the first place they'll look."

"Maybe," Rhience said, "but isn't this the hall where the bedchambers are? Do you plan to hide him in your wardrobe?"

"That sounds worse than the stove wood," Ywain said.

"Here it is. Now, you two wait in the shadows while

73

I make sure it's empty." Luneta hurried to the door and knocked. After a moment of silence, she pushed it open and looked in at Lady Laudine's bedchamber. No one was there. "Come on!" Luneta called to the others. "In here!"

They entered the room and Ywain whistled. "This is your room? They treat their guests well here, don't they?"

"No, it's not mine."

"You want Ywain to hide in a lady's bedchamber?" Rhience asked with exasperation. "Of all the witless—"

"You know, it's not such a bad idea," Ywain said. "Last place they would look, and all that. But I don't see any very good hiding places."

"I don't care where you hide," Luneta said sharply. "We're only here to get something. Take off your gauntlet."

"My gauntlet?"

"Yes, your gauntlet. That thing on your hand. Take it off." Luneta opened Lady Laudine's jewelry drawer and began rummaging among the gems.

"I hear voices down the corridor," Rhience said. "Can you crawl under the bed in your armor?"

"Here!" Luneta said, taking up the faery ring triumphantly. She turned to Ywain, who had just finished taking off his armored gauntlet. "Put this ring on, and make it fast!"

"Put on this ring?"

"Do it now!" Luneta snapped, and Ywain took the ring from her and put it on his finger. At once he disappeared.

"By all the gods," whispered Rhience.

Ywain's voice came from the air. "And now, where should I hide?"

"You *are* hidden," Luneta said, taking a deep breath. "It's a magic ring. You're invisible."

For a moment there was only silence. Luneta supposed that Ywain was confirming Luneta's words. At last his disembodied voice said, "Lud!"

"All right," Rhience said with an exaggerated sniff. "I'll grant you that this is a *little* bit better than the stove wood idea." The voices in the hallway were closer. "And just in time, too."

The door to the bedchamber burst open and Malvolus the steward and five armed soldiers rushed into the room. "Where is he?" Malvolus snapped at them.

"Where is who?" Luneta replied.

"One of the soldiers saw you running away with the knight who has slain my master!"

"Is Sir Esclados dead?" Luneta demanded.

"As if you didn't know. You probably planned the whole thing, the three of you."

Luneta thought quickly. "Your soldier may have seen this knight running the same way we did, but as you can plainly see, there is no knight here."

75

"You've hidden him!" Malvolus snapped. He waved to the soldiers. "Look under the bed! In the wardrobe!"

"Be careful!" shrieked Rhience, in a voice of abject horror. "You almost stepped on my imaginary friend!" He looked earnestly at Malvolus. "His name is Asinus, and nobody can see him but me."

"Begone, knave! I've no time for your foolishness!" Malvolus roared furiously.

"Very well, I'll tell Asinus to *step back into a corner where no one can accidentally bump into him,* shall I?" Rhience said this very slowly and clearly.

Luneta heard the faintest scrape of metal beside her, and she guessed that Ywain was taking Rhience's advice. Malvolus wasn't through with them yet, though. While his soldiers poked their swords and spears under the bed and behind hanging tapestries, he scowled at Luneta and demanded, "If you weren't hiding the knight, then why are you here?"

"I was looking for my lady, of course. Do you know where she is?"

Malvolus glowered at her. "With her husband, I would imagine!"

Luneta met his gaze without flinching. "Then I should go to her at once! Come, Rhience!"

"Should my imaginary friend stay here?"

"Yes, of course," Luneta said. When Rhience started

76

to leave, Malvolus glared at him with pure hatred, and Rhience hesitated, but Luneta grabbed his hand and pulled him out into the hallway. "I see what you mean," she said, once they were well away from the door. "The steward doesn't seem to care for you, does he?"

"No, he doesn't. It's very strange. Do you suppose he had an unhappy childhood?" Rhience replied.

"I certainly hope so," Luneta said. "Look, we need to figure out what to do next."

"I should think it would be easy from here," Rhience replied. "We wait until everyone is done searching—which may be several hours. Then, once they've given up, we can smuggle Ywain out during the night. I wonder if his horse becomes invisible when he gets on it. After all, his armor disappeared along with the rest of him."

"But he has to leave the ring here," Luneta pointed out. "It's not his—or mine, for that matter."

"Hmm. Well, that's awkward, but it can still be done. We just have to get him away and over a hill before he returns the ring to you."

"But how—?"

Rhience patted her hand. "We don't know yet, my lady. But we can't do anything until they've stopped looking for him anyway, so there's no rush. Now, don't you think that we should find Lady Laudine?"

The next several hours were as trying as any that Luneta had known. She had never herself experienced the death of someone close to her, so she didn't know exactly how it would affect her, but she still couldn't help thinking that she would deal with it better than did Lady Laudine. By the time Luneta found her—in the small chamber where the soldiers had carried the body of Sir Esclados—Lady Laudine was already stiff with hysterical grief. She sobbed and screamed and fluttered her hand in front of her breast in a gesture that meant nothing to anyone but herself. She would not respond to any of the ladies-in-waiting who stood around her offering timid and barely audible words of consolation. There were a few manservants standing over Sir Esclados's body, and two of them were taking off their dead master's armor one piece at a time, but even they were distracted by Lady Laudine's display of inconsolable sorrow.

Clearly, the first thing to do was to get Lady Laudine away from the body, and Luneta felt a stir of frustration that none of the attendants had had the wit to remove her from the bloody corpse. "Come, my lady," Luneta said firmly, nearly shouting so as to be heard above Lady Laudine's wails, "you should leave this room now."

Luneta's voice caught Lady Laudine's attention, and

her eyes focused on Luneta. "Oh, Luneta! He's dead! He's dead!"

"I can see that," Luneta said firmly, although she was carefully not looking at the form on the bed behind her, "and I'm very sorry, but staying here won't bring him back. Come with me and let Sir Esclados's servants attend to him."

"No, no, he wouldn't want me to leave!"

Luneta started to retort that she doubted that Sir Esclados cared one way or the other now, but she caught herself in time and replied instead, "I am sure that he would want you to take care of yourself, too. My lady, it is very sad, and of course you must grieve, but let me take you away from here."

Luneta kept her voice firm and even and practical, and her tone as much as her words seemed to calm Lady Laudine. She looked forlornly up into Luneta's face and said, "Oh, Luneta, you're just like your mother."

"I most certainly am not!" Luneta exclaimed angrily.

"Have you no *feeling?*" Lady Laudine asked forlornly. "I've lost my love, my heart, my being this day!"

Luneta could only stare, quite dumbfounded. Was that really what she felt for the surly Sir Esclados? Fortunately, Rhience, who had come in behind Luneta, chose that moment to speak. "We understand, my lady. But you must respect his wishes in death as well as in life." Lady Laudine burst into another gust of sobs at the word "death," but Rhience continued. "Would you have disturbed Sir Esclados's privacy when he was alive?" Lady Laudine's eyes widened, and Rhience pursued his advantage. "Then you should allow him time alone now, don't you think? Come away now."

With Luneta at one hand and Rhience at the other, Lady Laudine slowly rose from her chair and took a step toward the door. Then she stopped. Luneta held her breath, but then one of the footmen, a thick middle-aged man that Luneta had seen at dinner, stepped between Lady Laudine and the body and said, "I am sure that they are right, my lady. You may trust us to care for your lord, and if we need you, you may be sure that we will call."

Lady Laudine nodded. "Thank you, Rufus. I will leave you now."

Luneta looked over her shoulder at the servant, Rufus, and they mouthed "Thank you" to each other at the same moment. Then she and Rhience had Lady Laudine out of the room and into the fresh air of the courtyard.

For nearly three hours Luneta and Rhience followed the restless Lady Laudine, who seemed, once she had been dislodged from the chair beside her husband, to be unable to stop anywhere for longer than a few minutes. She wept at the least provocation, and since every chair that her husband had ever sat in seemed to qualify

80

as provocation, she cried nearly without stopping. At last, she appeared to have exhausted both her strength and her supply of tears, and the two were able to conduct her to her own room. Rhience waited in the hall while Luneta took Lady Laudine in and bundled her, fully clothed, under the covers of her bed. Luneta couldn't help wondering if Ywain was still in the room, but she obviously couldn't call to him.

Lady Laudine was asleep in seconds. Luneta stood and watched for a moment, then whispered, "Ywain? Come out into the hall. We'll get you out of here."

But no one came. She and Rhience stood in the corridor for an hour, waiting for Ywain to appear and talking in low tones about ways to smuggle him out of the castle, but until he showed up nothing could happen. At last, after midnight, Luneta could not hold her eyes open any longer and went to bed.

When she awoke, Ywain was at the foot of her bed. "Oh, there you are," Luneta said. "Thank heavens. We've got to get you out of the castle."

Ywain ignored her. His eyes held a distant, dreamy look—even worse than when he had been lost in visions of knightly glory. "I've seen an angel," he said.

"An angel?"

"The most perfect creature in all the world! Pray, who is she?"

"An angel?" Luneta repeated.

"The woman you led to the bedchamber last night! Who is she?"

Luneta swallowed and asked warily, "Why do you want to know?"

Ywain sighed. "I love her," he said.

IV

THE WOOING OF
LADY LAUDINE

Luneta sat up, rubbed her eyes with her hands, and said, "I beg your pardon?"

"I'm in love," Ywain said. "As soon as I saw her, I knew. At first I thought I was dreaming, because so much beauty could hardly be real, but then I heard her crying, and I knew that all my dreams had come true. Pray, why was she crying?"

Luneta stared at him, then answered slowly, "That would be because her husband just died."

"The poor thing!" Ywain said. Then he brightened. "Then . . . she's not married?"

"Not currently, no," Luneta said dryly.

Ywain closed his eyes rapturously. "I stood by her bed for hours, watching her sleep, longing to take her in my arms."

"You didn't, did you?" Luneta demanded quickly. She was suddenly glad that she hadn't bothered removing Lady Laudine's dress before putting her in bed.

"No," Ywain replied. "I may have been lost in a dream, but I had enough of my wits to realize that it might be uncomfortable for her to wake up in the arms of an invisible man."

"Good thinking," Luneta replied.

"So her husband died," Ywain said tenderly. "From her tears, I see that she loved her husband very much."

Luneta didn't answer. She was still wondering about that herself.

"How did he die?" Ywain asked.

For someone who wasn't at all stupid, Ywain could say some very dense things. Luneta took a breath, then said bluntly, "You killed him."

Ywain's eyes grew still, and Luneta watched as comprehension, then despair, flickered across his countenance. "Of course," he said. "That was your Lady Laudine."

Luneta rose from her bed, pulling a gown over her underdress and averting her eyes from her cousin to give him a moment to compose himself. "I'm sorry," she said at last, "but, as you see, you've fallen in love with the one woman who can never love you back."

"It doesn't change anything," Ywain said. "I still love her and always will."

"Ywain—"

"But why shouldn't she love me one day?" he demanded suddenly. "I didn't do anything dishonorable. Her husband attacked me, and I fought back."

Luneta decided not to point out that he had incited the attack to start with. Neither was it the time to suggest that it didn't matter a great deal to Lady Laudine whether Ywain had killed Sir Esclados honorably or dishonorably. Arguing would accomplish nothing, and her mind was bent on a different task: persuading Ywain to leave the castle.

"Perhaps you're right," Luneta said. "In time, once she is over the shock and grief, she may be interested in marrying again. What you should do is leave now, and wait for her to finish her bereavement. Then you could come back, you know, to visit me, your cousin, and I could introduce you. How does that sound?"

"I can't leave the woman I love while she's in such distress."

"Distress that you caused, Ywain!"

"All the more reason that I should stay."

"And do what? Look, Ywain, your hands are tied. If you show yourself, you'll be killed by the guards, and if you stay invisible, you can't do anything for her. As you yourself said, she might not find an invisible knight comforting. In fact," Luneta added, with a flash of inspiration, "if you touch her or make any sound or do anything at all while you're invisible, she'll probably think it's her husband's ghost, which might drive her completely mad. You don't want that, do you?"

Ywain pursed his lips thoughtfully.

"So you see: the only thing for you to do is to go away for a while. You can come back later, when she will be more willing to receive visitors. And besides, once you're away, you might decide that you don't love her as much as you thought."

Luneta knew this last statement was a mistake as soon as she said it. Ywain's face tightened, then set in a mulish expression, then disappeared along with the rest of him as he put Lady Laudine's ring back on. From the empty space, his voice said firmly, "I will not change, and I will not leave." Then Luneta's door opened and closed.

Luneta was thoroughly disgusted with Ywain, but even more with herself. She felt sure that until her ill-judged suggestion that his love might fade, Ywain had been about to yield to her persuasion, and she had no one to blame but herself. Her frustration was not helped by Rhience's response upon being told the new state of affairs.

"You're joking," he said, his eyes widening and his lips parting in a huge smile. "The poor sod's gone and fallen in love with her?"

"It isn't funny, Rhience," Luneta said sternly.

"Then I don't know what *is* funny! Come, Luneta, it's a rollicking farce!"

"Maybe to you, but it's madness for Ywain. As long as he stays here, he's in danger. You don't think that dreadful Malvolus will stop looking for him, do you?"

Rhience's smile faded slightly. "Unlikely," he said. "I've been checking the doors and gates, and Sir Stiffus Rumpus has guards at every one, night and day. It was going to be hard enough to get Ywain out when he *wanted* to leave. As it is, I don't see what else to do but wait and hope that Ywain stays out from underfoot."

Luneta had to be satisfied with this, and before long she had little time to worry about Ywain anyway. Lady Laudine awoke and, spurning the comfort of all her elegant ladies-in-waiting, she sent for Luneta to hold her hand as she wept for her husband. All that long day, Lady Laudine cried and refused to eat and sniffed at a vinaigrette and told Luneta her memories of Sir Esclados.

"I always knew that I was safe with dear Esclados," she said as they sat together in her room that evening. "You're too young to realize it yourself, but it's such a comfort to belong to a man who will care for you. I never had to worry about anything once we were wed. But now I . . . now I . . ."

Luneta had already learned to recognize the signs of an impending gust of tears, and when Lady Laudine trailed off, Luneta handed her a clean handkerchief. Lady Laudine wiped her eyes and sniffed into the cloth for a moment, then continued, "And he was so caring, so tender, so concerned for my comfort." Luneta couldn't help frowning at this, but she said nothing. Lady Laudine sighed deeply and said, "In all our time together, I never had a harsh word from him."

It was all Luneta could do not to point out that she'd met Sir Esclados only once, for a few minutes, and she had heard several harsh words from him, but with an effort she kept even this observation to herself. Instead she tried to change the subject. "How . . . how did the two of you meet?"

Lady Laudine smiled tearfully. "I loved him as soon as I saw him," she said. "And he me. It was just like a French minstrel's romance! He invited my parents and me for a visit—he had some business with my father—and at dinner I could hardly keep my eyes from him. He was so strong, so manly. I was no child—indeed, I was nearly an old maid, being quite twenty years old—but whenever he looked at me, I'm afraid that I blushed like a little girl fresh out of the nursery." She sighed again. "He was my first love."

Luneta blinked with surprise. It seemed very odd to her to find that Lady Laudine had been twenty years old and still unmarried. Luneta knew of girls who had been married at fourteen, or even younger. "Your first love?" Luneta asked. "But with your beauty, you must have had dozens of young men at your feet."

Lady Laudine shook her head. "Indeed I did not. But I admit that I was an awkward girl and not very attractive when I was younger."

"Why then, you improved remarkably," Luneta said. "For I don't believe I've ever seen a more beautiful woman than you." Luneta didn't enjoy saying this, feeling that this was not the time to talk about superficial things, but she had already discovered that the subject of Laudine's personal appearance was one of the few things that could distract Lady Laudine from her grief. It worked, and Lady Laudine brightened perceptibly and, for a time, abandoned her imaginary memories of her kind husband.

Luneta thought periodically about Ywain, wondering if he were perhaps looking over her shoulder or standing in a corner listening, but she heard no sound and saw no sign of him. Neither did the steward, Malvolus, who continued his vengeful search for his master's killer for three full days. On the second day, a guard discovered Ywain's armor under a pile of straw in the stables, and for several days the steward went about staring suspiciously at all the men of the castle, imagining that his master's slayer was still in the castle in disguise. He was especially suspicious of Rhience, and if the fool hadn't been with Lady Laudine at the time that Sir Esclados left the castle, he would have been locked up without hesitation. Malvolus grew more dictatorial daily, but the one time that Luneta brought up the matter to Lady Laudine, suggesting that now that she was sole mistress of the castle she could get rid of her husband's steward, Lady Laudine dissolved in tears and begged Luneta, "Please, don't ask me to think of such things now! You can't understand how comforting it is for me to know that Malvolus is running the castle just as my dear husband would want."

Only when Lady Laudine was asleep did Luneta have any time to herself, and at these times she usually sought out Rhience. On the evening of the second day after Sir Esclados's death, she found him reading in the sitting room where Lady Laudine had first received them, and sank exhaustedly into a chair beside him. "Any sign of my cousin?" she asked.

"Maybe," Rhience said. "I heard a kitchen maid complaining about some missing food. She had just set it down for a moment, and then it was gone."

"He's not starving, anyway," Luneta said. She closed her eyes wearily.

"Have you put your child down for the night?" Rhience asked.

Luneta allowed one side of her mouth to smile, and she replied without opening her eyes. "If you mean

Laudine, yes. And if I don't go back to my own room, then maybe no one will be able to find me to fetch me to her when she rings her bell rope."

"Is it so bad?"

Luneta shrugged. "I try to remind myself that she really is suffering. Her husband died just two days ago, and that would be a shock for anyone. And I must admit, she seems to have really loved her husband."

"Is that what you think?"

Luneta opened her eyes at this. "What else would explain all this moping around and crying all over the castle? Anyway, she told me so. It was love at first sight for both of them. Her father was visiting him on business, and they met at dinner and fell in love at once."

Rhience began to shake with laughter. "She told you that?"

"Yes."

"Did she, by any chance, tell you what the business was that Sir Esclados had with her father?"

"No. I doubt she even knew. She doesn't seem much interested in business."

"She'd have been interested in this. Their business was to arrange her dowry."

"What?"

"No joke, Luneta. Sir Esclados and Lady Laudine's father had this marriage all arranged before they even met."

Luneta stared at Rhience for a moment, then

shrugged again. "I suppose you had this from the servants, and they usually know, but it doesn't mean that they didn't fall in love."

"Did you see any sign of love at dinner the night Sir Esclados died?"

Luneta shook her head. "No, I didn't. He didn't look as if he cared for her much, and as for her, she was terrified of him. In fact, when she first started talking about how much they loved each other, and how gentle and considerate he was, I could hardly believe she meant the same fellow I met, but I can't deny that she's pretty desperately broken up by his death."

"Maybe he's easier to love dead than he was alive," Rhience commented. "I've known people like that." He looked thoughtful for a moment, then added, "In fact, I know some people I'd be willing to try it on. Take Malvolus, for instance. I find him very difficult to love just now, but I'm willing to give it a try, even if it means that I have to kill him first."

"Yes, I know," Luneta said, grinning ruefully. "A real piece of rotten fruit, isn't he? I tried to persuade Laudine to turn him out, but she won't hear of it. She says he's a comfort."

Rhience shook his head sadly. "She's quite mad. Malvolus a comfort?"

Luneta nodded. "But then, she also says that she never heard Sir Esclados utter a harsh word."

Rhience whistled softly. "Let's hope she recovers her wits after the funeral tomorrow."

Sir Esclados's funeral did not seem to help Laudine, though. The service itself took almost three hours, mostly because it was interrupted so often. No fewer than four times the priest had to halt the proceedings until Laudine had finished a hysterical outburst. At one point, she even had to be restrained from throwing herself on her husband's body, and Luneta came very near to slapping her hostess. Naturally, most of the people in the county were at the funeral of their feudal lord, and from the rapt expressions on their faces, Luneta could tell that they were enjoying the spectacle of Laudine's displays very much indeed. It angered Luneta that Laudine should be so oblivious of others, but grabbing her and shaking some sense into her would hardly help matters, so Luneta contented herself with holding her chin high and pretending to ignore everything except the Latin service that the harried-looking priest kept trying to complete.

When it was over and Laudine had gone to lie down, Luneta sought out Rhience to unburden herself, but when she found him, he refused to enter into her disgust.

"I think it was a splendid service," he announced, interrupting her furious tirade. "Marvelous!"

"You're mad! With all that shrieking and wailing? I daresay half the people forgot Sir Esclados was even there."

"Exactly! I cannot sufficiently describe my admiration for her."

"For Laudine?"

"Of course! As a performer myself, I—"

"Oh, shut up!" Luneta snapped.

"Never have I seen someone rise to an occasion as she did. Why, the audience was spellbound!"

"Yes, if it had been her intention to put on a show." Rhience only raised one eyebrow, and Luneta said, "I think I know Laudine better than you do, and I'm sure she had no such idea in her mind."

"Or any other, for that matter," Rhience contributed.

"Look, Laudine may not be the cleverest—"

"I think she's adorable."

Luneta stared at Rhience for a moment before it occurred to her that his lips had not moved. Rhience glanced around, then grinned and said, "How nice to hear from you, Ywain. So sorry I didn't greet you properly when you came in—unless you were here before me, of course."

"Poor Lady Laudine," Ywain's voice said. "She's so frail, so tender."

"But she has stamina," Rhience pointed out. "You have to give her that. Why, she must have cried for—"

"How much I longed to take her under my arm and comfort her. She needs someone to protect her."

"Look, Ywain," Rhience said suddenly. "I don't suppose you could take off the ring while we talk, could you? It's a bit disconcerting having a conversation with the air."

A moment later, Ywain appeared. He was wearing a sober suit of black velvet.

"You're wearing mourning?" Rhience asked.

"But of course," Ywain replied. "The woman I love is grieving. How could it be otherwise?"

"Even though you're the one who brought about her grief?" Luneta asked.

"It's not as if anyone will see you," Rhience added. "Where'd you get the black suit anyway?"

"Sir Esclados's things, of course. We're nearly the same size."

"This is getting strange," Rhience complained.

"Well, I couldn't keep wearing my armor. It clinks when I walk. And you wouldn't expect me to run around naked, would you?"

"Why not? You're invisible."

"It's cold," Ywain replied practically. "That's why not."

Luneta broke in impatiently. "I don't care where you got your clothes. The important thing is that we've found you again and can get you out of the castle."

"But I told you. I don't want to leave."

Luneta ignored him. "Rhience, do you know where they've put Ywain's armor?"

"Sure. It's in Malvolus's rooms."

"It doesn't matter," Ywain said. "I'm not leaving."

"Look, Ywain, you saw how grief-stricken Laudine was at the funeral. Can't you see how hopeless it is for you to stay? She'll never consider marrying again."

"She doesn't mourn for Sir Esclados," Ywain said simply.

"She doesn't? What do you call all that at the funeral?"

"She's frightened," Ywain said with confidence. "I've been watching her."

"You have, have you?" Luneta said suspiciously.

"Not when she's dressing or anything like that, if that's what you're thinking," Ywain said. "What sort of a cad do you think I am, taking advantage of her own ring to spy on her?" Luneta looked away, conscious of a sense of relief. She *had* wondered, when helping Laudine to undress, if Ywain were in the room. Ywain continued, "She doesn't act like someone who's lost a loved one. She's only afraid of what's going to happen to her now."

"Are you telling me that all that ghastly display at the funeral was fear?" Luneta demanded impatiently.

"Yes."

Then, to Luneta's surprise, Rhience came to Ywain's support. "Much as I hate to agree with our friend here, he's partly right. I too think that most of our lady's tears come from self-pity."

96

"Not self-pity. Fear for her future."

"As you wish," Rhience said agreeably. "That doesn't change the fact that you're wasting your time here. You can't show yourself, and you can't court the lady while you're invisible."

"That's why I came to find you."

"Why?" Luneta asked.

"Well, I couldn't help but notice that you've become her chief companion," Ywain said. "She trusts you."

"And?" Luneta asked.

"Do you think you could put in a good word for me?"

Luneta and Rhience looked at each other. "He's mad," she said.

"*Insanus*," Rhience said, nodding agreement.

Ywain shrugged. "Thought it wouldn't hurt to ask," he said. Then he was gone.

Laudine continued to live a life of ostentatious mourning, and Luneta continued to play the role of chief comforter, but she couldn't help remembering what Ywain and Rhience had said and wondering if they were right. Could all this excessive display of grief be prompted by fear (or, as Rhience would have it, self-pity)? Luneta began to notice that Laudine's most frequently expressed sentiment was "What's going to happen to me now?" Luneta adjusted her words of comfort accordingly, stressing how loyal the castle servants were to her and how well they would take care of her. These assurances seemed to help, but not a great deal. Finally, one day, Luneta asked Rhience to see if he could help her. He arrived escorted by two manservants, but Laudine gave him one glance and turned away.

"No," she said faintly. "Take the fool away."

Rhience turned to the two men. "Do you hear her? Take the lady away."

The men looked hesitantly at each other, and Laudine said, "I suppose you mean that I'm a fool, but if that's the best you can do, I'm afraid that your wit has dried up."

"Very true, my lady," Rhience replied at once. "But that's easy enough to fix." He looked at the servants again. "Ale, my good men. That's what we need."

"Please go away," Laudine said. "This is no time for foolishness."

"Exactly what I say, my lady. It is time to put away foolishness."

Laudine looked out the window, and Luneta said to Rhience, "This is your idea of cheering her up? Calling her a fool?"

"Do you think I'm joking? Come, let us see which one is the fool. But I shall have to catechize you. I shall ask, and you answer." Laudine didn't speak, but she hesitated, and that was enough for Rhience. "Tell me, my lady, why do you mourn?"

"I mourn for my dead husband, fool."

"Ah, yes. And this is because his soul is in hell, is it not?"

Laudine looked up sharply. "What?"

"I think Sir Esclados is in hell."

"I know his soul is in heaven, fool!"

"Why, if that's so, then the more fool are you to mourn for him. Take away the fool, gentlemen."

Laudine's perfect face contracted in an angry scowl, and Luneta quickly guided Rhience to the door. "Do you know, Rhience, I'm not sure that this was such a good idea."

"She stopped crying, didn't she?"

"And you think angry is better?"

"It's a change, anyway," Rhience pointed out. "Variety's good, isn't it?"

By this time Luneta had Rhience and the servants out the door. She said, "I'm about to find out, I think."

As she closed the door between them, she heard Rhience saying to the gentlemen, "Now, about that ale. You heard your mistress say I was dry, didn't you?"

Luneta turned slowly back to face Laudine, an apology on her lips, but Laudine's face no longer looked angry but rather was thoughtful. "Luneta?"

"Yes, my lady?"

"Do you think I mourn too much?"

Luneta stared at the stone floor between them. "I cannot say, my lady."

"It's just that . . . I'm so afraid." Luneta looked up quickly and for a moment saw the most genuine expression she had ever seen on Laudine's face. She looked like a little girl.

"For years, I was sure I would spend my life alone. My father was not wealthy, and no one wanted to marry me. By the time Sir Esclados came into my life, I was at my last prayers."

This was unfathomable to Luneta. Laudine was impossibly beautiful. How could no one have wanted to marry her? Ywain had fallen in love with her at one look, hadn't he? But Luneta held her tongue, and Laudine continued.

"My father was old, and he had no sons. When he died, my cousin would inherit our home, and then I would have nothing. Then my father grew ill. I came back to his bedside."

"Came back?" Luneta asked.

Laudine faltered. "I had been away, visiting . . . visiting some ladies. Like you are visiting me. That was where I met your mother, in fact. But I had to leave early because of my father's illness. Then, from nowhere, Sir Esclados invited us to visit and asked for my hand, and all my fears were taken away." Laudine twisted a handkerchief in her hands. "I know you think . . . thought . . . that he was too old for me. But that didn't bother me. Really, it didn't. He was a great knight, and with him I was safe at last. Even when my father died, I knew I would be cared for. And now . . . now I don't know what will happen."

Laudine began to cry, but with quiet, heartfelt sobs instead of the dramatic keening and wailing of the past week. Luneta's throat tightened, and she repented of all the irritation she had felt toward her hostess. "Laudine?" she asked tentatively. "What if . . . what if you were to remarry?"

Laudine looked up, her eyes bright with tears. "How could I? I have . . . I have thought of it, but it's impossible. Remember the magic of the Storm Stone? I'm now the mistress of this castle, and I must remain here until I wither away, an old maid."

"Don't do it," Rhience said. They were alone in the sitting room that evening. "Don't get involved."

"But Ywain is right. She needs someone to take care of her."

"Let her learn to take care of herself. Look, if you'd been married to Sir Esclados and he died, would you be in a big rush to find someone else to take his place?"

"It's a pointless question," Luneta replied promptly, "because I never would have married Sir Esclados to begin with."

"That's just the point! She needs to stop asking other people to do everything for her, or she'll end up in the same basket as before."

"Ywain's not like Sir Esclados."

"Don't be deceived, lass. Any man who marries a simpering, helpless ninny like Laudine can end up like Sir Esclados."

"Even you?" Luneta asked.

"It's a pointless question," Rhience replied with a sniff. "Because I wouldn't marry a simpering ninny like that to begin with."

"Perhaps Laudine is a little bit too helpless . . . all right, so she is. She's not going to change now. The best thing for her will be to marry again to someone who will love her as Sir Esclados didn't."

"And who are you to decide what's best for Laudine?" Rhience demanded.

"It's not just what I think; it's what she thinks, too. Look, Rhience, I know that she can be irritating and silly, but she has a good heart, and I like her. And when you like someone, you can't just let them suffer when there's something you can do to help."

Rhience shook his head sadly. "I still think it's wrong to meddle, but I'm not going to convince you, am I?"

"No."

He sighed. "My only consolation is that you won't be

successful. I know you cherish the illusion that you can get anyone to do anything you want, but remember that Ywain is the man who killed her husband. No one could bring those two together, not even you."

The next morning, when Luneta went to Laudine's room, she took a sword with her. Laudine stared at her. "What are you doing with that sword?"

"I thought that if you were feeling up to it later, I could give you some pointers."

"Some what?"

"I've never actually been trained in swordplay myself, but as you know, my uncle is Sir Gawain, one of the greatest knights in England, and I've watched him practicing. I should be able to get you started. Later on, of course, you'll need to spar with some of your soldiers. Do you know if any of them have been trained with the broadsword?"

"I . . . no . . ."

"So many soldiers these days are taught only how to use the pike and the longbow."

"What are you talking about, Luneta?"

"Pikes and longbows. Pikes are these long spears—"

"But why? I have no interest in weapons."

Luneta looked thoughtful. "Hmm. That makes it harder." Then she shrugged. "But it doesn't change anything, does it? You'll just have to develop an interest."

"But why? Why would I ever want to know about weapons?"

Luneta stared at her with exaggerated astonishment. "Don't tell me it hasn't occurred to you!"

"What hasn't occurred to me?"

"What will happen when the next person disturbs the Storm Stone, of course!" Laudine's face went blank, and Luneta pressed on ruthlessly. "You told me yourself that you're now the mistress of this castle. Well, aren't you bound by oath and custom and magic to defend the land against those who disturb that stone? Here, let me show you how to hold the sword."

"Luneta! You don't mean that you think . . . . but *I* can't defend the stone!"

"Not if you won't learn how to hold a sword. Now, are you right- or left-handed?"

"No! I'll send one of the soldiers out if something happens."

Luneta shook her head sadly. "If that were possible, don't you think that Sir Esclados would have done it? No, it's got to be you."

"It can't be!"

"But it is. There's no point in arguing about it. You may not know this, but my father is also the king's sheriff in Orkney, and so I know something about the law. If there's no heir, then the rights and duties—this is what you would call a duty—pass to the widow."

Laudine began to cry, but Luneta set her jaw against her welling sympathy and said, "Come on, Laudine. Maybe it won't be so bad. For all you know, the next knight who comes along may be a bad swordsman."

"It's impossible! I can't do it!"

Luneta sighed. "It seems as if everything is impossible to you. Just yesterday you told me it was impossible for you to marry again." She broke off and added thoughtfully, "Of course, if you did that, we could avoid all this, couldn't we? Oh, well, never mind. Perhaps it's too soon to begin with the sword. I'll put it away for now. We'll start sparring tomorrow."

Luneta left, well satisfied with the morning's work. She took care to stay out of Laudine's room for the rest of the day, leaving her to her own reflections, and the next morning when she went back she found her hostess looking very hollow-eyed and sober. "Why, good morning, Laudine! My goodness, you don't look at all comfortable! Are you ill?"

Laudine looked up quickly at Luneta's voice. "Oh, Luneta! Where have you been? I've so needed to talk with you."

"Shall I fetch a doctor?"

"No, no, I'm not ill. I just haven't slept all night," Laudine said. "I've been thinking about what you said."

"Then you're ready to begin studying the broadsword?"

"No, not that," Laudine said hurriedly. "I was thinking about what you said . . . about my marrying again."

"But you said that was impossible."

"That's what I wanted to talk to you about. Is it really impossible?"

"I shouldn't think so, but you seemed so certain."

"Oh, I can't believe I'm thinking these thoughts!" Laudine wailed. "My husband is barely a week in his grave!"

"You're afraid of what people will think?" Luneta asked. Laudine looked down but nodded. "But that needn't be! I'm sure that everyone who lives near the castle knows how things stand with that Storm Stone. They will know that you're marrying in order to protect them. I would imagine that they'll all cheer when they hear you're engaged."

"Won't they . . . wouldn't they think me fickle?"

"What, after seeing you at the funeral? Don't be silly. No one will think that your feelings are shallow after that! Everyone knows how much you loved Sir Esclados."

"But then what will they think?"

"What should they think but the truth? That you've made a marriage of convenience, out of duty to your people. Who will think ill of you for that? It's really quite a common arrangement, you know. Why, I've known such cases myself."

Laudine blushed self-consciously, and Luneta knew

then that Laudine had never held any real affection for Sir Esclados. All that talk about love at first sight and all her ghastly excess at the funeral had been for form's sake. She had been behaving as she thought she was supposed to behave—or, rather, as the French minstrels who sang syrupy love songs thought she was supposed to behave. Luneta said, with an air of decision, "No, I don't think you need concern yourself with what others will think. Provided you marry someone who is able to protect the land against the storms, you'll probably be regarded as a public benefactor."

"But that's the thing," Laudine said immediately. "Wherever will I find someone like that, cloistered away in this castle as I am?"

"Hmm. It's a puzzle, isn't it?" Luneta said pensively. "I don't suppose you'd be interested in marrying one of your own soldiers, would you? There's one very powerful-looking sergeant who seems as if he'd be a fierce fighter. Maybe you know the one I mean. I don't know his name, exactly, but his soldiers call him the 'Ape of Araby.'"

"The what?"

"The 'Ape of Araby.' He seems most formidable to me."

"Why do they call him that?"

"I'm sure I don't know why soldiers give their little names for each other," Luneta said primly. "And besides, I imagine that once he's married he'll shave more often. And bathe sometimes."

"No!"

"No, perhaps you're right. How about the Captain of the Guard—Regivald or something like that. He's not half so niffy as the Ape of Araby, and in his day he was probably quite as good with his weapons. I wonder, Laudine, do you insist on your future husband having all his teeth?"

"Teeth?"

"Never mind. As lord of the castle, he can have someone make him some new ones. Perhaps even dye his hair. Without all that gray, he'll look decades younger!"

"Decades? How old is this fellow?"

"Oh, I couldn't say for certain. He's very well preserved, and besides, there are advantages to marrying an experienced man. They know so many interesting stories about how things were in our grandfathers' days—"

"Stop! I won't hear any more!"

"Well, there's always Malvolus . . ."

"No!" Laudine shrieked.

"No, you're right. None of these men will do the trick, will they? What we need is a knight, and not just any knight, either. I'll have to think about this some more."

With an air of deep concentration, Luneta turned and left the room, closing the door behind her. When it was latched, she allowed herself a smile.

"I've clearly underestimated you," came Rhience's voice from the shadows by the door.

"Oh, were you listening in? Not very chivalrous of you."

"I refuse to acknowledge a rebuke from someone who's manipulating her friend into a marriage."

Luneta lifted her chin high. "And are you absolutely certain that Ywain and Laudine are ill suited for each other?" Rhience didn't reply. "Tell me so, and I'll stop."

"No, on the surface it seems as if they were made for each other," Rhience admitted. "All I'm saying is that if they get together, they should do it without your help."

Luneta smiled triumphantly and, ignoring this last comment, returned to her room. All was going according to plan.

Laudine looked even more miserable the following morning, and Luneta was more glad than ever that she was doing what she could to help Laudine. When Luneta entered, Laudine looked up with a faint gleam of hope in her eyes. "Have you thought of anything yet?"

Luneta shook her head dejectedly. "I'm afraid not. You see, there are few knights in England who are even close to Sir Esclados in strength and skill, and none of them are available. My uncle Sir Gawain is not interested in marrying, and he's far too old for you anyway. You want a young and handsome knight. Then there's

Sir Lancelot, but he doesn't seem interested in romance either, from what I've heard. He lived alone as a hermit for years, you know. He can't be that interested in women. There just aren't many who are as great as Sir Esclados." Luneta smiled wryly, then shrugged and added, "And if it were possible, we would want someone who was actually a *better* knight than Sir Esclados. After all, Sir Esclados was defeated, wasn't he?"

"But are there any such knights?" Laudine asked despairingly.

Luneta assumed an awestruck expression. "Well, there's one." Then she shook her head sharply and said, "No, no. Forget I said anything. That's impossible!"

"What's impossible?"

"I'm sorry, my lady. I should have remained silent."

"Why? What are you thinking? Tell me! I beg you!"

Luneta sighed. "There is one knight who I know is a greater warrior than Sir Esclados, but it's hopeless. You would never marry him."

"Why not?" Laudine demanded. Then she sat up straight. "Does he have all his teeth?"

"Oh, yes, very toothsome indeed. But my lady, don't tease yourself about this knight."

"No one calls him Ape Boy or anything?"

"Not that I'm aware of," Luneta said cautiously. "He's really quite good-looking, I suppose."

"How old is he? Not a friend of your grandfather's or anything, is he?"

Luneta grinned at this, but only said, "I would think that he's about your own age, my lady."

"So young? Then how could you possibly think that he's a stronger knight than Sir Esclados?"

Luneta smiled hesitantly, watching Laudine. "Because you see, my lady, he was the one who defeated Sir Esclados."

Laudine's face grew still and pale.

"But you mustn't think ill of him, my lady," Luneta said hurriedly. "What was he to do when Sir Esclados attacked him? On his honor, he could do nothing but stand and fight!"

Laudine stared for a moment at the floor, then lifted expressionless eyes to Luneta. "You know this knight?"

Luneta nodded.

"Is he a good man?"

"I believe so, my lady."

"And can you produce him? Where is he?"

"He's . . . been in hiding, my lady, not wanting to slay any more of your men."

"Where is he?"

"I don't know, exactly, at least not now, but—"

"I am here, my lady," said Ywain's voice, and then he appeared from the air just behind the chair where

Laudine sat. She whirled around, but Ywain was already walking in front of her and kneeling at her feet. "My lady, I beg your forgiveness for causing you such grief. Had I seen you before I fought your husband, I would have permitted him to kill me rather than cause you one second of the pain that you have felt."

"But where have you . . . ?" Laudine began, but then she looked into Ywain's face, and the words died on her lips. Her eyes widened, her lips parted, and her cheeks began to glow.

"I do not know if you can ever forgive me or give me the joy of calling you my own, but whether you do this or not, I must have you know this: I have loved you since the moment I saw you. I love you more now than I did then. I will serve you, honor you, and protect you if you will do me the honor, grant me the joy, of possessing this hand and this heart." Ywain raised Laudine's hand to his lips and kissed it fervently.

Luneta nodded appreciatively. A very pretty speech. Perhaps a little flowery for her own taste, but she could tell that Laudine saw no fault in it.

"My love, my heart, my life, may I call you my own?"

Laudine didn't hesitate. Clearly all her qualms about what others would think had been forgotten. "Yes. Yes. Though I do not even know your name or station. I will marry you though you were the son of a goatherd."

Ywain laughed softly. "I am sorry to disappoint

you, but I'm afraid that I'm rather the son of a king. I am Ywain, son of Ywain, grandson of Uriens, King of Scotland."

Laudine's eyes grew round, and for a moment Luneta thought she was actually going to faint, but just at that moment the sky grew dark and a great crash of thunder shook the castle.

"The Storm Stone!" shrieked Laudine.

V

LAUDINE THE LAUGHLESS

Ywain didn't hesitate. Pausing only long enough to place a firm hand on Laudine's shoulder and say, "Don't worry, my heart. I'll take care of it," he strode from the room. Another crash of thunder came, followed by the sound of glass breaking down the corridor, and Laudine began to tremble and whimper. She reminded Luneta of a dog she'd once had who had always crawled under a bed during storms, but Luneta decided to keep this reflection to herself and instead held Laudine's hand in what she hoped was a reassuring manner.

As before, the storm ended in a few minutes, and Laudine recovered her composure, for a moment, at least. She took a deep breath, let it out in a sigh, then— to Luneta's surprise—began to cry again.

"What's wrong now, my lady?"

"I'm afraid something will happen to my beloved, Y— . . . What was his name again?"

"Ywain. Nothing will happen to him. Remember that he's already proven himself once."

At that moment the door burst open, and into the sitting room came one of the most ridiculous sights Luneta had ever seen. It was the steward, Malvolus, dressed in an odd assortment of various pieces of armor. "I have come, my lady!" he announced grandly.

"Come? Whatever for?" Laudine asked.

"The Storm Stone, my lady!" he declared. "Do you not remember the charge that lies on this castle?"

Rhience slipped into the room behind Malvolus, grinning with delight, and Luneta had to look away from him to keep her own expression under control.

"What do you mean?"

"When the storm breaks over the land, one from this castle must defend it!"

"Oh!" Laudine said, with a sudden understanding. "And you're offering to fight?"

"It is the least I can do for you, my dear mistress," the steward replied, executing a very correct, though mechanical, bow. "You must be protected."

"That's so kind of you!" Laudine said, evidently moved. "I had no idea you were that loyal to me!" She hesitated, then added, "But why . . . forgive me, why does your armor not fit?"

Malvolus flushed angrily and didn't answer, but Rhience explained for him. "Because he's such a spider shanks, of course. None of the armor in the castle will fit such a paltry fellow as our Malvolus."

The steward's eyes blazed with fury, but he didn't respond to the fool's remarks. "I shall have armor made for myself later, in the correct size," he said austerely.

"Why would a steward need armor?" Laudine asked, confused.

Malvolus's face grew even more rigidly furious, and he replied in a controlled tone, as if explaining something to an idiot. "To defend the castle after the storms, of course."

"Oh, but that's not necessary!" Laudine said.

"It is the law, the custom, and the enchantment of this castle! We are bound to do so for our very lives by the magic of the stone!"

"Yes, yes, I know that," Laudine said quickly. "I didn't mean that it didn't have to be done. I only mean that I've already sent a knight to do so."

"What?" Malvolus's face grew pale.

"I do believe our steward's going to faint," Rhience said dispassionately. "Good thing he's in armor. Maybe he won't hurt himself too badly when he falls."

"I've already sent a knight out," Laudine repeated.

"What knight?" Malvolus demanded.

Luneta deemed it time to step in. Assuming a bright

116

and cheerful voice, she said, "Isn't it the most fortunate thing? My cousin Ywain had just arrived to visit me, and we had barely finished telling him about the curse of the castle when the storm broke and he offered to go fight for Lady Laudine."

"You fool!" Malvolus shrieked.

"Yes? You called?" asked Rhience.

"Don't you know what you've done?" Malvolus stammered. His face had recovered its color and more, to the extent that he was quite purple. "The enchantment that was laid on this land says that when there is only a mistress over the castle, then whatsoever knight defends the Storm Stone and marries the mistress becomes the new lord!"

Startled, Luneta glanced at Laudine and saw the same astonishment in her eyes. Evidently Sir Esclados had never mentioned this part of the castle's curse. The shocked silence was broken by Rhience's sardonic voice. "Ah, so that's why you were so eager to deck yourself out in borrowed armor and rush out to fight. You were thinking to raise your station in life. But what if Lady Laudine didn't *want* to marry you?"

Malvolus glared balefully at the fool and for several seconds struggled against his rage. At last, he controlled himself and bowed stiffly to Laudine. "I assure you, my lady, that my only intention was to protect you."

117

"Indeed, I'm very grateful to you," Laudine replied warmly. "Why, you could have been killed!"

Malvolus bowed again, stiffly, then stalked toward the door with as much dignity as was possible for a man who had just had an ambitious plot exposed while wearing a silly outfit. Just before he left, Rhience said casually, "By the by, Luneta, where did your cousin get armor? I thought his visit was going to be social only and that he wouldn't be wearing armor when he came."

Luneta understood at once and flashed a grateful smile to Rhience. His quick thinking might save an awkward scene. Ywain had undoubtedly rushed off to put on his own armor, which he knew was in Malvolus's room. When Malvolus saw that armor, he was sure to recognize it and to ask some bothersome questions. "Yes, that's true," she replied. "But one of the servants told me that there was a suit of armor in Malvolus's room, so I told him he should try that." She smiled sweetly at the steward. "I hope you don't mind, Malvolus. My cousin's bigger than you and so that armor might fit him."

The steward ground his teeth, but he bowed again. "Of course not, my lady. By all means, send people to my private chambers whenever it is convenient for you."

Luneta smiled even more brightly. "That's very kind of you. Thank you."

Malvolus left, still seething. Rhience listened at the door until he heard the steward's clanking steps disappear, then turned back to Luneta. "So," he said carefully, glancing at Laudine. "Your cousin is here?"

"Laudine knows about Ywain," Luneta said. "They are betrothed, in fact."

Rhience gave Luneta a swift, shrewd look, but then bowed deeply and graciously to Laudine. "I felicitate you, my lady. I have known this man Ywain before, and I believe he is a good man who will love you well."

Laudine blushed and looked very self-conscious, but happy. "You don't . . . you don't think ill of me for getting betrothed so soon after my husband's death?"

"No, my lady."

"And nor will anyone else!" Luneta declared as a sudden thought came to her. "Because I'll wager that everyone in the district knows that the one who defends the Storm Stone becomes the lord of the castle! When they hear that Ywain has defended the stone, they'll all assume that you had no choice but to marry him! Just as, I suppose, you would have had to marry Malvolus if he'd gone out to fight." Laudine blanched at the thought, and Luneta continued, "Why, it's perfect! No one will question your decision at all."

It took two or three repetitions before Laudine grasped all the implications of this new idea, but when she did she was even more enthusiastic than Luneta.

"Then everyone will think that I *had* to marry Ywain, and no one will think that I've been disrespectful to Sir Esclados!"

"Quite true, my lady," Rhience said.

Laudine's face brightened. "Then I can go ahead with the full six months of mourning, just as I ought!" she exclaimed joyously.

Rhience raised one eyebrow, but said only, "You can grieve as long as you want, if that's what will make you happy."

Laudine missed Rhience's irony and sighed with relief. "That was the part that bothered me the most. I just couldn't help feeling that it was wrong not to have the proper time of mourning. Ywain and I can be betrothed now, then married in six months after I've put off my blacks!"

"And I thought it was only men who went into mourning before they got married," Rhience commented.

"My lady," Luneta said, "is this really necessary?"

"I was taught that a proper time of mourning was *very* necessary," Laudine said primly.

"What a curious expression!" Rhience said thoughtfully. "I wonder what the opposite of 'very necessary' is? Mildly necessary? Somewhat essential?"

"Whatever do you mean?" asked Laudine.

"Shut up, Rhience," said Luneta.

* * *

120

Luneta had been afraid that she would have to explain to Laudine a great many awkward details—such as where Ywain had been hidden for the past two weeks—but it appeared that once Laudine had grasped that she could marry the young and handsome knight Ywain and still go through the socially correct time of mourning for her deceased husband, her happiness precluded all other thoughts. She sighed over Ywain's beauty and courtesy for nearly an hour—which Luneta found very tedious indeed—until the footman Rufus entered their room and announced that a host of knights had approached the gate and the knight at the head had asked for her by name. It was Ywain, of course. He had defended the stone and returned to claim his betrothed, and behind him rode a small army of knights from Camelot, including Gawain and Terence.

It was some time before Luneta understood all this, since the next few hours were spent helping Laudine and the castle servants prepare rooms for their illustrious and unexpected guests, but she did finally learn what happened at the Storm Stone. After leaving Laudine and Luneta, Ywain had put on his armor, saddled his horse, and departed through a seldom-used side gate, all without arousing the least suspicion, since he still had the faery ring. Once in the magical copse, Ywain had removed the ring, lowered his visor, and galloped off to challenge whoever had disturbed the stone. Arriving in the clearing, though, he had found not one wandering knight but a host of knights from Camelot.

It was Gawain who told Luneta what happened next, as he and Terence were sitting with Luneta in her room late that evening. "It was Agrivain's own fault, of course," Gawain said. "Back in my chambers that night, when your friend Rhience told about this magical basin, Agrivain had been boasting about how he wanted adventures, too. So, when Kai mentioned the Storm Stone at the next meeting of the Round Table, Agrivain must have felt obligated to back up his words, and he demanded that this adventure be given to him." Gawain grinned ruefully. "Poor Agrivain."

"Why *poor*?" Luneta asked.

"Letting alone what happened to him at the copse, which is enough, he got much more than he asked for. Nearly everyone at the table wanted to see the magical storm, and the end of it was that nearly a dozen of us came along. I doubt Agrivain really wanted to fight at all, and I'm certain he didn't want to do it in front of a crowd, but he was trapped. When we found the stone, he brought on the storm, then mounted up to wait for a fight while half the Round Table sat around watching.

"A minute later, along comes this knight. We were all expecting an angry, rude fellow like the one Rhience described, but this knight comes into the clearing, stops his horse, and calls out, 'Who disturbed the stone?'

Agrivain says, 'I did,' and gets ready to charge, but the knight only explains that these storms are a curse on the land and that he is sworn to protect the land. Then he says, 'If every knight here will take a solemn vow never again to pour water into the magic basin, then we shall have peace between us.' "

"What a sensible thing to do!" Luneta said approvingly.

"Except that it didn't work," Gawain said. "I suppose Agrivain took this as a sign of fear, or maybe he didn't hear what Ywain said."

"He heard," Terence said.

Gawain shrugged. "For whatever reason, Agrivain charged, and Ywain popped him off his horse as neatly as you could wish. Then he dismounted and held his sword to Agrivain's throat. As I said, poor Agrivain."

"Did anyone help Uncle Agrivain?" Luneta asked.

Gawain looked surprised. "No, why would they? It was a fair fight. If anything, Agrivain was the one in the wrong for attacking a knight who was offering terms. Then Ywain asks again for everyone to take a vow to leave the stone alone in the future, and we all promised."

"Even Uncle Agrivain?"

Gawain nodded. "Not, perhaps, very gracefully, but he did it. So then, as the chief knight present, I asked if I might know the name of the knight who had defeated my kinsman, and Ywain put away his sword and without

123

a word slowly loosened his helm, took it off with a flourish, and said, 'Your kinsman, of course.' Very dramatic, our cousin."

"A silly ass, more like," Terence contributed mildly. "He couldn't have done anything that would have more thoroughly embarrassed Agrivain."

"I suppose that's true," Gawain said. "Ywain's young, though. And he *had* just impressively beaten a knight of the Round Table before everyone he most wished to impress."

"Is Ywain really that good?" Luneta asked.

Gawain nodded. "And more. I don't think I've seen a knight so gifted so young." Then he added loftily, "Barring myself, of course."

Luneta giggled, and Terence closed his eyes wearily. "I wonder if Ywain bashed the wrong relative."

Gawain grinned again. "To be honest, the boy might be able to do it. He's a natural. As I said to him on the way to the castle, he could clean up prizes at any tournament in the country. I was telling him about the Lincoln Tourney that's just been announced. I think all the best knights in the land will be there, and the prize is a crown studded with rubies. He tried to act as if he weren't interested, but I think he is."

Luneta smiled to herself. What Gawain didn't know was that, with her help, Ywain had found something more precious than any tournament prize. Ywain would hardly be attracted by such baubles now that he had won the love of Laudine.

Luneta was wrong. The next time she encountered Ywain, the first words out of his mouth were about the upcoming Lincoln Tourney. "But Ywain," Luneta said reproachfully, "you've just gotten betrothed."

But Ywain was ready for this. "Yes, of course. And if there were any chance of my marrying my dear Laudine at once and settling down with her, I would do it. But haven't you heard Laudine's plan? She wants to put off our wedding for six months, out of respect for Sir Esclados."

"Stuff!" Luneta snapped. "She has no more respect for Sir Esclados than for her horse!"

"Well, out of respect for social conventions, then," Ywain conceded. "And you can't deny that she has a great deal of respect for those."

No, Luneta could not deny that, but she was still unsatisfied. "You can't get engaged to a lady and then trot away the next day."

"Not normally, perhaps. Usually, I'd take her with me, but there's this silly curse about the lord of the castle having to stay right here to guard the stone as long as it might be disturbed. I'm going to be stuck here for the rest of my life once we're married, you know. I need to see the world while I can."

Luneta hadn't thought about that. "Aren't you already the lord of the castle, since you defeated the stone?"

"No, only after I marry Laudine. I checked with everyone, even Laudine, and they agree."

"Laudine agrees?" Luneta repeated. "You mean she's approved this plan?"

Ywain looked mildly effronted. "You didn't think I would do this without discussing it with Laudine, did you? We love each other, and lovers talk about things like this. She says she has no objections."

Luneta stared at Ywain, then took her cousin by the hand and dragged him off to Laudine's sitting room. "What is this nonsense about Ywain going away?" Luneta demanded of her hostess as soon as they were alone.

Laudine allowed a slight but audible sigh to escape. "But my dear Luneta," she said, "surely you don't expect him to stay here, kicking . . . kicking his heels and doing nothing while he waits for the mourning time to be finished."

"There, see?" Ywain said. "Just what I told her."

"I'm well aware that it's just what you told her," Luneta replied with asperity. "Listen to me, Laudine. Don't just repeat what Ywain said to you; tell me what *you* want."

"But my dear," Laudine said with a trembling smile. "He is to be my husband. I want whatever he wants."

Luneta stared at Laudine, aghast. "Bleah!" she said.

"I beg your pardon?" Laudine asked.

"That's appalling! Don't you have any preferences of your own? Good Gog, if that's how you acted with Sir Esclados, no wonder he treated you like a spaniel! If you *will* lie down on the doorstep, then you can't be surprised if people wipe their feet on you!"

"I don't know what you're talking about," Laudine said coldly.

"You're going to let my cousin here pledge his love to you, then turn around and ride away? And for six months? Or longer, until he's done playing games? Are you willing to sit here for the next two years, wondering when he'll think of you again?"

"Cousin Luneta!" Ywain said sharply. "I think of Laudine every minute of every day. It is that very thing that makes it such torture to stay here beside the most beautiful woman in the world but unable to claim her for my own! I will count the days until I am permitted to marry my heart, my life, my love—"

"Oh, stow it, Ywain," Luneta interjected. "What about the Storm Stone? Who's going to be here to protect the stone if you're gone?"

But again Ywain was ahead of her. "It should hardly be a problem now that King Arthur's knights have sworn to leave the stone be. And, I've taken the liberty of posting two armed guards by the stone, just to make sure nothing happens." Ywain smiled smugly at Luneta, then knelt at Laudine's feet and took her hand in his own. "You may trust me, my dearest Laudine," Ywain went on. "I shall be back in six months. I vow it, as a pledge of my love for you."

"And I grant you leave to go, my dearest Ywain," Laudine said, her chin lifted proudly. "Your own cousin may not trust you, but I do. Always. Forever."

"Bleah!" Luneta said again.

Luneta didn't give up, but despite her best arguments, Ywain left two days later with the rest of King Arthur's company. He bid a tender goodbye to Laudine, promising to think of her every second and renewing his vow to return before six months had past, and it all would have been extremely moving had Ywain been leaving reluctantly, out of duty, to fight for England or something. Since he was going off by choice, however, for no better reason than to see if he was a better jouster than the other knights in some tournament, Luneta was easily able to withhold her sympathy.

"It's all so stupid!" she complained to Rhience later that day. "Laudine doesn't want him to go, but she won't admit it. She seems to think it's unladylike to have opinions."

Rhience frowned, as if concentrating very hard, and

said, "And you . . . wait, don't tell me . . . you *do* have opinions, don't you?"

Luneta rolled her eyes expressively, then set her mouth in a small prim rosebud and said in a little-girl voice, "I really couldn't say. What do *you* think? Just tell me, and I'll agree with you."

Rhience grinned, but he didn't let the opportunity pass. "I believe that Ywain is actually a French minstrel in disguise, and he left in order to pursue his calling in the county fairs of the north."

Luneta fluttered her eyes and, still in a child's voice, said, "I've often thought so myself!"

"Or else he's a beautiful princess who's under a strange enchantment!"

"How clever you are!" Luneta trilled admiringly.

"Or a three-headed pig."

"Very true!"

"How long can you keep this, ah, ladylike compliance up?" Rhience asked.

"Without vomiting? Not much longer."

"Then I'd better stop. It won't do for you to go comfort the forlorn Laudine if you're already feeling queasy."

Luneta sighed. "She *is* the most appalling milksop sometimes, isn't she? Has she been asking for me?"

"All morning."

"Why didn't you tell me earlier?"

"I didn't think her request very urgent. Why? Do *you* think you'll make her feel better?"

"I doubt it," Luneta admitted. "Still, I suppose I'd better get it over with."

Rhience laughed. "What a silly thing to say! As if her need for someone to hold her hand will ever be 'over'!"

"Now, that's not fair," Luneta said. "When has Laudine been anything but kind to you?"

"When she doesn't laugh at my jokes, of course," Rhience replied promptly. "It hurts my feelings."

Luneta lifted her chin and looked down her nose at Rhience. "Perhaps she doesn't laugh because your jokes aren't funny."

"Now you're hurting my feelings, too. I liked you better when you were being ladylike."

"I'm sure you did," Luneta replied. "You should take on Laudine as a challenge. Make her laugh! If you do, then you can truly claim the title of Greatest Fool in England."

"And if I don't?"

Luneta smiled sweetly. "Don't worry, you'll always be the Greatest Fool in England to me." With that, Luneta tripped up the stairs to Laudine's sitting room.

Luneta arrived in Laudine's room to find her hostess propped up in bed on several pillows and attended by three ladies-in-waiting and two manservants— one of them the steward Malvolus—but as soon as

Laudine saw Luneta she said reproachfully, "Where have you been?"

"I'm sorry, Laudine. I didn't know that you were asking for me. Was there something you needed?"

"I told that fool that I wanted you, oh, ages ago! I've been expecting you for this hour and more! What can have kept the fellow?" Laudine asked peevishly.

From the shadows at the far side of the room, Malvolus said smoothly, "He is a most undependable knave, my lady. I should not repose any further trust in him, if I were you."

Luneta glared at Malvolus but spoke to Laudine. "I am here now, my lady. How may I help you?"

Laudine sighed. "I just needed someone to be with me. I've lost my betrothed for six long months, and I hardly know what to do."

"You don't know that it will be all of six months," Luneta pointed out. "He may be back as soon as this tournament is over. But as for what to do while you wait, why, I think you should get up and go about your life."

Laudine smiled at Luneta wanly. "Your mother was always very energetic, I remember. You are very like her. I don't suppose either of you has any idea what it is like to be sensitive to atmosphere the way that I am."

Luneta had a vague idea that she had just been insulted, but she wasn't sure how to respond. If being "sensitive to atmosphere" meant lying around feeling sorry for oneself, then Laudine was right: Luneta had never had any patience with such behavior. It was clear from Laudine's tone, though, that she considered it an admirable trait to always have fits of the vapors. For the first time in her memory, Luneta was glad to be like her mother.

Malvolus spoke again. "You are all too delicate, my lady. My late master always told me so. 'Malvolus,' he would say to me, 'you must be gentle with Lady Laudine. She is like a flower that must be given the greatest care.'"

Laudine's eyes grew misty, and she dabbed at them with a cloth.

Malvolus continued. "I assure you that my master— who must have been slain by some treachery, as no knight alive could have beaten him fairly—would never have left you disconsolate as this new knight has done."

Luneta stared at the steward. "Why are you trying to turn Laudine against her betrothed husband?" she demanded bluntly.

"Oh, dear," Malvolus replied humbly. "Have I spoken out of turn? It's just that I am still loyal to my late master—as would be anyone who had *truly* cared for him."

This was so clearly directed at Laudine that even she caught the implication and began to sob. Luneta spoke abruptly to the steward. "Poppycock! Your late master treated Laudine like a stable cur. If she owes him any loyalty, I don't see why."

"I'm sure you don't, my lady," Malvolus said. "Loyalty is not natural to some people, I believe."

Luneta's mouth dropped open, but before she could reply, the door swung ajar and in walked Rhience, carrying an armload of pots and pans and a broom handle and a coil of rope. "Lady Laudine!" he announced grandly, without preamble. "I have come to bring cheer to your heart, to delight your day, to while away your hours, to make you laugh again. I say 'again' because I assume that you *have* laughed before."

Laudine shook her head sadly. "Not today, fool. I am in no mood for laughter."

"I understand perfectly. You're bilious, aren't you? Well, how could you help but have an upset stomach? Would you like me to remove him?"

"What are you talking about?" Laudine asked.

"Malvolus, of course. He's turned your stomach."

The steward glowered angrily at Rhience, but Laudine answered firmly, "Malvolus has *not* turned my stomach."

"He hasn't?" Rhience asked in patent astonishment. "Extraordinary! No, really! Look at that hangdog face of his! Hasn't it made you even the least bit queasy?"

"You are not funny, fool," Malvolus said menacingly.

"I must say, it's very curious," Rhience continued, ignoring the steward. "But that's not why I'm here. I've come to engage you with a pantomime."

"A what?" Laudine asked.

"Ah, it's an ancient art," Rhience replied loftily. "I will tell a story, but without words. I will act out a great adventure, and you must guess what story I am telling."

Laudine looked mildly interested, but she said only, "I don't know many stories. What if I don't recognize it?"

"You shall have to ask your ladies and Luneta and, er, this fine steward to help you," Rhience said, and immediately he launched into his act.

He began by walking about in a very feminine way, fanning himself and arranging his hair. Laudine already looked lost. "Whatever is he doing?" she asked.

"I believe he's supposed to be a beautiful lady," Luneta said.

Rhience nodded and immediately took the hand of one of the ladies-in-waiting and drew her into his act. Placing her before the imaginary mirror where he had been primping a moment before, Rhience drew back behind a wardrobe and watched the lady closely, a malevolent sneer on his lips.

"Oh, what is he doing now?"

"He's someone else, now, my lady," said one of the other ladies-in-waiting.

"Ooh!" chimed in the third one. "He's a wicked man who wants the beautiful lady!"

Rhience nodded again, then stepped out of his hiding place, holding an imaginary tray in one hand. He walked very stiffly over to the lady he had selected and, bowing deeply, pretended to serve her some wine, then strutted back to his corner.

Luneta couldn't help sneaking a glance at Malvolus, who was glaring at Rhience with a seething fury. Rhience's peculiar walk was exaggerated, but Luneta had no trouble recognizing the steward's pompous gait. The ladies all smothered giggles, and the other manservant cleared his throat in an awkward attempt to hide a laugh. Only Laudine appeared not to know whom Rhience was imitating.

Now Rhience, still in character as Malvolus, walked back to the wall and began preening himself before yet another pretend mirror, but this time he preened for much longer than he had when he had been the lady. He posed before the mirror and flexed his muscles and pretended to pluck hairs from his nostrils until the ladies-in-waiting were nearly bursting their seams from laughing. Luneta gathered that Malvolus had a reputation for vanity among the servants.

Then Rhience cupped his hand to his ear, listening to something, then began shaking as if he were in an earthquake. The shaking stopped, then began again, then stopped. Rhience raised one finger in the air and assumed a cunning expression. Immediately he leaped over to the pile of kitchenware and rope that he had brought with him. For the next few minutes, the ladies laughed helplessly while Rhience tied bits of crockery to his legs and put an iron pot on his head as if it were a helm.

Luneta glanced nervously at Malvolus. Rhience was obviously aping Malvolus's mismatched suit of armor, and Luneta was afraid that he was going too far. Now Rhience drew his broom handle and began to strut about practicing swordplay with it, but since his cooking pot helm kept falling over his eyes and he kept running into walls, this display only had the servants laughing harder. Now even the other manservant was roaring with laughter, no longer paying the slightest heed to Malvolus's furious glares.

"Whatever is he doing?" Laudine asked. She alone was not laughing but was staring at Rhience with the consternation of one watching a madman.

"I'm sure I couldn't say," Luneta replied.

But this question gave Malvolus the chance he needed. Stepping between Laudine and Rhience, he asked suavely, "Is this barren fool annoying you, my lady? Shall I remove him?"

"But I don't know what story he's presenting," Laudine said.

Malvolus gave the ladies a quelling glare. "Nor does anyone else, my lady. I shall take him away with me now, as there is some business that I must attend to anyway."

Rhience walked into a wardrobe with a crash, then removed the pot from his head. "Wait," he said. "I hadn't gotten to the part where the brave knight of the silly armor tries to seduce the beautiful lady while her betrothed is away."

Malvolus's self-control snapped. "I've heard enough!" he roared. "I will endure this no more! Choose your weapons! I shall fight you in the courtyard!"

The room grew still. Rhience looked amused, but he shook his head. "My dear fellow, nothing would give me more pleasure than to knock you around a bit, but I can't."

"Afraid?" Malvolus demanded.

"Disappointed, actually. You see, I've given my word not to take up arms against another man for another ten months or so."

Malvolus's face suddenly lit up with triumph. "Of course! You're the knight my master defeated on the Fool's New Year! He told me about the vow he forced you to make! He thought it was a grand joke!" Rhience bowed in mute acknowledgment, and Malvolus let out a sneering laugh. "Come with me, fool. You're bothering the ladies." Then the steward took Rhience firmly by the arm and led him away.

"Was it one of the stories of Aesop?" Laudine asked. She never had laughed.

Rhience was gone. When Luneta went to look for him later that day, he was nowhere to be found. His small room in the servants' quarters was empty, and no one could tell her anything about him. Finally she checked the stables, and his saddle and gear and great white horse were not there. She was staring at the empty stall for a moment, feeling curiously alone, when a voice spoke behind her.

"If you're looking for your foolish friend," came the smooth, triumphant voice of Malvolus, "I am desolated to tell you that he's gone. For good, I'd say. He ran off like a frightened cur because I told him to leave."

"Frightened?" Luneta replied scornfully. "Of you? I don't believe it."

The steward glanced significantly at the empty stall and said, "Then why, I wonder, is he gone?" With that, Malvolus strutted away, leaving Luneta to her thoughts.

These were bleak. Even if Malvolus was lying about the reason for Rhience's departure, it was obvious that he had gone, and without bidding her goodbye. Luneta remembered something he had said the day they arrived at Laudine's castle: *I'm free to leave when I want.* After all, she admitted, it was true. No one at Laudine's castle had any claim on him.

Life at Laudine's manor was less enjoyable without Rhience, and for all she had protested at the time, Luneta came to realize that Rhience had been right about one thing. Laudine was caring and pleasant and even smiled sometimes, but the one thing that she didn't do was laugh. And, with Malvolus ruling the castle more firmly with every passing day, there were precious few others who would laugh either. Luneta's life would have been dreary indeed if it hadn't been for her lessons.

These began two days after Rhience left. Laudine had allowed Luneta to coax her out of her bed that morning, and though she still repeatedly wondered aloud what Ywain was doing at that moment, she seemed to have a little more energy. Luneta skillfully guided her to her dressing table, succeeding in distracting Laudine with her morning toilette for more than an hour, and was just casting about in her mind for some other diversion when Laudine said, "Let me see your hand, Luneta."

Ready to encourage interest in anything, Luneta held both hands out to Laudine, who took her left hand and examined its back. "How long have you had this mark?"

Luneta glanced politely at the small dark spot on her hand. "As long as I can remember. It's just a birthmark."

"I wonder what Lynet's thinking, sometimes," Laudine said to herself. Then, more loudly, she said,

"Come here." Standing, Laudine pulled back an embroidered tapestry that hung along one wall of her room, revealing a small door. "Now you mustn't tell anyone about this room," Laudine said, "but it's all right to show you. I'm sure that you have the look."

"What look?" Luneta asked.

"Why, the look of an enchantress, of course."

"An enchantress? Me?"

"Yes, indeed," Laudine replied, opening the door and pulling Luneta in after her. "I can't always tell, the way some people can, but I've been watching you, and I'm quite sure of it now."

"But I've never done anything magical," Luneta protested.

"Why, my dear, none of us do until we've been taught. No one is born with the ability to do magic; it's just that some of us are born with the ability to learn. Now this," she said, gesturing at the small room behind the door, "is where I make my own enchantments."

Luneta gazed around her with awe. Except for the mirrors that lined every wall, it looked very much as she would have expected a witch's workshop to look: dark and filled with bottles and mysterious vials. Laudine was busy lighting dozens of candles.

"I wish that I could have more sunlight in here," Laudine said. "Often after working here I have to go

140

out into the daylight to see the effects, but there are certain potions and brews that must be done in darkness. So I just use a lot of candles."

Luneta took a blue bottle down from a shelf. "What's in here?"

"That removes warts," Laudine said. "You don't have any warts, do you?"

"No," Luneta said, mildly disappointed. Ointments that removed warts were hardly her idea of magic. Even her mother had some wart cream.

"Here it is," Laudine said. "Now, stretch out that hand." Laudine opened a tiny vial and dipped a delicate brush inside. She painted Luneta's birthmark with the lotion and muttered, "Melifelet telefilem," or something like that, and Luneta's birthmark was gone.

Luneta examined the spot. "It wasn't bothering me, really," she said.

"I know what you mean," Laudine said. "A birthmark can be very attractive, if it's in the right place. I have several myself. But you don't want them on your hands. They'll look like those horrid dark spots that *old* people get. Now," she continued, "have you ever wished that you were different than you are? In any way?"

"I used to wish I were a boy," Luneta said.

"Oh, I couldn't do that!" Laudine said. "Very advanced magic, that would be."

"It's all right," Luneta hastily assured her. "I don't want to be a boy anymore. That was just when I was younger and wanted to wear breeches."

Laudine looked shocked and muttered, "Breeches."

"For riding, you know. I'd much rather wear a silk gown now." This appeared to reassure Laudine, so Luneta tried again. "I sometimes wish I were taller," Luneta said.

Laudine shook her head. "Don't even think about that, my dear. No one ever looks at a tall girl."

"I would think that they'd look at her rather *more* often," Luneta said. "I mean, she'd be more evident, wouldn't she?"

"I meant boys," Laudine said. "Nothing is more fatal to a girl's chances than to be taller than the boys. Trust me on this. It positively terrifies boys to be introduced to a girl who towers over them. Next time you're at a ball, take a look around and you'll see that all the tall women are standing at the edge of the room watching the shorter women dance. No, you are a very acceptable height." Laudine peered closely at Luneta's face. "You're probably too young, but it doesn't hurt to ask: Do you have any wrinkles? Even little ones? I can smooth them out."

"No, I don't think so."

"Good. I didn't really think so, but I felt I should ask because—forgive me, dear—your mother has a pronounced tendency to wrinkle. You may have noticed this yourself."

"Not really," Luneta said.

"What? Haven't you seen those wrinkles at the corners of her eyes?"

"Oh, those. Yes, of course. I think she gets those from laughing. She always crinkles her eyes up when she laughs, you see."

Laudine nodded soberly. "That's what she told me when I saw her last. It only goes to show that you can't be too careful. Even things that seem completely innocent can have horrible ill effects. That's why I don't ride anymore."

"I beg your pardon?" Luneta asked, bewildered.

"Riding has a terrible, er, *flattening* effect on certain parts of your body. And, of course, one must take into account the dreadful effects on the skin of being out in the wind and the sun." Laudine shuddered expressively.

"So you don't ride because it might hurt your complexion and flatten your, your other parts?"

Laudine nodded.

"And you don't laugh because—"

"Your mother's wrinkles should be a caution to every lady."

"I never thought that her wrinkles looked bad," Luneta pointed out.

Laudine sighed tolerantly. "I suppose you were just

143

used to them. One can only hope that your father has also grown reconciled to them." She didn't sound very hopeful, though.

"What else do you have here?" Luneta asked.

"I'll teach you," Laudine said, with more energy than she had shown since Ywain left.

And so began Luneta's lessons in enchantment. Every morning for the next several months, the two of them would disappear into Laudine's private room and discuss various potions and charms. Most of these seemed rather trivial to Luneta, as they had no goal but to enhance one's own personal appearance, but she was not immune to the delight of a charm that made rubies glow like fire or a lotion that completely erased a sunburn or a complex charm of Laudine's own devising that, when uttered over silk, made it sheer and diaphanous and impossibly beautiful. In the afternoons, Luneta rode out of the castle to gather herbs and plants with magical properties to use the next day. She had no trouble finding these plants—her mother had taught her about herbs almost as soon as she could walk—but she took her time on these rides. It was her only time alone and away from Laudine's constant prattle, which, though it was always good-natured, did pall on one after a time.

In this way, learning some elementary magic and riding alone in the fields, time passed fairly quickly for Luneta, and since Laudine gradually stopped asking so often for Ywain, Luneta paid little attention to the passage of time. Summer came, then cooled into autumn, but with beautiful clothes to wear and new things to learn each day, Luneta barely noticed. Thus it was a surprise for her when she walked into Laudine's room one morning and found her prostrate on her bed, surrounded by her lady attendants. The sneering, joyful face of Malvolus gloated over his weeping mistress. Luneta demanded, "What have you been doing to Laudine, you plague of boils?"

"Is it possible," the steward replied smoothly, "that you, like my mistress, are unaware of what day it is?"

"What difference does the day make?" Luneta snapped.

"I see," Malvolus said. "Do you know, I believe that you really aren't pretending. I'm quite surprised. I had thought that you at least would be more careful."

"What are you talking about?" Luneta demanded.

"I am desolated, my lady, to be the one to inform you, but yesterday was the day that your cousin promised, as a proof of his love, to return to marry my mistress. It has now been six months *and one day* since Sir Ywain left."

VI

THE MADNESS OF YWAIN

Huddled in her long winter robe, her fingers numb, Luneta rode gratefully up to the gaily colored encampment around the Oxford tournament fields. Guiding her horse through the outer ring of tents, she found herself at once in a busy crowd of brightly dressed courtiers and ladies. Normally she would have been enthralled by the sumptuous furs and fashions that surrounded her, but this day she hardly noticed. "Excuse me," she said to a passing lady-in-waiting, "is the tournament over yet?"

"Oh, no," the lady replied. "The final joust for the prize won't be until tomorrow afternoon."

Luneta sighed with relief. She had ridden nearly eighteen hours straight, trying to get to this tournament before it ended. "And, forgive me, my lady, but do

146

you by any chance know of a knight by the name of Ywain?"

The lady gaped at her with incredulity, then shrieked with laughter. "Zounds, girl! Wherever have you been for the past few months? *Everyone* knows Sir Ywain! He's the greatest knight in England!"

"Is he?" Luneta asked, without much interest. "And is he here?"

"Of course he's here," the lady said. "I told you. He's the greatest knight in England. He'll be competing for the prize tomorrow—and winning it, too!"

"Thank you so much," Luneta said, with determined politeness. "And, if I might trespass on your good nature one more time, do you think that you could take me to Ywain?"

The woman shrieked again, as if Luneta had said something uproariously funny. "I wish I *could* get a private visit with Sir Ywain! But I certainly wouldn't bring you along! He's *so* handsome!" she added dreamily.

"I'm sure that he'll see me," Luneta said.

"Child," the lady said, shaking her head. "The most beautiful women in the court wait outside his tent every morning, just hoping to catch a glimpse of him, and if he didn't have five guards who went everywhere with him, they'd be crawling into the tent as well."

"But I'm his cousin," Luneta explained.

"Dear child, if that would work, we would all be his

cousins," the lady replied. "Why don't you find a nice boy closer to your own age?" With that, the lady walked away, still chuckling.

"She's telling the truth, you know," said a familiar voice behind Luneta. She whirled around in her saddle and stared with a mixture of delight and indignation at Rhience the Fool. "No one can get in to see his famousness. I've been trying for nearly a month now."

"Where have you been?" Luneta demanded, indignation winning the struggle for a time. "Why didn't you tell me you were leaving?"

"I thought you'd figure that out yourself," Rhience replied.

"Was it something that I said?"

"More like something *I* said," Rhience answered. "Malvolus told me that if I didn't leave at once he would have his soldiers kill me." He pursed his lips thoughtfully. "You see, in retrospect, I suspect I shouldn't have told him about my oath not to raise arms against any man." Luneta understood, and her indignation faded. She should have known. Rhience said, "But you aren't here looking for me, are you?"

"No," she said.

"Ywain missed his wedding date. How did Lady Laudine take it?"

"Badly," Luneta said. She slid from the saddle and shook her head at the memory.

148

"And now she's sent you to fetch him back?" Rhience asked.

"Not exactly," Luneta admitted. "She sent me to tell him that he needn't bother returning."

Rhience raised one eyebrow. "A perfectly understandable response, but somehow it doesn't sound like Lady Laudine. Has the lap dog learned to bark?"

Luneta shook her head. "No. I've no doubt that Malvolus told her what to say. I know for a fact that he told her to send me with the message."

"I see," Rhience said softly.

"It's Malvolus who rules the castle now. I suppose he always did, behind the scenes, but now it's out in the open. He's the one who kept track of Ywain's six months, and when Ywain didn't show, he convinced Laudine that Ywain had never loved her but was only after Sir Esclados's castle. He said it was all a plot hatched by Ywain and his wicked ally."

"You?"

Luneta sighed. "Who else? What else was Laudine to believe? It all fits together. First Ywain kills Sir Esclados, then I persuade her to marry him, and finally it turns out that we're cousins. I think at heart she knows I wouldn't do her harm—we've grown a little closer the past few months—but she's not strong enough to contradict Malvolus."

"And so you were sent to deliver Laudine's rejection

to Ywain," Rhience said. "To punish both of you at once."

Luneta nodded. "I think, though, if I can just persuade him to come back, I might be able to talk Laudine into—"

"Haven't you done enough persuading?" Rhience asked with a hard edge in his voice. "Why don't you leave it be, Luneta? It wasn't your fault that Ywain broke his promise, you know. Let him face the results himself."

"Let his life be ruined because he forgot a date?" Luneta asked. "Anyone can forget a date. I forgot it myself. So did Laudine. She doesn't even have a calendar and would never have known that the time had passed if Malvolus hadn't told her. If you're so good with dates, why didn't you remind Ywain?"

"I told you, I've been trying," Rhience said. "I've been hanging about for weeks now, but you can get an audience with the king more easily than with your precious cousin these days. Except in the tournament arenas, I've barely been able to catch a glimpse of him, he's been so surrounded by guards and fainting women."

"Fainting women?" Luneta repeated. Then, a bit fearfully, she asked, "He hasn't . . . he hasn't found another—"

"Another love? No, as far as I can tell from the gossip, he's been faithful to Lady Laudine. But that only

150

makes it worse. He's called 'The Unattainable Knight' or some such rot. It gives him an air of mystery, and every lady in the land imagines how famous she would be if only she could be the lady who finally wins his heart. He's had to hire some men to keep all his admirers at bay."

"Then how am I to . . . but I have to speak to him! I've been riding almost without a rest for two days."

"How did you know to look for him here, by the way?" Rhience asked.

"I just asked around until I heard of a tournament," she said. "Isn't there any way to get to him? Could Gawain get me in?"

"Sir Gawain's not here. Nor is King Arthur, if that's your next thought. I gather they don't go to many tournaments themselves."

"Well, I have to get to him somehow," Luneta said.

"You can try, but you won't succeed," Rhience said.

By noon the next day, Luneta was nearly ready to admit that Rhience was right. She spent all that morning pushing through the crowds that encircled Ywain's tent, tramping in puddles of old snow and being pushed about by the flocks of women (and quite a few men) who gathered wherever Ywain went. She succeeded once in getting to the front of the throng and even handing a note to one of Ywain's guards, but a moment later she saw her note, crumpled into a ball, tossed into a dirty snowbank. Not once did she even glimpse her cousin.

"No wonder he lost track of the days," she moaned to Rhience over a meager luncheon. "With all those ladies and courtiers screaming his name all day and night, he probably hasn't slept in months. By the way, why do you suppose those men are out there with the ladies?"

Rhience looked uncomfortable, but after a moment he replied. "Well, there are some who have suggested that there's a private reason that Ywain has never shown any interest in the ladies," he said.

"Oh."

"I believe it was your uncle Agrivain who first proposed this theory," Rhience added. "I hesitate to speak ill of your family, lass, but—"

"What a toad he is," Luneta said, but she was too tired even to work up a good anger at Agrivain. "Isn't there *any* time when Ywain is alone?"

"Only when he's jousting," Rhience said. "And I'm not sure you can call that alone, since there's a crowd watching."

Luneta looked up, then lowered her eyes quickly so that Rhience wouldn't see that her interest had been caught. "Then there's nothing to be done," she said, with studied despondency. "When is the final joust for the tournament anyway? This afternoon, isn't it?"

"Yes," Rhience said. "You want to watch?"

Luneta shrugged and said, "I suppose."

The final event of the weeklong tournament was to take place at midafternoon, but Rhience and Luneta went as soon as they had eaten. Though it was still hours early, they were lucky to find a place in the rough wooden benches behind the palisade that ringed the jousting area. Luneta scanned the arena closely and soon found what she was looking for: a small gate in the fence, by which the servants who cleaned up after the horses went in and out. Having found this entrance and marked how to get there, Luneta sat demurely beside Rhience, talking with him about all the places he had visited over the past six months.

The crowd grew more dense around them as the time for the final joust approached. It became much harder to move and see, but in one important respect the crowd was a good thing: it made it easy for her to slip away from Rhience. A few minutes before the joust was to take place, she ducked into the press and began moving toward the gate.

She almost didn't make it. She was still ten yards from the entrance when she heard a roar from the crowd, the pounding of horses' hooves, and the clang of lances on shields. Fortunately for Luneta, though, neither Ywain nor his opponent was unhorsed, and by the time they had drawn back for a second pass, she had reached the door and stepped into the arena. The first thing she saw was Ywain, still using the same armor (though it was polished to an astonishing degree) and riding the same horse she had come to know on the journey from Scotland months before. The knights were just beginning their second pass, so she moved quickly. Picking up her skirts, she ran to the middle of the field, right into Ywain's path. She heard shouting and glimpsed figures leaping over the fence and coming after her, but she was able to intercept Ywain and halt his charge. His horse reared abruptly, and Ywain shouted, "Get back, girl! You'll be hurt!"

"Ywain!" she called back. "It's me! Luneta!" But Ywain was busy calming his mount and didn't hear. Hands grasped her arms and started pulling her away, and Luneta screamed, "I've come from Laudine!"

Ywain had already started moving again, head down and lance leveled, but when Luneta called Laudine's name, he jerked his head around sharply and pulled up. His opponent hit him square in the chest, and Ywain flew from the saddle and landed in a shiny heap in the dirt. The crowd roared with angry disapproval, and wrenching herself free from the hands that held her, Luneta ran to his fallen figure.

Ywain was already climbing to his feet, unhurt but indignant. Jerking his helm from his head, he glared furiously at Luneta. "You made me lose the tournament!" he shouted.

Luneta met his anger with a boiling anger of her own, too long suppressed. "You've lost more than that, you stupid gapeseed! You've lost Laudine!"

"Laudine?" Ywain repeated, his furious expression fading to a haughty indignation. "What do you mean? Why, you're Luneta! What are you saying? Lost Laudine? Do you mean that she's been unfaithful? I will never believe that she could—"

"Shut up, blitherwit!" Luneta snapped. "No, she hasn't been unfaithful. If anyone's been unfaithful, it's you!"

"No!" Ywain cried. "Never!"

"Don't you have any idea what month it is? You stupid, foolish peacock—strutting around in your shiny armor! 'The Unattainable Knight'! You promised Laudine you'd be back within six months, promised it as a pledge of your love!"

Ywain's mouth dropped open, and the color drained from his face.

"That was six months and one week ago, Ywain. Six months and one week."

"Laudine," Ywain whispered.

Luneta's own fury faded, and all she felt was a horrible sadness. In a quieter voice, she said, "I've been sent to tell you that you needn't come back now."

Ywain fell to his knees, his chin on his chest. Then he raised blank eyes to the heavens and emitted a long, fierce, wrenching howl of despair that echoed eerily over the tournament field, then died away. He sounded like a wounded animal, and Luneta took an involuntary step back. Ywain leaped to his feet, screamed once more, and ran wildly from the field. Then he was gone, and Luneta was alone under the gaze of hundreds of amazed eyes.

"While I have your attention," came a voice from her side, calling loudly to the crowd, "would you like to see me juggle?" It was Rhience. "No? Well, then, we'll just be off." Taking her arm, Rhience led her briskly away.

Ywain's armor was found at the edge of a nearby forest, his sword driven deeply into the trunk of a tree, but no one could locate Ywain himself. A few search parties went out looking for him, led by Sir Lamorak, the knight who had defeated Ywain in the tournament and won the prize, but there was no sign of him. Luneta found herself very popular immediately after the tournament, as everyone was agog to know what she had said to Sir Ywain to cause such a display, but when she refused to tell details, her fame swiftly became notoriety. Having no explanation for Ywain's shocking behavior, people began to make up their own stories, usually with Luneta in the role of the villain.

"The way I hear it," Rhience said on the fifth day after Ywain's disappearance, "you're in love with Ywain yourself, but he wouldn't look at you, so you found out who his secret ladylove is and murdered her. Not very clever of you, lass," he added disapprovingly. "I mean, having killed his true love, how could you possibly expect him to fall in love with you?"

Luneta nodded glumly. "That explains some of the looks I get when I go out."

Rhience dropped his bantering tone and asked, "Bad, is it?" Luneta nodded. "Do you know, Luneta," he said, "I've begun to wonder if I could escort you somewhere."

"Where?"

"Anywhere but here," Rhience replied.

Luneta nodded again. He was right. "I need to go back to Laudine as soon as I'm able," Luneta said. "I can't just leave her in Malvolus's power. But I'm also worried about Ywain. I've stayed this long only to see if the searchers find him."

"Then we can leave anytime," Rhience said. "No more search parties are going out. I heard Sir Lamorak say that it was useless."

"They're giving up?" Luneta exclaimed. Rhience nodded. "But he's out there somewhere with no horse or weapon or armor!" She scowled angrily at the ground for a moment, then looked up. "They all called him the greatest knight in England! He was their hero! What happened to the admirers of 'The Unattainable Knight'?"

"Ah, that," Rhience said. "Well, that's gone off a bit. You see, he was unhorsed, which always takes the shine off a knight. You can't deny that it looks rather silly. Then there was all that screaming business. Not very courtly at all. And finally, it turns out that Sir Lamorak—who defeated him—is also unattainable. He's told everyone that he, like Ywain, loves an absent beauty and can never look at another woman. So you see? From the court's perspective, they've just traded even up. Some of the ladies are already swooning when Lamorak walks by."

"Ladies can be so stupid," Luneta said.

"Your words, not mine," Rhience said.

"I've got to go find him," Luneta said. "It's partly"—she cast a look of warning at Rhience—"*partly* my fault that he's in this mess."

Rhience raised one eyebrow but kept his lips tightly closed.

Luneta met his gaze squarely. "Will you go with me?" she asked.

Rhience smiled. "Sure," he said. "I'll get our horses."

They started where all the other search parties had begun, at the edge of the forest where Ywain's armor had been found. It had been snowing earlier but now was just cold and dreary. Rhience looked into the trees. "Most of the searchers have gone right into the woods," he said. "The idea is that he took off his armor so as to climb more easily over tree trunks and so on. They haven't found anything, but that's hardly surprising. You could lose a village in this forest."

Luneta stared glumly into the shadows. Looking for one man's trail in those woods did seem futile. Ywain had been missing almost a week and could be in the next shire by now. She was about to say so and to suggest going home when a movement within the trees caught her eye. She squinted at the spot where she had seen the movement and made out a vaguely human shape—but it was much too small to be Ywain. She cocked her head and listened intently, the way that she had trained herself to listen at the fireplace at home. A soft voice said, "I don't suppose you can hear me, can you, Luneta?"

Luneta sat bolt upright in her saddle. The voice continued, "Good heavens, you can, can't you? Fascinating!"

Luneta's mouth dropped open, and she glanced involuntarily at Rhience, who was examining the trail. He clearly hadn't heard anything. The voice, really more like a whisper that sounded right in her left ear, spoke again. "Do you know, my dear, I'm acquainted with some full-grown elves who can't use their inner ears like that. Full-grown as elves go, of course. Most of us don't grow all that—"

"What's wrong, Luneta?" asked Rhience.

"Nothing," Luneta said, rubbing her left temple. "Something in my ear. Maybe a snowflake fell in it."

"It stopped snowing an hour ago," Rhience pointed out.

"But you aren't interested in elves, are you?" the voice in Luneta's ear said. "You're looking for your witless cousin. And let me assure you, I don't mean 'witless' as an insult. The fellow's really lost his wits."

Luneta stared at the woods, but the small figure she had first seen had disappeared. Only the voice continued. "If you want to find Ywain, you need to go south a bit, just past a frozen stream, and there you'll find a cow path. Follow that path to the east, except of course when it doesn't go directly east. Sometimes it goes more southeast, and once or twice it actually goes due south. When that happens, you'll want to stay on the path and not keep going east. Or maybe not directly on the path itself. Beside the path is just as good, and considering some of the things that are in the path itself, maybe beside the path is better. You know, I've never understood cows, the way they don't even step aside out of the path when they have to unload. Do you understand what I mean by 'unload'? I don't want to be indelicate."

"I know what you mean," Luneta said.

Rhience said, "I didn't say anything."

The voice in Luneta's ear broke into a merry giggle. "Got you!" it said.

Luneta reddened and said to Rhience, "I'm sorry. I was thinking of something else."

160

"Were you thinking about calling this off?" Rhience asked. "Because if you were, I agree. We have no hope of finding one man in that forest five days after he disappeared."

Luneta glanced once more at the woods. She licked her lips, hesitated a moment, then said, "Let's try going south."

"South?"

Luneta nodded. "Er, which direction is that?" she asked.

Rhience blinked, then pointed to their right, across a meadow. "That's south. Why that way?"

"Because . . . no one else has looked in that direction?" Luneta said hopefully.

Rhience raised one eyebrow and said, "Do you know something I don't?" just as the voice in her ear said, "You sound like an absolute clodpate, Luneta!"

"I don't either," Luneta snapped.

Rhience threw up his hands in mock surrender. "All right, so you don't."

The voice began giggling again and Luneta said hurriedly, "I didn't mean you, Rhience." Rhience only stared at her, so she said, "Here, let's go south for a while and see if we find a cow path or something that Ywain might have followed."

Rhience continued to look at Luneta curiously, but he turned his horse and headed across the meadow. A few minutes later, when they crossed the frozen stream and came to a clear cattle trail, he looked at her even more curiously. "Which way now?" he asked.

"East along the path," Luneta said.

"Whatever you and your snowflake say," Rhience replied, turning his horse left and following the path.

The voice laughed. "What a clever fellow! But Brother Matthew was always clever. It was one reason he didn't fit in at the monastery. He's already figured out that you have a friend."

"Are you my friend?" Luneta whispered under her breath. "Who are you?"

"Didn't you hear Brother Matthew? Call me Snow-flake." Then the voice disappeared in an explosion of mirth.

They followed the cattle trail for two hours, and when that trail ended, Snowflake directed Luneta around a field of bracken to a small stream and told them to follow that stream. Rhience asked Luneta no questions but turned wherever she said to turn. At last, when the sun began to set, Rhience pulled up and said, "Here's a good place to camp. Are we almost there, or should we stop for the night?"

"How should I know?" Luneta demanded.

"Ask, why don't you?"

Luneta felt herself turning red, but she said, "Well?"

"You'd best camp," Snowflake replied in her ear. "You won't come up on Ywain for a day or two yet."

Luneta looked up to Rhience's patient gaze. "Er, I think . . . he says we should camp."

Rhience nodded and dismounted. For the next half-hour they were both occupied in rubbing down their horses, building a fire, and opening the packs of dried food that Rhience had brought with them, but when at last they were seated by their fire, eating, Rhience said, "You want to explain this to me?"

Luneta nodded, but she felt very self-conscious as she said, "It's a voice, right in my ear. Do you think I'm mad?"

"I've thought so for months," Rhience replied. "But hearing a voice isn't necessarily a sign of it. What does your voice tell you?"

"He says that we won't come up on Ywain for another day or two."

"Does your voice have a name?"

Luneta reddened again and, in a small voice, said, "He says to call him Snowflake."

Rhience began to laugh. "Ah, a spirit with a sense of humor. My favorite sort."

When Rhience said "spirit," Luneta looked up sharply. "It *is* a spirit, isn't it? Do you think it's leading us to our death or something?"

Rhience cocked his head and thought for a moment. "I shouldn't think so. I've a notion that evil spirits would take themselves too seriously to call themselves Snowflake. Can you imagine it? Satan and his demons gathered in council—Marduk, Mephisto, and the wicked Snowflake?"

Luneta began to laugh. "True. And I must say that Snowflake doesn't *sound* evil."

Snowflake's voice said, "I thank you, my dear. And please tell Brother Matthew that his insight into the spirits is quite accurate."

"Who's Brother Matthew?" Luneta asked.

Rhience stared at Luneta. "Where did you hear that name?"

Luneta tapped her ear. "Snowflake says to tell Brother Matthew that his insight into the spirits is accurate. Is it you?"

Rhience nodded, grinning. "I think I told you once that at one time I was planning to enter a religious life." Luneta nodded. "It was a bit more extreme than that. I was a novice at a monastery, nearly accepted into the cloister. While there, I took the name Matthew. It seemed more religious to me."

"As you did when you were a knight. Sir Calosomething, wasn't it?"

"Calogrenant," Rhience said. "Yes. Just like that."

"What happened at the monastery?"

"I was quite a success there," Rhience said, leaning back against a boulder and giving Luneta a lopsided smile. "I'm good at numbers and figures, and I know something of land management. Before I left to join the church, I was practically running the family estates. I think Father Abbot was grooming me to be overseer of the monastery lands."

"Would you have liked that?" Luneta asked, a little surprised.

"I think so," Rhience said. "The problem was that I wasn't as suited for the rest of monastic life. Not serious enough, you see. They were forever trying to heal me of my levity. Once my preceptor caught me telling faery stories to some of the orphans. He took me by the ear off to the scriptorium, where he made me read an improving book about some old fellow named Simeon Stylite. This chap ate only once a week, slept only a couple of hours a night, and to top it off lived the last half of his life up on top of a tower, all to prove his devotion."

"This was supposed to cure you of laughing too much?"

Rhience grinned. "Yes. And it just made me laugh, which got me two days of solitude. When I got out, I packed and left."

"So then you changed your name to Sir Calogrenant and became a knight."

"And now I've taken back my real name and become who I really am."

"A fool?" Luneta asked.

"Just so," Rhience said. He unrolled his blankets and stretched out on them. "Tell Snowflake good night for me."

They rode off before sunrise the next morning, still following Snowflake's whispered directions. It was growing late when they came to the first human they had encountered since leaving Oxford: a thick-waisted shepherdess with rosy cheeks and freckles. She was sitting on a fallen tree surrounded by her flock, but she was paying the sheep no attention, and although the winter wind was cold, she was fanning herself and making odd clucking noises. Rhience glanced quizzically at Luneta, then rode close to the shepherdess, who jumped to her feet. "Oh, lawks!" she said.

"Lawks, indeed," Rhience replied politely, inclining his head. "Truly you say so."

The girl blinked and asked, "Say what?"

"Lawks. A truer word has never been spoken."

"Lawks?" she asked.

"Lawks," Rhience repeated gravely.

"Shut up, Rhience," Luneta said. "Don't mind him. He's a fool."

The shepherdess looked at Luneta, eyeing her fine

gown with admiration, then dropped a rough curtsy. "Indeed, your ladyship. I beg your pardon for being forward, and for not speaking respectful to ye when ye come up, as my mother would be shocked to hear of me not doing. But I *have* had such a shock!"

"Lawks," said Rhience.

"What gave you such a shock?" Luneta asked, ignoring him.

"That man! Did ye see him?"

"We saw no one," Luneta said. "Did a man threaten you?"

"Nay, your ladyship. He no more than took one look at me and he run off, which isn't hardly a surprise, considering."

"Considering what?" Luneta asked.

"Well . . . ." The girl glanced nervously at Rhience. "I hardly like to say, miss."

"You can trust us," Luneta said.

The girl leaned forward. "It's that he weren't . . . didn't have . . . well, it was all just right there!"

"All what?" asked Luneta.

The girl clamped her lips shut. "That, your ladyship, I won't say for no persuading."

Luneta glanced helplessly at Rhience, but the fool only grinned. "Do you mean that this man was naked?" he asked the girl. Her face brightened to a shiny cherry color, but she nodded expressively.

"It must be him," Luneta said. "Snowflake said that he'd lost his wits." She turned to the girl. "Did you see which direction he went?"

"Yes, ma'am," the girl said. She pointed at a thick clump of bushes at the edge of a wooded area. "He saw me and just jumped up, turned around, and run off that way. He went right through those gorse bushes."

"Ouch," said Rhience.

"Just there by that big oak!" she said, pointing. "I'll never forget it! The last thing I saw as he jumped into the shrubbery was . . . was . . ."

"His lawks," Rhience supplied.

Luneta struggled to keep her countenance, thanked the shepherdess for her help, and led the way to the wooded area. "He must be frozen," she said.

"Not to mention scratched," Rhience said. "Shocking!"

"Well, and so it was to that poor girl!" Luneta said. "It wasn't very nice of you to make fun of her, you know."

"Don't be silly. She's just had the time of her life and will bore her friends and family for many years to come, telling the story every chance she gets. Now, what do you think is back in those woods?"

They found out twenty minutes later when they rode into a clearing where a stocky man in a heavy fur robe was turning a whole haunch of venison on a spit over a cheerful fire. "Welcome, travelers!" he called. "Come and share my bounty!"

"We thank you, sir," Luneta replied, "but we must—"

"Just a minute, lass," Rhience said. "It's almost dark, and we won't be able to look much longer anyway. And perhaps this gentleman can help us." More loudly, Rhience said, "We thank you indeed, Father. 'Bounty' is the right word. That's a lovely piece of meat. The hermits of this country do well by themselves."

"God provides, my son," the old man replied, laughing. "But all I have is yours to share. How did you know I was a hermit? I didn't get around to putting on the old sackcloth this morning."

"A bit chilly for sackcloth, I would think. No, I noticed your beads on the bench by the door, and besides, who else would live in such a cottage alone like this?" Rhience dismounted and led his horse to the well while he talked.

"Who else indeed? But I must say, it's not such a bad life as I'd expected. I'm new here, you know. The last hermit in this hut died—some think of starvation."

"Indeed?" asked Rhience, casting another glance at the haunch of venison.

"But as I said, God provides."

"Do you hunt, sir?" Rhience inquired.

The hermit shook his head and beamed at them. "I'll tell you all about it while we eat, if you like."

At last able to fit a word in, Luneta said, "Before you begin, we need to ask you—"

"Let's listen to the good holy man first, Luneta," Rhience said. "I've a feeling we may learn all we want to know."

"I came here to keep a vow," the jovial man said over a delicious meal of perfectly roasted venison. "I didn't start out a hermit, as you might have guessed. I'm a butcher by trade, and to tell the truth, I haven't been a very good Christian, what with one thing and another. I don't mean I was dishonest—ask anyone and they'll tell you Godwulf the Butcher has the fairest scales anywheres about—but I do like my food and beer and I did go on the occasional spree, so that it most drives our priest up a tree when he thinks on my sins. Well, it pleased God to let me come down deathly ill last month so that I thought I was about to cock up my toes, and here comes Father Richard saying that I might be healed if I would just make a vow to obey him for three months. Like I said, I thought I was dead anyway, so I decided to give him a bit of pleasure before I died, and I took his vow. Then, what do you think happened? I got well!"

"How disappointing," Rhience said sympathetically.

"Well, it was! Not at first, of course; I mean, I didn't *mind* God healing me."

"That's big of you," Rhience said.

"But it was right downheartening to think I'd just given three months of my life to that priest. And I didn't know the half of it, either. As soon as I was well, Father Richard tells me that for my three months, he wanted me to live in this forest hermitage that's just come open and say prayers all day and eat only what God provided for me."

"I knew a preceptor in a monastery once who sounds a bit like your Father Richard," Rhience commented.

"Sour bloke, eh? But then what do you think happened? Three nights ago, on my first night here, I'm just sitting by the fire listening to my gut rumble, and out of the woods crawls this young man as naked as a skinned rabbit."

Luneta shot a quick glance at Rhience, who only nodded and said, "Indeed?"

"Well, I wasn't feeling so well myself, as I said, but at least I had some clothes, and so I thought to help him. I spoke to him, but he didn't seem to understand me. Mad, you know. I'm a big fellow and handy with my fists, so I wasn't rightly afraid of him, and I soft-talked him over by the fire and put a thick fur robe over his shoulders. He went to sleep right there, and the next morning I wake up and there's a brace of rabbits, fresh killed, lying on the doorstep."

"The madman gave them to you?"

"And a fine game hen the next morning, and a whole deer today. By now we've got it all worked out regular, even if we never say a word. Every night, sometime around midnight, he comes and drops off whatever he's killed during the day and curls up in this robe by the fire and eats whatever I've cooked and left for him. I never ate so well in my life! When Father Richard said I was to eat only what God provided, you could tell he didn't expect God to provide much, but I'll tell you this—God provides like the merry dickens! I may just decide to stay a hermit!"

By this time, Rhience was shaking with laughter, clearly enjoying their jovial host very much indeed. He talked with Godwulf in high good spirits for another hour while Luneta waited. At last the best-fed hermit in England went inside to sleep off his penance.

"It sounds as if all we have to do is wait here, and Ywain will come to us," Luneta said.

"True," Rhience replied. "But let me ask you this. What will you do with him once you find him?"

Luneta had already been wondering that. "I know," she said. "When we came after him, it was because I was afraid he was in danger."

"I suppose living naked in the forest in winter could be considered danger," Rhience said.

"True. It wouldn't be *my* choice, anyway. But he does

have a place to get warm, and he seems to be able to get food."

"You think we should leave him here?" Rhience said.

Luneta shrugged. "Even if we could drag him away by force, which I doubt, where would we take him?" Rhience nodded thoughtfully. "I don't want to make any decisions now, though," Luneta said. "I need to see him first and try to talk with him."

Luneta never got that chance. An hour or so before midnight, as she stood in the shadows of the trees, watching the fire and waiting for Ywain, a now familiar voice spoke to her, not at her ear but from beside her. "Lady Luneta," it said.

Luneta looked down to see a little bearded man with leafy hair and an impish grin. "Snowflake?" she said.

"It's as good as most of my names," the little elf replied. "I've come to fetch you."

VII

In the Other World

Luneta stared at the little man. "Fetch me where?" she asked.

"Come and see."

"Why?"

"You'll understand when you're there."

"I have to be back at midnight or so to talk to Ywain. How long will it take?"

The little man giggled. "That's a nonsense question. There's no answer."

"Why?"

"Come and see."

Luneta glanced over at Rhience, who had his back to them and was kneeling over the fire. "Why should I go anywhere with you? Why should I trust you?" she hissed.

"You've trusted me this far. It's a bit late to start

wondering that now," the man replied. "As for why you should go with me, you'll come because as long as you can remember you've dreamed of getting away from your ordinary life, and I'm not ordinary."

He was right, and Luneta no longer hesitated. Pulling her cloak around her shoulders, she stepped into the woods behind the green man. After a few steps, she said, "By the way, I ought to know what to call you. Snowflake isn't your real name, is it?"

"All my names are real," Snowflake said.

He led Luneta through the forest, down trails that seemed perfectly obvious in the night but that Luneta had seen no trace of when she and Rhience had ridden over the same ground in daylight. They didn't go far. After only a few minutes, Snowflake led her to a pond. It could hardly have been more than twenty paces across, but in its center was an island, smaller around than King Arthur's Round Table, and on the island stood a tiny hut, barely large enough for one large adult to stand in.

"Here we are," Snowflake said.

"Are we going into that shack?" Luneta asked. Snowflake nodded, and Luneta said, "Good thing we're both little. How do we get there? Jump?"

By way of answer, Snowflake took Luneta's hand and stepped into the pond, pulling her in after him. At the very first step, they both plunged into water over their heads—indeed, Luneta never did know how deep the pond was, since she never touched bottom—and began paddling forward. Oddly, there was more light under the surface of the water than there was above in the night; a pure blue-green glow illuminated the water around Luneta, and she saw that the pond was much larger than she had thought. Snowflake pulled her hand to hurry her, and she paddled harder, looking around with wonder. They swam together for a long time—time itself seemed larger below the surface than it was above—and never once went up for air. It didn't occur to Luneta that she ought to breathe, and so she didn't bother. Instead, she swam through the warm, clear, beautifully lit water, enjoying the journey and forgetting everything else.

At last they came to land, and Snowflake pulled her out of the pond. They stood dripping on the shore of the island for a moment, outside the shack, while Luneta looked back to the shore where they had started. It was only about three or four paces away, across a narrow strip of black water. She could have flipped a stone to the opposite shore with her thumb. "The pond is bigger on the inside than it is on the outside, isn't it?" she said, half to herself.

Snowflake giggled. "That's impossible, and you know it," he said.

Luneta nodded, then said, "I think over there—on

that shore, where we started—it would have been impossible. But there are different rules here, aren't there?"

Snowflake beamed at her. "You astonish me again, my Luneta. Oh, yes, I think we're right about you." He still held her hand, and now he pulled her toward the hut and opened the door. "After you, my lady."

After her experience in the pond, Luneta was only mildly surprised to find herself in a vast stone room with high, vaulted ceilings. There were no windows, but candles lined every wall, and a great fire roared in a huge fireplace. By the fire sat her aunt, Morgan Le Fay.

"I've brought her," announced Snowflake.

"That much I can see for myself," Lady Morgan replied wryly. "Why don't you save your words for when you have something to say?"

Snowflake giggled and swept a bow. "If I spoke only when I had something important to proclaim, then I'd be as boring as you are, my most revered ladyship."

Lady Morgan turned her eyes to Luneta and examined her from head to toe. Luneta felt like a fish at the market, but she waited in silence. When Morgan spoke again, though, it was to Snowflake. "Are you sure of this, Robin? I see no more mark of the enchantress in her than I did six months ago at Camelot."

The elf met Lady Morgan's gaze with a limpid smile. "She has the inner ear, my lady. She heard me speak in her ear in a voice that no one else could have heard.

Moreover, when we made the crossing just now she knew at once that we had entered another world, one with different rules than the one she came from."

Now Lady Morgan looked at Luneta with more interest. "Tell me, child, have you ever heard people speak of the Other World?"

Luneta shook her head. "Not exactly," she said.

"What does that mean?" Lady Morgan demanded.

"Not when I was awake. But I used to dream sometimes about going to another world, where magic wasn't magic, because it was normal, and where life was much more interesting than in my own world." Lady Morgan's eyes widened, and she shot a sharp glance at the elf. Luneta added, "I thought that was just wishful thinking, though. You see, my own life was so wretchedly ordinary that anything sounded better. You'd have to know my parents to understand."

"You forget, child, that I've known your father since he was in short coats, and I'm perfectly willing to agree that he is depressingly dull."

Luneta felt a stir of anger. "Actually, I wasn't thinking of my father so much as my mother," she said.

Lady Morgan almost smiled, which made her face appear more human. She glanced at Snowflake, whom she had called Robin. "Have you asked her yet?"

"No, my lady," he responded.

"Then how do you know she—?" Lady Morgan began.

178

"Lady Morgan," Luneta said firmly. "I am right in front of you. If you have anything to ask me, you may do so."

Again, Lady Morgan looked slightly less forbidding, as a trace of amusement flitted across her face. "Very well," she said. "I am here to train you to be an enchantress, if you wish it. If you do not, of course, you will be returned to the World of Men."

Luneta started to mention that she had already received some training as an enchantress, but she had a sudden hunch that Lady Morgan would not be impressed by the beauty lotions and oils that Laudine had taught her. Luneta hadn't decided whether her aunt was good or evil, but whatever she was, she wasn't trivial. Instead she said simply, "I would like to learn."

Lady Morgan nodded briskly. "Very well, then. We shall begin at once—"

But Luneta shook her head. "No," she said. Both Lady Morgan and Snowflake-Robin looked at her with surprise. "First I must know: Why me?"

"You're very pert for one of your years, girl," Lady Morgan said austerely.

"Why me?" Luneta repeated.

Lady Morgan looked at her in silence for a moment, then said, "You heard what Master Robin said just now. You appear to be attuned to things of this world in ways that others from your world are not."

"I don't want to be disrespectful to either of you," Luneta said. "But when you step into a tiny pond and find that under the surface it is as large as a great lake, it doesn't take special powers to realize that you've entered a different sort of world than you're used to."

Snowflake-Robin said with a gentle laugh, "Actually, you would be surprised at the amazing shifts that humans will use to deny the evidence of their own eyes when they don't choose to believe something. Nineteen out of twenty humans who stepped into that water and saw what you saw would have convinced themselves they had simply misjudged the size of the pond."

"Quite true," Lady Morgan said.

Luneta shrugged doubtfully. She still didn't feel that she was anything special, but she was willing to accept that she was at least more perceptive in some ways. "And why you? Why are *you* the one to teach me?"

A spark of anger glinted in Lady Morgan's eyes. "Is the arrangement unsatisfactory to you?" she asked in a withering voice.

Luneta swallowed but answered forthrightly. "I don't know that yet. It might be. I just don't see you as the sort of person who would be a patient teacher."

"No one said I would be patient, child. You'll do well to remember it," Lady Morgan replied, her face stony.

There was an uncomfortable silence as Luneta and Lady Morgan gazed at each other. Then the elf said, "I suppose I can answer that. You see, you are now in what Lady Morgan just referred to as the 'Other World.' This is the world of faeries and magic and the sorts of things that in your world you generally find only in stories. This world is divided in two. There is the Seelie Court, made of benevolent faeries, and the Unseelie Court, made up of the rest. Everyone in this world and everyone from your world who traffics here must choose which side will be theirs."

Luneta took this in, then said to the elf, "Yes, I see. You're from the Seelie Court, aren't you?" He bowed, and Luneta added thoughtfully, "And so is Gawain's squire Terence."

Snowflake-Robin giggled. "Oh, dear me, yes. His Grace, the Duke of Avalon, is very much of the Seelie Court."

That explained a few things, Luneta thought. Then she looked at Lady Morgan. "But I can't tell about you."

"As Master Robin said," Lady Morgan said, "everyone must choose. That doesn't mean everyone must choose at once, however. I am—ah—still undecided."

"And that," said the green man, "is what makes her the ideal instructor. As her student, you will see both sides."

"That sounds pleasant," Luneta murmured to herself.

"And now," the elf said with another bow, "I'll be going."

Luneta turned to him. "Will I see you again?"

"Assuredly, my dear."

"And when I see you, I believe I should call you by your real name. It's Robin, isn't it?"

The little man shrugged. "I am called that as often as anything. Call me as you will, but for myself, I believe I shall always think of myself as your Snowflake." Then he was gone. Luneta stared at the space where he had stood a moment before; then, calm on the outside but shaking within, she turned to face her teacher.

"Before we begin, I must know," Lady Morgan said imperiously, "if you have ever been taught any magic at all. Did anyone show you any potions or oils when you were a little girl?"

"Not when I was a girl—" Luneta began.

Shaking her head, Lady Morgan said, "I wouldn't have believed it."

"But I did learn a few things when I was staying with Lady Laudine of Salisbury."

Lady Morgan covered her eyes with one hand. "Laudine," she repeated, with a slight moan. "Don't tell me that was who you were off to visit when you stopped at Camelot."

"It was."

"What was your mother thinking? Of all the flitter-wits to whom to hand over one's daughter!"

"Laudine has a very kind heart," Luneta said defensively.

"I am indifferent to the quality of her heart. It can be as kind as she likes, but it will never change the quality of her mind. What did she teach you? Creams for your complexion? Lotions to give you thick, lustrous hair and repair those irritating dry ends?"

Luneta couldn't help grinning. "Mostly, yes."

"You will oblige me by forgetting all such foolishness," Lady Morgan snapped.

"But Lady Morgan—"

"And you will oblige me even more if you will not argue with me."

"I was only going to point out that you yourself have an unearthly beauty that must be the result of magic, so it seems that—"

Lady Morgan's eyes widened. "What do you mean, 'must be the result of magic'? Is it not possible that I am this beautiful without any magic at all?"

"No."

Lady Morgan's lips parted, and she stared at Luneta in shocked amazement.

"For beginners, you're my great-aunt. I don't know how old you are, but you must be at least fifty, and very likely older, so—"

"If I, in years past, enhanced my beauty with magic," Lady Morgan said in a perilously calm voice, "you may be certain that I was already a beauty to begin with. It was a very different story with your precious kindhearted Laudine, I assure you! When I began teaching her, she was a tall, awkward, ungainly, and extremely plain girl!"

Luneta looked at her fuming great-aunt for a moment, then nodded slowly. "That explains it, then. That's why she's so obsessed with keeping her beauty. Poor thing."

"Believe me, child. Laudine is an object for contempt, not pity."

Luneta looked into Lady Morgan's stormy eyes for a long moment. In them she saw a barely suppressed anger, and so Luneta turned her own eyes demurely to the stone floor and said, "I beg your pardon for distracting you, my lady."

In an awed voice, Lady Morgan said, "Good Gog, child. You're patronizing me, aren't you? 'Let's not get the old lady all wrought up.' That's it, isn't it?"

Luneta hid a smile. "I don't know what you mean, my lady."

"I have trained a dozen enchantresses," Lady Morgan said, "and not one of them has ever made me lose my temper or has ever driven me to defend myself. Not *one* of them has dared to interrupt me. And I assure you that not one of them would have dreamed of patronizing me."

"That must have been dull for you," Luneta commented.

Slowly, Lady Morgan's icy mask melted. "It was, in

184

fact, you abominable child. Come, let us begin. The first step in magic is to gain control over physical objects . . ."

Luneta couldn't have told how long she was in the stone chamber with Lady Morgan. In that windowless room, days and nights seemed irrelevant, and besides, without ever being told, Luneta knew that time itself was different in that world than in the one she was used to. She learned how to manipulate physical objects, even distant objects, without touching them, how to make a piece of wood give off more light than any torch, and how to start a raging fire with a pinch of dust and an incantation. She learned how to hasten and to delay natural processes—so, for instance, she could touch a caterpillar and make it go through its cycle and become a butterfly all in a matter of seconds. She learned to make potions that would either sicken or heal, and various oils and lotions and unguents of more practical value than Laudine's beauty aids—such as the lotion that would soften untreated iron or another that made steel nearly unbreakable. She even learned how to control her own senses and experiences. For example, she could make herself feel no hunger, and she learned a spell that made hot feel cold and cold feel hot.

"This will be useful the next time I drop something in the fire," Luneta commented.

"Not so useful as all that," Lady Morgan replied.

"The fire may feel cold to you, but it will still blister your skin. Feelings are not reality, child."

Luneta also learned the limits of magic. Lady Morgan told her, for instance, that no spell could force a human to do something against his or her own will. "People speak of the philosophers' stone," Lady Morgan said, "that will turn lead into gold. But that's nothing: a mere parlor trick. The true quest of all sorcerors is to gain control over the human will, and hundreds have sacrificed all in the attempt to learn that skill."

"And failed?"

"Always. Oh, I don't mean that it's all that difficult to get people to do what you wish, especially men"—the beautiful enchantress smiled to herself—"but it has to be done with guile, not with magic, and even then"—she glanced wearily at Luneta—"it doesn't always work."

Luneta knew what Lady Morgan meant. One thing that had become clear to both of them during their time together was that they were both used to getting others to do what they wanted, and they had both expended a great deal of energy working on the other. But, since they were both skilled manipulators, they recognized each other's tricks and only ended up frustrating themselves. Luneta had always been proud of what she thought of as her "persuasive" arts—for instance, inducing Laudine to betroth herself to the man who had just killed her husband—but in Lady Morgan she had met her match. Judging from Lady Morgan's frequent mutterings about "mule-headed chits," her mentor felt the same way about her.

At last, one day—if it was, in fact, day—Lady Morgan said suddenly, "I've done."

"I beg your pardon?"

"I've done. Your training is over. You know as much as any enchantress should know as she begins, and far more than many ever do."

"I don't know as much as you do," Luneta pointed out.

"Nor will you ever," Lady Morgan said.

"I might someday! I don't think I'm so bad as all that!"

Lady Morgan gave Luneta her almost-a-smile. "If ability were all that mattered, you could be quite as powerful an enchantress as I am. I admit that freely. But you won't, because you don't care enough about magic to devote yourself to it as I have. And even I don't devote myself to it as some." Luneta looked questioningly at her, and Lady Morgan continued, "My sister, Morgause. She cares for nothing but power, both magical and earthly. Thus she devotes her whole life to learning the techniques of power and is a very powerful enchantress indeed."

Luneta nodded. "But you care for other things more?"

Lady Morgan turned a direct gaze on Luneta. "Yes," she said. "And I am the weaker for it. I would not use my powers, for instance, to hurt King Arthur—even if by doing so I could rule the world." Then she looked away, to a small cabinet by the fire. "But we have one more lesson. Go to that shelf, Luneta, and bring me the three bottles you find there."

Luneta did as she was told, bringing her teacher three small crystal vials.

"These," Lady Morgan said, "are the final lesson of your training. Each of these contains a higher and more powerful sort of magic than any you have yet learned. You may take one of these with you when you return to that other world."

"What's in them?"

If Lady Morgan had been less majestic, she would have rolled her eyes. Instead, she said, with only a trace of sarcasm, "Actually, I was about to explain that to you, even without your helpful prompting."

"I'm sorry, my lady."

"No, you're not," Lady Morgan said with a sigh. She picked up the first of the bottles. "This vial contains a love potion. Place a drop in a man's drink, and the very first person he sees after drinking it he will love forever."

"That doesn't make sense," Luneta said promptly.

Lady Morgan bowed her head in mock humility. "I do beg your pardon. Indeed, I beg pardon on behalf of the entire magical realm for not meeting your approv—"

"No, listen," Luneta said. "Haven't you taught me that we can't use magic to influence other people's wills? Well, then, how can we make someone fall in love?"

"You are confusing two similar things, my dear. It is true that we cannot change a human's will, but we certainly may change that person's emotions. As you grow more knowledgeable, you will learn that there are any number of potions and spells that can cause humans to have certain feelings. But feelings are not the same thing as decisions."

"That's just splitting hairs," Luneta said.

"Is it? Let me give you an example. Suppose a man were attacking me. I could, by means of magic, make that man suddenly feel terrified. What I could not do is make him run away; that would be his own choice. A strong-willed man would continue in spite of fear."

Luneta thought about this for a moment. "So this potion could make someone feel desperately in love with someone else, but it couldn't make him, for instance, keep a promise to the person he loves."

"That is correct."

Luneta wrinkled her nose with distaste. "Sounds pretty useless to me. What's the next bottle?"

"This potion, once taken, will give you—ah, how did I hear you phrase it one time?—will guarantee you an *unearthly* beauty."

Luneta smiled, slowly at first, then more broadly. "I see," she said, glancing once, quickly, at her great-aunt.

"Yes, you impertinent scamp, I did choose this one, if that's what you're wondering."

"Well, I was, a bit."

"And so does nearly everyone else, I might add. How do you think your kindhearted bosom-bow Laudine overcame her adolescent plainness?"

"Yes, of course," Luneta said, taking the vial and turning it slowly in her hand. "She would." She looked up suddenly. "But this potion guarantees that the one who drinks it will have great beauty, doesn't it?"

"That *is* what I said, I believe."

"Then all of Laudine's messing about with complexion creams and eye brighteners—it's all silly and unnecessary, isn't it?"

"Just so. Laudine would be beautiful dressed in rags and with no beauty lotions at all."

"What an ass she is, to be sure," Luneta said. "What's in the third bottle?"

"A healing potion."

"Healing? That sounds useful."

"Not as useful as all that. It has some limits. It cannot bring anyone back from the dead. It can only be used on a person once—no one cheats death forever—and, most unfortunate of all, you cannot use it on yourself."

Luneta looked at the three bottles for a minute. The love potion just sounded stupid, and she ruled that out immediately. The beauty drink was a little better, but whenever she looked at that vial, all she could think of was silly Laudine and her fixation on beauty. As for the healing potion, Lady Morgan was right: it had bothersome limitations, and Luneta didn't like having limits. In the end, though, she took up the third bottle and said, "I'll take this one."

For the first time in Luneta's memory, Lady Morgan allowed herself a real smile. "I was almost certain that you would, although it's rare enough for anyone to do so. Indeed, in all my years of training enchantresses, I've known only one other who did."

"Only one?"

"That's right. Your mother," Lady Morgan said.

Luneta bid farewell to Lady Morgan with genuine gratitude and even, to Luneta's surprise, a certain amount of affection, but her mind was elsewhere. Even when Robin appeared to escort her back to the World of Men, while she greeted him with pleasure, her thoughts were far away. She was thinking of the chilly vastness of Orkney Hall, where her very ordinary mother kept home and estate together.

Mother, an enchantress?

It was impossible, but Luneta knew it was true. She remembered her mother riding out in her little cart, drawn by a fat old mare, to visit the sick on the estate. She remembered her mother's exhaustive knowledge of herbs and medicinal plants. She even remembered the tiny windowless room behind the kitchen where she kept these herbs to dry—and no doubt brewed her own potions and prepared her own enchantments. Of course she was an enchantress. *The most boring enchantress that has ever lived*, Luneta thought bitterly, but as soon as she thought this, she had to admit that her mother no longer seemed as dull as she had used to.

"Robin," Luneta said to her elf friend as they walked back through the forest away from the tiny pond, "I don't suppose you know my mother, do you?"

The little man giggled. "My dear, I've known Lynet since she was your own age. Oh, yes, I know your mother quite well."

"It seems that everyone does," Luneta said. "Except for me, of course."

"Quite a promising girl, your mother was," Robin said reminiscently. "I've only known one who showed more potential." Luneta glanced at the elf from the corner of her eye. "Ay, that's right. You." The elf stopped and swept a deep bow to her, and when he spoke again, his voice was earnest. "My dear Luneta, I expect nothing but great things from you."

Luneta felt a warm glow inside, but she allowed nothing to show on her face. "Instead of talking nonsense, why don't you explain to me why it's so warm? It was early December when we left for the Other World. How long have I been gone?"

"Just three months, my dear."

"I see," Luneta said slowly. "And where are we going now?"

"Why, back where you started, of course, to the good fool Rhience and the right holy Hermit of the Hunt."

"Is that how Godwulf is known?"

"It's how I think of him."

"And are you sure that Rhience is still there? Why would he wait so long?"

"He *was* a bit concerned when you disappeared," Robin admitted, "so I took the liberty of speaking to him after I left you with Lady Morgan. I let him know today that you'd be back this afternoon, and he's expecting you."

And so he was. When Luneta stepped out of the trees into the warm, grassy area before the hermitage—sensing as she did so Robin fading away from her—there was Rhience, leaning against a wooden post in the sun, idly stirring a great cauldron. "Hallo, there, lass," he called.

"Hello, yourself," she replied, suddenly self-conscious. "Listen, Rhience, I'm sorry about leaving you without warning back—"

"By what that little green fellow said, you really didn't have much choice."

"But I did," Luneta replied. "No one made me go with him. Did Robin frighten you?"

"Not really," Rhience replied. "You see, we'd met before. He was the shepherd boy who directed me to the Storm Stone last April. He seems to be behind rather a lot. And now I suppose you've been off somewhere magical that I wouldn't understand and that you can't tell me about?"

Grateful to Rhience for not asking her directly, Luneta said, "I . . . don't know if I can or not, but if it's all the same to you, I'd rather not. Have you been well? It can't have been very pleasant, spending the winter at a hermitage."

Rhience grinned. "It hasn't been too bad, actually. When I left the monastery, I thought I had no taste for the religious life, but I might have a bit more inclination to holiness than I'd thought."

Before Luneta could reply, the hermit himself appeared from the forest carrying an armload of wood. "Ah, she's come back, has she? Welcome, welcome! Stay for dinner! Stay as long as you like! How's the brew going?"

"Look for yourself," Rhience replied. "I tried to keep the fire low."

The hermit leaned over the pot that Rhience had been stirring, then beamed at him. "Just right!" He looked back at Luneta. "Are you hungry? You don't look as if you've been eating well."

"I'm very well, thank you. Not hungry at all."

"Skin and bones is what you are! Good Rhience, if

you'll stir up another fire, I'll take over here. This batch is just coming to a ticklish bit."

"Oh, ay, a ticklish bit that will require you to taste it regularly just to make sure that it's doing what it should," Rhience answered good-naturedly. "Why don't I go make a fire?"

"Good man," the hermit said. "Remember that we're cooking for five, now that this lady's back."

"Five?" Luneta asked.

"Oh, yes," Rhience said. "The three of us, Ywain, and another guest, a knight from the Round Table named Bleoberis who's been with us this month and more. You might say that he's found a great affinity for the austere life of a hermit, too. He's off hunting just now, though I don't know what we'll do with his game. Ywain's still providing us with more than we can eat."

Luneta moved closer. "So Ywain's still living naked in the woods, hunting barehanded and bringing the food here to be cooked? He's no better at all?"

Rhience shrugged. "Can't say if he's healed any or not. He's not so jumpy as he used to be, but that might be just because he's gotten used to us."

At the word "healed," Luneta gave a visible start. Of course, that's what he needed: healing. And she had in her pouch a healing potion.

The hermit's voice boomed behind them. "The best batch yet! We don't want to waste any of this!"

"We never do," Rhience replied, grinning.

"Waste any of what? What is that stuff?" Luneta asked.

Rhience's eyes grew bright with merriment. "As it happens, before the good hermit Godwulf was articled to a butcher, he spent some time in apprenticeship to a brewer."

"That's beer?"

Rhience said, "Godwulf calls it 'Merry-Go-Up.'"

Luneta looked at Rhience, then at the hermit, then back at Rhience. "This is the austere life of a hermit that you were talking of?"

"All right, not austere, exactly," Rhience admitted.

"More meat than you can eat and more beer than you can drink?"

"If you want to put it that way."

"'The right holy Hermit of the Hunt,'" Luneta said slowly. "Holy indeed."

"To tell you the truth, I believe he is," Rhience said suddenly. "Oh, I know that such a life wouldn't be especially holy for most people, but our good Godwulf— my dear, you've never seen a man who was more thankful for what he has than our friend there."

"Why wouldn't he be thankful? He has everything he wants."

"But surely you've noticed that it hardly ever works that way. Those who have the most are nearly always the least grateful for what they have. Godwulf there, he spends his entire day giving thanks to God and sharing what he has with everyone who passes by. The local farmers and villagers are beginning to come to him for spiritual advice."

"Spiritual advice? What sort of spiritual advice does he give?"

"He says, 'Enjoy your food, enjoy your work, give thanks to God.' Then he usually hands them a pint of ale."

Luneta watched the burly brewer for a moment. Then her face clouded. "But Rhience, his bounty all comes from poor, mad Ywain. What would happen to him if Ywain were to be healed?"

Rhience thought about this briefly. "I shouldn't think it would bother him at all. Sir Bleoberis is already talking about building another cottage and staying on here—best hunting he's ever seen, he says—and many of the local people who come to visit the hermit bring gifts as well." Then Rhience's eyes narrowed. "Why? Do you think Ywain might get better?"

Luneta nodded. "I have . . . well, I have this lotion that might help him. And I have to try."

"Something from that magical place you'd rather not discuss?" Luneta nodded, and Rhience grinned. "We'll try it tonight."

Luneta had been afraid that Godwulf and the knight Sir Bleoberis might not be pleased at the prospect of their food source being healed, but she needn't have worried. No one could have been more excited than Godwulf about Ywain's being restored, and as for Sir Bleoberis—a bluff, enormously good-natured knight with rough manners and an open smile, whom Luneta liked at once—he seemed pleased at the prospect of going hunting more often.

So it was with great anticipation that four pairs of eyes watched the shaggy and nearly unrecognizable Ywain creep out of the woods that evening, eat his dinner, then curl up in the fur robe that was his nightly bed. When they were sure he was asleep, Luneta went to him, dropped a single drop of her healing lotion on his temple, and gently rubbed it into his skin.

"That's it?" whispered Sir Bleoberis when she had come back to the other watchers.

Luneta shrugged. "I hope so. I haven't actually done this before."

Then they were still. Ywain had moved. As they watched nervously, he sat up and looked about, his eyes blank and confused-looking. Luneta's heart sank; it hadn't worked. Then Ywain spoke.

"Luneta? Where are my clothes?"

"There it is, Luneta," Rhience said. "Now, one more time. Are you sure you want to go back?"

Luneta looked for a long moment at the towers of

Laudine's castle, just showing above the hill where they sat on their horses. It was true that she could summon very little excitement about rejoining her silly, malleable friend and no interest at all in returning to the realm of the steward Malvolus, but she nodded. "Laudine was good to me; I won't desert her."

"Like some have," said Ywain in a wooden voice.

"I didn't mean that, Ywain," Luneta said quickly. "I didn't mean to rebuke you."

"I know. I rebuke myself" was the reply. Taking a deep breath, Ywain turned his eyes away from the castle, his face expressionless.

"All right, then," Rhience said. "You should be able to get there on your own from here."

Luneta nodded, a lump in her throat. She didn't want to leave Ywain and Rhience, whose company she had enjoyed very much over the past few days as they had ridden together to Laudine's castle. Ywain was quiet, but he was a much more thoughtful companion than he had been the previous year. He would still occasionally lose himself in his own thoughts, but it was clear that he was no longer dreaming of glory. More likely, from his rigid countenance, he was brooding on his betrayal of Laudine, but when he did speak, it was never about himself. Besides having a different attitude than before, Ywain simply looked different. He rode Sir Bleoberis's horse, and he wore a scarred and dented suit of armor that Rhience had found for him at a shop in Winchester, and most striking of all, he had trimmed neither his hair nor his beard. He looked like a wild beast in shabby armor. Ywain was no longer the callow youth who had ridden beside them from Orkney; even less was he the love-struck courtier who had knelt at Laudine's feet; perhaps least of all was he the "Unattainable Knight" who had been the idol of the court ladies.

"I'll be fine," Luneta said to Rhience. "You?"

"Fine," Rhience replied. "I think I'll just trail along with His Shagginess here for a while. Every fool dreams of one day working with an animal act."

Luneta suppressed a giggle, and even Ywain granted this sally a perfunctory smile. Luneta turned back toward the castle, but before she could begin, Ywain spoke. "How long will you stay?"

Luneta hesitated. "I don't know," she admitted at last.

"We'll come back to check on you in a few weeks," Ywain said suddenly. "If you're ready to leave, we'll take you away."

Luneta's heart felt suddenly lighter. "Take me where?"

Ywain's eyes, which seemed oddly older than his face, met hers. "Wherever you like, Luneta. I think you no longer need your parents' permission to do what you wish."

Maybe I look older, too. Luneta nodded to Ywain, then urged her horse forward over the hill. Ten minutes later she was at the front gate of Laudine's castle, where not only was the portcullis closed but the great wooden gate behind it as well.

"Open up!" she called. A face appeared in one of the bow loops in the tower above. "Come on! It's Lady Luneta! Open the gates!"

For several long minutes there was no sound. Luneta banged on the gate with increasing vehemence, until at last the portcullis rose slowly and the gate swung out toward her. There, in the courtyard, was a company of armed guards pointing spears at Luneta, and at their head was Malvolus.

"My dear Lady Luneta," he purred. "I quite thought you had forgotten us."

"I was delayed," she said. "Take me to Laudine at once."

The steward made no move to obey. "If only I had known that you would be returning," he said, "we shouldn't have had to hold the trial without your presence."

"Trial?"

"I'm very much afraid that you've been found guilty of treason," he said. "Guards, take her to the prison in the woods. At once."

VIII

The Knight of the Lion

Luneta's prison was a squat, newly built structure surrounded by trees, and judging from the fact that the dirt floor inside was still loose, she was its first occupant. Everything was stone except the ceiling and door, which were solid oak that might as well have been stone. A thin slit of a window beside the door and a slightly larger barred window on the back wall were the only sources of light.

The soldiers had taken her horse and her baggage—which of course included all the herbs and powders that she had so recently learned how to use—before locking her in. From the window Luneta could see a solitary guard sitting by a fire across a small clearing from the door. She called once, but the guard ignored her. She sat in the fresh dirt and thought over her surprising change of circumstances. Clearly, Malvolus was in control of the castle, and Luneta should not expect help from Laudine. If Malvolus had actually held a mock trial of some sort and convicted Luneta of treason in her absence, then he must have poisoned Laudine's mind against her. It was odd, though, that Luneta had been imprisoned in a secret cell away from the castle instead of in one of the dungeon rooms inside. This alone gave Luneta hope, because it might mean that Malvolus didn't want Laudine to know what he was doing, which could imply that he didn't have Laudine completely under his thumb.

After considering these things, Luneta turned her mind to her situation. If she had her bags, she would be able to escape by any of a number of means. With one powder, she could make a fierce fire and burn the door down. She had a lotion that would soften the iron bars in the back window so that they could be pushed aside like string. She had sleeping powders for the guards, if she could get them to eat something, but without her bags she could do none of these things anyway. Without any magical aids, all she could do was control her own senses so that she felt only what she wanted to feel, make a few small objects fly about, and by touching some living thing speed up or slow down its natural growth. All this was helpful in certain situations and excellent for producing butterflies, but it was not as useful for getting through stone walls.

Night came, then morning. Luneta slept beautifully, having told her body to feel the hard ground as if it were a feather bed, but when she awoke she was no nearer to knowing what to do. Faint voices in the distance drew her to the window by the door, and through the narrow slit she saw two soldiers approaching through the woods. Focusing her "inner ear," as Robin had called it, she heard the first one saying, "His Grace wants her dead, but he wants it to look an accident, see."

"Why?"

"Her ladyship's still being stubborn, and he figures if he hangs the girl in public it'll make her angry at him. So what we do is give 'er this poisoned food, see? Then he takes 'er body to Lady Laudine and tells 'er that she was found in the woods dead."

"I don't much like poisoning," the other guard said. "It makes a body scream and thrash about so."

"Stop up your ears. That's what I always does. Here, fill up the bucket at this stream. We got to give 'er some water, too."

"Why, if she's just going to die?"

"So she won't suspicion the food, of course. Do I have to do all your thinking for you?"

The two soldiers came near, greeted the guard in the clearing, then put two buckets inside Luneta's door and left. Luneta watched one of them take the other guard's place, stuffing some wads of cloth into his ears; then she

204

turned to consider the buckets. The water was all right, having just been scooped out of the stream, but how would she eat? Clearly any food that was brought to her would be deadly. She could enchant her body to feel no hunger, but that wouldn't stop her from dying of starvation. How long would Malvolus keep her here? Having no answer, she drank some water and buried the food in the loose dirt at a corner of the cell. When she began to feel the first hunger pangs, she used magic to suppress them, but no charm would take away her sense of foreboding.

It was midafternoon when Malvolus arrived in person. He threw open the prison door and stepped carelessly inside, then stopped at the sight of Luneta standing against the far wall. "You?" he exclaimed.

"You were expecting someone else?" Luneta asked. "I'm terribly sorry to disappoint you, but if you'd like I could go now."

Malvolus looked at the empty food bucket, then back at Luneta, then gritted his teeth against his anger. "Did you like your breakfast, my dear?" he asked.

"It was lovely, thank you."

His lips twisted in a thin, vicious smile, and he said, "Excellent. I'll see that you get *extra* tomorrow." Then he turned and left.

This pattern was repeated the following day, with the same result, except that Malvolus was even more incensed at finding her still alive. The third day he didn't even come himself but sent a guard to check on her. Luneta still felt fine, but she had begun to notice that her dress hung more loosely on her, and she knew she had to find something to eat. Looking through her barred window, though, all she saw was trees, most of them just beginning to leaf out after the winter. On the fourth morning, the nearest of the trees showed a small white blossom, and Luneta almost gasped with delight. An apple blossom. Using magic she coaxed a limb over to the window, touched one of the nodes on the twig, and muttered a few words. Immediately the node burst into flower, then dropped its petals and began to swell up. In less than a minute, Luneta was holding a large red apple. She ate the apple quickly, then began to experiment. Most of the other trees were oaks, and though she could produce acorns she wasn't able to muster much appetite for them, but there was also a walnut tree. Between apples and walnuts, she should be all right for a while—and Ywain had said they would be back to check on her in a few weeks, if Malvolus would wait that long.

Malvolus wasn't good at waiting, however. After two weeks of finding Luneta not only alive but obviously feeling very well indeed, he changed his approach. One afternoon he rode alone to the prison in the woods, dismounted, then dismissed the guard in the clearing.

Luneta watched this new development apprehensively. When the guard had gone, Malvolus stepped into Luneta's room, holding a long, thin dagger in one hand. "So, my dear. You appear to be stronger than I'd expected."

Luneta said nothing.

"Quite remarkable, really. A woman this strong should not be a prisoner but a princess."

"Well, if you want to be technical, I already am," Luneta said. "My grandfather was a king, you see. So is my great-uncle. You may have heard of him—his name is Arthur, and I'm sure he's wondering where I am by now. I was supposed to be at Camelot by—"

"Spare me your lies, my dear. You're very good at it, but I saw through your plot from the beginning."

"You mean the plot to steal Laudine's castle?"

"That's right."

"You don't really believe that, do you? I thought that was just a story you concocted to fool Laudine."

Malvolus shook his head sadly. "Please do not try to act the innocent, when I know that you are a manipulator worthy of . . . well, worthy of a man like me."

Luneta fought back a wave of nausea. "I thank you for the compliment, sir, but you do me far too much honor."

"Together we could rule much more than just these few lands, you know. I could make the plots, and you could make people believe them. The way you cozened up to poor, stupid Laudine! Why, she still can't quite believe that you were against her! I must take my hat off to you. Think what we could do as associates."

"I believe that you would be happier with a different associate," Luneta said. "A snake, perhaps. Or a spider."

Malvolus's leering smile disappeared. "I believe that you shall regret that. What you do not choose to offer willingly may be taken by force."

He raised his dagger threateningly, and Luneta saw anger and madness in his eyes. She didn't hesitate. Staring hard at the dagger, enunciating clearly a few words, and waving her hand, she made the blade leap from Malvolus's grasp and sink itself into one of the ceiling beams. Malvolus's face went white and he staggered away, slamming the door behind him. Luneta heard the lock click, and she stepped up to the window by the door.

"So that's it!" Malvolus said. "You're a witch! Do you know what the laws say about witches? They shall be burned!"

"Does Laudine know about those laws?" Luneta asked mildly.

"I'll be back with my full garrison tomorrow morning! We shall have a burning at noon!" Malvolus cried out, his voice cracking like a boy's. Then he turned and ran.

"Oh, bother," Luneta said.

* * *

Malvolus must have made no secret of his discovery that Luneta was a witch, because no guard returned to sit outside her prison that night. Luneta tried for a while to retrieve Malvolus's knife from the ceiling beam but only managed to break the blade. She was sitting in the dark turning over plans for escape when she heard voices, two men passing through the woods, and a wave of relief swept over her. Leaping to the window, she called out, "Rhience! Ywain!"

A moment later her two friends were at the window. "Don't tell me. You've decided to start your own hermitage," Rhience said.

"Quiet, friend," Ywain said. "This is a prison."

"No good asking for a beer, then? When I go to a hermitage, I expect—"

"Who has done this to you, Luneta?"

"Malvolus."

"Does Laudine know?"

"I don't think so. Malvolus is plotting to take over her castle and kill her when she no longer serves his purpose, I think."

"Have you been here since we left you?" Rhience asked. Luneta nodded. "How are you? Do you need food?"

"Something besides apples and walnuts would be wonderful," Luneta said, "but that's not the most important thing. You see, I had to use a bit of, um . . . well, Malvolus has decided that I'm a witch."

"You don't say," Rhience said.

"And he intends to burn me at the stake tomorrow."

"Can't you turn him into a frog or something and be done with it?" Rhience asked.

"This is no time for jokes, Rhience," Ywain said sternly.

"Actually, that time I wasn't joking," Rhience replied. He looked back at Luneta, "Can't you?"

"Not without my things," Luneta said.

Ywain stared at her. "Do you mean that you *are* a witch?"

"We don't use that word. The polite term is 'enchantress.'"

"I beg your pardon," Ywain said. Then he said, "Really? Like Aunt Morgan?"

"How do you suppose you were healed from your madness?" Rhience asked. "So, it looks as if you need someone to help you out. Let's get this door open."

For almost two hours Rhience and Ywain cut and dug and pried at the door and ceiling, but the prison was too well made, and at last they gave up and returned, panting, to Luneta's window. "No good," Rhience said.

"Are the two of you alone?" Luneta asked. "Because

210

while you were working I thought I saw a shadow moving in the woods."

"That'll be Lass," Rhience said. "We've picked up a pet while we were traveling. She's shy of strangers, though. So what should we do? Wait here and attack Malvolus when he comes to take you to the stake?"

Luneta thought for a moment. "Malvolus said he'd be bringing his whole garrison. Is that asking too much?"

"Probably," Ywain said. "Do you know when or where this burning is to take place?"

"He said at noon, but I don't know where."

Rhience said, "It won't be hard to find out. Witch burnings are always proclaimed publicly. They serve as a warning to people—plus, of course, they're great fun for the family."

"Then our best plan is to find out the details, then ride in just before you're tied up, when all his men are scattered about in the open, and take you away."

Luneta wasn't excited about waiting until the last minute, but she saw the force of Ywain's arguments and had to be satisfied. They talked for a few more minutes, and then her friends rode away to make preparations for the next day's rescue.

It was nearly noon before Malvolus came for her, and from the number of tight-faced soldiers who accompanied him, Luneta could see that her magical powers had not been understated in the telling. She went with the soldiers peaceably, having decided that to resist might get her run through by a nervous spearsman. The soldiers nearest her never took their eyes from her, and once when she stumbled slightly on the path, those closest to her leaped away. Malvolus rode near and cursed them roundly as cowards.

"Lovely day, isn't it," Luneta said to the steward. If she thought about it, she was as terrified as the soldiers, and with far more reason, but she would not grant the steward the satisfaction of seeing her fear.

"It will be a bit too warm for you soon, I fear, my lady," Malvolus said with sneer.

"Come, Malvolus, that's very good. It's almost like a joke. Not so good as the time that Rhience did the pantomime of the servant who wanted to be a knight, but—"

"It is a pity that your fool is not here," Malvolus interrupted bitterly. "So long as we have the fire, it would be thrifty to cook two pieces of meat."

"Yes, it would be like a reunion. Will Laudine be there?"

Luneta had expected Malvolus to make an excuse, explaining why Laudine could not be present, but he replied, "Yes, indeed. She is very shocked, I must say. When I told her that you were a witch and had to be burned, she almost fainted. I think you can expect no more support from your friend Laudine."

They led Luneta to an open field outside the castle gates. A stout post had been driven into the ground on a small hillock, and bundles of brush and twigs were stacked nearby. Malvolus wasted no time but directed two sweating soldiers to tie Luneta to the post while he read from a sheet of parchment. "Inasmuch as this lady, Luneta of Orkney, hath been seen performing unnatural acts and hath changed her shape sundry times, being made into a black dog, a spider, and a huge, unnatural crow—"

"I did all that?" Luneta asked.

"You did, as witnesses have sworn."

"I wonder why I didn't escape from my prison while I was a spider. Stupid of me."

Malvolus returned to his parchment while Luneta looked quickly around. There was no sign of either Rhience or Ywain, but she saw the slender form of Laudine sitting on a wooden platform beneath a canvas shelter.

"—having also had unnatural discourse with the devil and having brought many an illness onto the village and made the milk in John Farmer's dairy spoil all at once, and most of all for having caused an unnatural blade of Hell to appear and throw itself at my own person, she is condemned by this tribunal to die at the stake, as unanimously approved by all present here."

"Not by all," said a voice. Luneta looked around joyfully, but it wasn't Rhience or Ywain. It was Laudine. Under the shocked eyes of the crowd, Laudine stood to her feet. "I challenge this court. It is not legal. I am the mistress of these lands, and I never gave permission for such a trial. I demand that the Lady Luneta be released at once."

Luneta smiled with delight. Knowing Laudine as she did, she could guess how hard it had been for her to stand before everyone and oppose a will stronger than her own. Luneta's smile faded at once, though. The steward called out immediately, "You see the witch's power! She has bewitched your own mistress, forcing her to speak against her will! Soldiers! Restrain your mistress, lest this wicked woman enchant her further!" Four soldiers leaped forward and grasped Laudine's arms. One tied a cloth over her mouth.

Malvolus kicked the piles of brush and twigs over toward Luneta, then took a torch from a waiting servant and tossed it at her feet. The brush caught fire at once. Luneta looked again over the crowd. Still no sign of Rhience or Ywain. Then there was a whisper in her ear. "Sorry I'm a bit late, lass."

"Rhience?" She looked over her shoulder, but there was no one there.

"Ay, but don't twist about so. I'm trying to untie your bonds."

"Where are you?"

"Untying your bonds. I thought I'd mentioned that already. You see, your friend Laudine lent me her ring."

"Where's Ywain?"

"Ah, well, there was a bit of a holdup. He's busy just now but should be along soon."

"Busy?" Luneta exclaimed with, she thought, pardonable indignation.

"That or dead, I'm afraid. We'll hope he's just busy. There we go. You're free. Now I'm going to kick the fire up. You step away from the post. I'll take off the ring and you put it on. Ready?"

The brush before Luneta gave off a shower of sparks. A strong hand pulled her down behind the flames. For a fleeting second she saw Rhience holding her hand, and then she saw only Rhience. She was invisible. Together they backed away from the post.

"Sorcery!" shrieked Malvolus. "The witch has changed her shape. She has become this man!"

The crowd stared open-mouthed, and Rhience said, "Now that would be daft of her, wouldn't it? A beautiful girl like Luneta changing herself into a gawky fellow like me?"

"Where is she?" demanded Malvolus.

"Where is who?" Rhience asked.

The steward looked around furiously, but balked of his intended victim, he seemed willing to make an exchange. "Your life is forfeit, fool!" he declared. "I told you what would happen if you ever came back to this castle. And you have no weapons, I see."

"Well, I did take a vow not to raise weapons against any man, you recall," Rhience said apologetically.

"And you still keep that vow? It will be your death," Malvolus said, drawing his sword and licking his lips. "Today I shall feed you to the dogs."

Luneta stared fixedly at the sword and raised her hand, preparing to make it drive itself into Malvolus's own breast, but before she could utter the spell, Rhience glanced at her—or rather, through her—and said, "Ah, there you are, Lass. Can you handle this fellow for me?" A tawny lightning bolt seemed to fly past Luneta onto Malvolus. The steward screamed once, then gurgled, and then was silent. Luneta stared, dumbfounded, at an actual lion, who sat with bloody jaws beside the sprawled and mangled body of the steward.

"Don't eat him, Lass," said Rhience. "He's sure to disagree with you."

And then, in the deathly silence, there came a clang of arms from across the field, and there was Ywain, riding straight into the mass of assembled soldiers, slashing right and left and dropping men on every side. The melee was over in seconds. Most of the soldiers threw down their weapons and scattered, screaming in terror, and they were quickly followed by the rest of the gathered crowd. In the confusion, Luneta removed the magic ring and went to Rhience's side. In ten minutes, the field was clear, and Ywain was cantering over to where they stood together by Malvolus's body. "Did Rhience tell you I was held up?" he asked. "I hope you aren't too angry at me."

"You have a lion now?" Luneta asked, fixing on the most incomprehensible part of the recent events.

"Lioness," Rhience corrected her. "No mane, see? She's a real pussycat, too. Want to pet her?"

"Your pussycat just killed a man."

"Only Malvolus. You're not going to hold that against her, are you?"

"Of course not," Luneta said. "It was quite the best thing to do, I know, but I'd rather not pet her just now, if you don't mind."

Rhience reached over to the great cat and scratched her head. She rolled her ears under his fingers. "Very well," Rhience said. "Another time."

"Rhience," hissed Ywain suddenly, looking over the fool's shoulder and lowering his visor over his face. "Speak for me."

Following Ywain's gaze, Luneta saw Laudine stumbling across the field. Luneta hurried up and took her arm. "Laudine, I want to thank you. Your courage . . ."

Laudine shook her head briskly. "No. If I had not believed Malvolus's lies about you and about . . . do not thank me. Forgive me."

"If there is anything to forgive, it is already forgiven," Luneta said.

"And you, friend Rhience, thank you for finding me this morning and telling me the truth."

Rhience bowed. "And thank you for the ring. It was most useful."

"Oh, yes, your ring," Luneta said. She pressed it into Laudine's hand. "Put it away somewhere, why don't you?"

Laudine ignored her, looking at Ywain's silent form. "And I thank you, Sir Knight."

Ywain inclined his head slightly but did not answer.

"My lady," Rhience said. "He will not speak. He's taken a vow."

Laudine acknowledged the knight with a deep curtsy, then said, "And may I offer this brave knight—and all of you—the hospitality of my castle?"

Rhience glanced at Ywain, who held up one gauntleted finger. Rhience nodded and said, "For one night, my lady, we accept your offer, but we must be left alone. It's that vow again."

Laudine nodded. "And may I know this knight's name?"

218

"You may call him . . . the Knight of the Lion," Rhience said. "I mean, Lioness."

"I want to know what business was so pressing that you were late to your own cousin's rescue," Luneta said, "but I want to know first how the devil you got a lion."

"Lioness," Rhience murmured.

They were alone in the palatial rooms that Laudine had assigned to Rhience and the Knight of the Lion, and it was nearly midnight. Luneta, ignoring Laudine's strict instructions that no one should disturb her guests, had strolled into their apartments a few minutes before. She had eaten three times already since noon, but the pleasure of eating something besides apples or walnuts was still strong, and she had brought with her a plate of ham and chicken.

She took a bit of ham now and said, "Lioness, then. How did you get her? I didn't know there were any lions—lionesses—in England at all."

"They aren't native here, perhaps, but those crusader chaps down in the Holy Land have brought some back as trophies," Rhience explained. "All I can guess is that Lass here is one of those, escaped from her captor."

Luneta looked at the lioness, stretched out asleep before the fire. She did look rather like a pussycat, albeit a very large one. "You call her Lass?"

"It was Rhience's idea," Ywain said.

"She reminded me of someone," Rhience said carelessly.

Luneta was pretty sure she knew who, but she decided not to press the point. "How did you come on her?"

"Well, it was only a day or two after we left the Count Alier," Rhience said. "We were riding through this unnaturally dark and spidery bit of forest, and we heard the sounds of a great battle—not between men, with swords and armor, but between beasts. There was roaring and screaming and thrashing about and all that. Ywain here didn't say a word but dived at once into the darkest part of the woods, leaving me by myself. I'm afraid of the dark, so I followed." Ywain rolled his eyes and shook his head, but he allowed Rhience to tell the tale as he chose. "In a moment we came on the fight, and there was Lass here, locked in mortal combat with a . . . well, it was rather a large serpent-thing, I suppose."

"A dragon?"

"I suppose so," Rhience said.

"Yes, a dragon," interposed Ywain. "The beast had the lioness trapped in its coils and was about to strike a final blow. So we jumped in and stopped it."

"Both of you?" Luneta asked.

Ywain nodded. "I attacked the worm's head, and Rhience began cutting through its coils."

"You had a sword?" Luneta asked Rhience.

"I always have a sword. You've seen it on my horse."

"Yes, but—"

"Dear, my vow was not to bear arms against any *man*," Rhience said. "Dragons are perfectly legal."

"Oh, of course. And you killed the dragon."

"After a bit, yes," Rhience said.

"It wasn't easy," Ywain said. "And had we not fought together, it would have killed us both. Rhience would have you believe that he is a coward who has no skill with a sword, but the truth is—"

"Ywain killed the dragon," Rhience said. "I may have helped a bit, but your cousin's a wizard with that weapon. Anyway, when it was over we had a dragon, now in three separate pieces, and a very irritated and wounded lady lion." At this point Rhience glanced at Ywain. "May I?"

Ywain nodded slowly. "You may tell what you like."

"Tell me what?"

"Well, it's a bit odd here. Ywain put down all his weapons and took off his armor and then . . . ah, I don't know exactly how to say it."

"I let the lioness know that we wouldn't hurt her."

"How?" Luneta asked.

"By my actions. I don't know exactly how I knew what to do," Ywain replied frankly. "I suppose it has to do with having been something of a wild beast myself until recently."

221

"All I can say," Rhience said, "was that they growled and sniffed about for a while, and in no time they were rubbing their heads together, and Lass was as tame as a fat kitchen tabby. Ywain and I bound up her wounds and gave her something to eat."

Luneta looked curiously behind her at the lioness and saw that she was awake and watching Luneta. A soft rumbling sound came from the lioness's chest, something between a growl and a purr, and Luneta instinctively shrank away.

"Do you want all your ham?" Ywain asked. "She'd like a bite if you don't mind."

"Of course," Luneta said. Ywain chose a thick slab from Luneta's plate and gave it to Lass, rumpling her ears gently as he did so.

Rhience grinned. "And so she adopted us. When we packed up to leave, Lass just came along. She was useful today, too. For that matter, we could have used her in Norison, but that was before we met her."

"Where is Norison?"

"That's the village we went to right after we left you," Rhience explained. "It's about a day's ride from here, and we happened into it just in time to help a noble lady there. You see, she was the daughter of the lord of that district, and when he died a few months back, he left everything to her. The Lady Norison is quite attractive, and so it happened that a gentleman by the name of Count Alier thought that he would be happy to marry her, even though marrying her would mean that he'd have to take possession of all her inheritance."

"I see," Luneta said dryly.

"Have you ever known a fellow who took longer to tell a simple story?" Ywain commented.

"No. So the Count Alier was wooing this Lady Norison?"

"Wooing," Rhience repeated thoughtfully. "Well, yes, I suppose you could say—"

"He had besieged her castle," Ywain explained. "He was going to start killing villagers every day until she consented to marry him."

"I didn't say it was a very *romantic* sort of wooing," Rhience said. "So, Ywain here told him to go away and stop bothering her, and after disagreeing at first, he finally agreed that he'd been very bad and promised to stop."

"You fought him?" Luneta asked Ywain.

"Yes, while Rhience set fire to his men's tents and drove off their horses and led the villagers out with their shovels and picks and pitchforks. Count Alier wasn't much without an army behind him, so I made him yield to Lady Norison and then, with her approval, let him go."

They sat in silence for a moment. It occurred to Luneta that the adventure at Norison had been just the sort of thing that the young Ywain had dreamed about doing less than a year ago. It was a very different Ywain who now spoke so indifferently about such a victory. Not the same Rhience she thought she knew, either. Luneta glanced curiously, but with a new respect, at the fool.

Rhience spoke suddenly. "Ywain's not going to tell you, but I suspect you should know one more thing. After he sent Count Alier off with a burr in his breeches, Lady Norison offered our Ywain her hand in marriage, by way of saying thank you, I suppose." Luneta looked at Ywain. His face was still, and his eyes were focused on nothing at all. Rhience said, "He turned her down."

Luneta thought about this for a moment, then changed the subject. "Ywain, why didn't you want Laudine to know who you were?"

"I don't want her to feel obligated to me."

"But you saved her from an enemy. This might be just the thing you need to make her forgive you for forgetting your appointment," Luneta said. Part of her mind was already weaving plans.

"No!" Ywain said sharply. "If Laudine should forgive me, it should be because she chooses to, not because she feels obligated to me."

"But Ywain," Luneta said, "couldn't I at least talk to her? Maybe she wants to forgive you anyway."

"I said no. People who feel they are in debt may do all sorts of things that they wouldn't do otherwise."

"Like Lady Norison offering to marry you?" Rhience asked.

"Yes, and Baron Montanus, too."

"Baron Montanus wanted to marry you?" Rhience demanded. "I hope you said no. He's far too old for you."

"He offered me his daughter."

Rhience grinned and nodded. "Of course he did. I should have expected it."

"Wait," Luneta said, confused by mention of this newest character. "Who's this baron?"

"That's why I was a little late to your rescue," Ywain explained. "After we left you last night, we rode to the nearest village and asked at the tavern there where you were to be burned. They told us, and we rode back up the road a couple of hours. We didn't want Malvolus to hear about two knights staying in the village.

"Anyway, we took a twisty forest path that didn't look as if it went anywhere in particular, but we ended up in a pretty little town with a manor house and everything in it, and the lord of the manor was named Baron Montanus."

"And he offered you his daughter?" Luneta asked.

"Not at first, no," Ywain said.

"He had other plans for Ywain," Rhience said. "You see, he was in a bind there. A band of outlaws had made their home on the mountain nearby, and the leader of the band was a huge fellow named Harpin. Harpin had been raiding all the country round about, but Montanus didn't have enough men to fight them, just him and his three sons. Well, the day before we arrived, this Harpin had taken a fancy to the baron's daughter, a pretty little thing, and had tried to capture her when she was out riding with her brothers. The brothers did well by their sister. They held off the outlaws long enough for her to escape, but they got captured themselves."

"What did this Harpin want with the brothers?" Luneta asked.

"A trade, of course. Just hours before we showed up, Harpin sent word to the baron that he'd swap even up, three sons for one daughter, but if the baron didn't trade, he'd bring the sons down the next morning and slit their throats in front of him."

"What a horrible choice!" Luneta said with a gasp.

"You see why I stayed late, don't you?" Ywain asked. "The baron was no fighter, and he had no one else."

Luneta nodded. "Of course. You couldn't just leave him."

"The only thing is," Rhience said, "we didn't know when Harpin was coming in the morning, and we were at least an hour and a half of hard riding from here. So we waited until just before ten, and then I mounted up to come back alone. Ywain was to come as soon as he had defeated Harpin. I didn't really think he'd make it in time, so I planned a rescue instead of a fight. I

226

sneaked into the castle and managed to talk to Laudine privately and get her ring. You know the rest."

"Except what happened with this Harpin," Luneta said.

"I killed him, along with a couple of the other outlaws," Ywain said with a shrug. "Lass helped a lot. Then we came here as fast as we could."

Luneta nodded thoughtfully. "So in the past two weeks you've rescued two villages, killed a dragon, tamed a lion, saved my life, and turned down two offers of marriage."

Ywain nodded soberly. "Something like that. Pity I couldn't have done any of this stuff a year ago. It might have mattered to me then."

IX
QUESTING

Luneta had let the matter drop when she saw how strongly Ywain felt, but she had not given up on bringing Ywain and Laudine together again. It was obvious that Ywain still loved Laudine, and Luneta suspected that Laudine still loved him. No, Luneta told herself, she couldn't just sit on her hands. One has to help a friend in distress, after all. She was pleasantly weaving plans for reconciliation the next morning when Rhience tapped on her door and entered.

"Good morning, Rhience," Luneta said, smiling.

"Good morning, Luneta. Did you sleep well?"

"Very well," Luneta replied. "And you and Ywain?"

"I don't know if Ywain slept at all," Rhience said calmly. "He and Lass left the castle about an hour after you went to bed last night."

"Left the castle?" Luneta repeated blankly.

Rhience nodded. "He asked me to stay and make his apologies to you."

"But why? Why did he leave?"

Rhience pursed his lips, then drew a long breath and said, "He said he didn't want to hang about while you plotted to get him back together with Laudine."

Luneta's mouth dropped open. "Because . . . but that's ridiculous!"

Rhience raised one eyebrow. "Do you mean to say that he was wrong? That you haven't been making such plans?"

Luneta turned red, but she met Rhience's eyes. "No, I mean it's ridiculous that he should leave for such a reason."

"Why do you do that, Luneta?"

"I don't know what you mean."

"Why do you try to arrange other people's lives?"

"I don't think of it that way," she replied.

"I'm sure you don't, but it's what you do all the same."

"Well, if I do, it's only because they do such a wretched job of arranging their own lives! Look at Ywain and Laudine. He loves her, but he feels too guilty about breaking that six-month promise to go tell her so and ask her forgiveness. As for Laudine, she loves him too, but because he's never begged for her forgiveness she thinks he doesn't love her, so she's just

229

sitting around the castle feeling miserable. If someone could just bring them together for ten minutes, everything would be fine!"

"And you're the someone?"

"It doesn't *have* to be me, but I'm a good choice—after all, I may be the only one who sees what both of them want."

Rhience's face was solemn. "And what about you? What do you want? Do you see that as clearly?"

"What?"

"What do you want from life?" Luneta stared blankly at Rhience, but she could think of no reply. Rhience shook his head slowly. "You don't know. So why should Ywain and Laudine, or anyone else for that matter, let you plan their futures?"

Luneta's mouth opened, then shut again. Angry as she was, she could think of no suitable reply. She contented herself with giving Rhience a withering glare.

"Nay, lass, don't hurt me," Rhience said, dropping his unaccustomed seriousness. "To say the truth, you're probably right about Ywain and Laudine. Proper chuckleheads, both of them. But they won't get out this mess they're in unless they do it themselves."

"But no one can help them now that Ywain's gone and left," Luneta pointed out disgustedly.

Luneta may not have been able to help Laudine with her love affair, but over the next two weeks she and

Rhience had ample opportunity to help their hostess in other ways. For the first time in her life, Laudine actually had to be concerned with the business of running a castle and a home. It appeared to Luneta that Laudine had never borne the slightest responsibility, having gone directly from the protective control of her father to that of Sir Esclados, and from there to the influence of Malvolus. Now she had a whole castle full of servants and guards waiting for her instructions, but there was no domineering man to tell her what to do. To Laudine's credit, she didn't try to shirk her new duties, and she even had some of her own ideas as to what should be done—mostly concerning the dismissal of servants who had been cronies of Malvolus—but the truth was that she was hopelessly inept as an administrator. Rhience and Luneta, being the two people Laudine most trusted, were called on to help their hostess with decisions ranging from whom to place in charge of the castle accounts to what sort of sauce she liked with roast lamb. And, when either of them turned the question back on Laudine—asking "What do *you* prefer?"—it only became clear again that Laudine wasn't used to having any preferences at all. Luneta found her hostess's eagerness to agree with anyone else's ideas to be infuriating, and it was fortunate for all of them that after a week Rhience was able to find just the right man to replace Malvolus.

Laudine's new steward was the footman Rufus, the one who helped Luneta separate Laudine from Sir Esclados's body on the day he had been killed. Rufus was blessed with just the right blend of competence, tact, and fatherly affection for his mistress. As soon as he had been installed in his new position, life became easier for all of them. Rufus managed the minor matters on his own and seemed to be able to make sense of even Laudine's most contradictory instructions regarding the rest. At last there came a day when Luneta and Rhience were able to escape for an afternoon ride.

"What a relief!" Luneta exclaimed with a deep sigh as soon as they had left the castle behind. "I think another day in there and I would have gone mad."

"*Insana*," Rhience murmured.

Luneta grinned. "You know, I haven't used my Latin in months. My father would be so disappointed."

"Your father is a scholar?"

"Not really. He's a farmer, if you think about it. He runs the family estates up in Orkney, even though I suppose they officially belong to Uncle Gawain. But he likes to read, and he was teaching me Latin by the time I was five." She smiled at the memory. "I'm afraid I wasn't very interested at first. It took me years to get past the simplest verbs, all that *amo, amas, amat* business."

"Ah, yes. 'I love, you love, she loves.' I've always had trouble with that bit myself."

"But if you've studied for the church, your Latin must be much better than mine. Didn't you say you had read some theology books?"

"Yes, but they never really told me what to do about *amo, amas*. Theology's frustrating that way. But enough about Latin. You just said that you were about to go mad at Laudine's castle."

"*Insana.*"

"Exactly. So why don't you leave?"

Luneta watched her horse flick his ears at a fly, then said, "I don't know where to go."

"Do you want to go to Camelot?"

"I used to."

"How about home? I could escort you to your parents."

Luneta nodded. "Yes, I think I'd like that. But not yet."

"When, then?"

"I don't know." Luneta peeked at Rhience's puzzled face. "It's just that . . . I left home to become my own person. I didn't know it then, but I was tired of being just my parents' daughter. If I go back now, I don't think I'll be any different. Nothing has really happened to me."

Rhience's shoulders began to shake. "I see," he said unsteadily. "No, I daresay you're right. You haven't changed a bit in the past ten months, except for the bit about becoming an enchantress, and you really haven't

233

had any interesting experiences except for being imprisoned and nearly burned at the stake."

"*Es asinus,*" Luneta said without rancor. "That's not what I . . . what's that?"

"What's what?" Rhience asked.

"That moan. Didn't you hear it? A woman."

"No, but I've grown used to not hearing all that you hear. Which direction?"

Luneta listened for a moment, then pointed to the left, and they booted their horses into a gallop. In a moment, Luneta heard another faint groan and altered her direction slightly. As they were jumping a marshy gully, Luneta saw a flash of blue cloth. Leaping from her horse, she pushed through the spring grasses and found a young woman, her back covered with blood, lying face-down in the ditch. "Quick! Rhience! The crystal bottle in my saddlebag!"

Rhience brought her healing potion, and a moment later the young woman was sitting up, dazedly feeling her back. "It doesn't hurt anymore," she whispered. "And where are the knife wounds?"

"Knifed, were you?" Rhience asked.

The woman nodded. "I feel the cuts in my gown and the dried blood on the fabric, but I'm unhurt!"

"Remarkable," Luneta said calmly. "Who knifed you?"

"Ruffians, perhaps from my . . . no, she wouldn't.

They must have been bandits. They took my horse and left me for dead." She felt at her waist, then began to sob. "And took all my money. Oh, what am I to do now?"

"Come with us," Luneta said. "We'll take you to the castle where we're staying. The mistress of that castle, the Lady Laudine, will be happy to shelter you."

"Lady Laudine? Oh, thank the stars! She's the one I've come looking for."

"For Laudine?" Luneta asked, mildly surprised.

"Well, not Lady Laudine herself. Actually, I'm looking for the Knight of the Lion."

"My name is Philomela," the girl began. She had been bathed and fed and was now sitting with Laudine, Luneta, and Rhience in Laudine's sitting room. "I am the second daughter of the Earl of Blackthorn. My older sister is named Philomena."

"I always wanted a sister," Laudine murmured, almost to herself. "I was an only child."

"Sisters aren't that great," Philomela replied. "We've never gotten along, you see. The only time Mena was ever nice to me was when Father was nearby. He always thought we were best friends. Father was a dear man, but he never saw beyond the end of his nose."

"Where was your mother?" Luneta asked. "Surely she saw how things really were between you and your sister."

"She might have," replied Philomela, "but she died

when I was three. Father never remarried, and then a few months ago he died, too."

"I'm sorry, Lady Philomela," Rhience said.

She nodded absently. "The past few years he seemed very far away, anyway. Before he died, he had his clerk write a will, saying that all his possessions should be divided evenly between Mena and me. He showed it to us and told us that his two loving daughters could share everything, as we always had."

Lady Philomela was silent for a moment. The three listeners waited.

"But when Father died, the will was nowhere to be found. Mena denied it had ever existed and, as the eldest, claimed everything for herself."

"What did you do?" Luneta asked.

"I confronted her publicly and told everyone about the will. I challenged Mena to go with me to the home of the clerk who had written the will. He would prove me right."

"That was good thinking," Laudine said.

Lady Philomela hunched her shoulders. "Mena had already thought of it. The clerk couldn't be found, either."

Rhience raised one eyebrow. "Would your sister actually commit murder to secure your half of the property?"

Lady Philomela gave a tight little shake of her head.

"I can't believe she would. But she might have paid the clerk to leave the country."

"Was there nothing else for you to do?" asked Laudine.

Lady Philomela nodded. "Yes, and I did it. I appealed to King Arthur."

"Worth trying, I suppose," Rhience said pensively, "but what could the king do? It was your word against your sister's."

Lady Philomela lifted her chin. "I appealed for a trial by combat!"

"A trial by combat?" Rhience asked. "Each of you chooses a champion, and the one with the best knight takes all? That's taking rather a chance, isn't it?"

Lady Philomela nodded. "It was all I could think to do, but you're right. Worse, I foolishly told Mena what I was going to do, and she hurried to Camelot ahead of me, telling everyone there how her younger sister was trying to steal half her lands. Mena can be very convincing. By the time I got there, she already had her own champion, and she had gotten promises from all the other competent knights at court that they wouldn't take my part."

"What a conniving weasel!" Luneta exclaimed.

"Yes, don't you hate manipulative people?" Rhience said.

"Hush," Luneta said. "So you're at a standstill?"

"Almost," Lady Philomela said. "Just when I was

237

about to give up, word came to the court about an unknown new knight who had done great deeds in this country."

Luneta understood at once. "The Knight of the Lion," she said. "Of course."

Lady Philomela nodded. "It's said that he slew a giant named Harpin—"

"A giant?" Rhience asked.

"Yes, and also that he rescued the Lady Laudine from a burning stake by defeating a huge army single-handedly. Is it true?"

"Sort of," Laudine said. "Except that he rescued Luneta from the stake, not me."

"And it wasn't really a *huge* army," Luneta said.

"Don't quibble," Rhience said. "If Harpin was a giant, then the army was huge."

"And does this knight really have a magical lion with a flowing mane that fights alongside him?"

"Flowing mane?" Luneta asked.

"The lion's a giant, too," Rhience contributed.

"This knight is my only hope! All the other great knights in the land have pledged their word not to help me. I must find him. Is he still here?"

"No, my lady," Laudine said. "But Rhience here has been his companion before and may be able to find him for you." She turned to Rhience. "Could you?"

238

Rhience looked at Lady Philomela. "When is the trial to take place?"

"King Arthur gave me three weeks. That was a week ago."

"I might be able to round up the Knight of the Lion for you in that time," Rhience said after a moment. "I can't promise he'll help, but I'll ask. You stay here, though."

"Stay here?" Philomela asked. "Why?"

"Because I don't want to have to guard you while I search. I don't know if the men who stuck knives in your back were common bandits or murderers sent by your sister, but either way, I'd feel better if you stayed in this castle and let Lady Laudine watch over you."

Laudine looked pleased at this prospect, and Luneta realized glumly that her stay at Laudine's castle was about to become even duller, with Laudine occupied with her new houseguest and Rhience away.

Rhience grinned at her. "Well, don't just sit there, Luneta. Go saddle up."

Luneta and Rhience rode first to Godwulf's hermitage, where the good hermit greeted them with open arms. "My friends!" he boomed across the clearing. "Welcome! Have you eaten?"

Rhience grinned and glanced at Luneta. "That's Godwulf's way of saying 'Bless you, my children.'"

Godwulf smiled at this but only said, "What good's a blessing if you haven't eaten?"

Rhience dismounted. "Still plenty of food?"

"Always. How many times have I told you, God provides like the merry dickens!" Rhience reached up a hand for Luneta. She didn't need help dismounting, but she took it anyway. The hermit continued, "Will you share a meal with me?"

"Assuredly," Rhience replied, "but we can't stay long. We need Ywain. Has he been here?"

"Of course he has. God sent him."

"God sent him?" Rhience asked, one eyebrow raised.

"Ay," Godwulf said contentedly. "Brother Bleoberis is joining me here in the hermitage, but he had to return to Camelot to ask the king's permission to leave the Round Table first. He left me with plenty of meat, but the day after he rode off, a band of minstrels and actors and such came through, and I fed them. Used up my whole food supply. The tales those fellows could tell! And there was this one boy who could bend himself up near in knots! I've never laughed so hard!"

Luneta looked at the hermit curiously. "You gave them all your food? Didn't you keep anything back for yourself?"

"Why should I? I've not been hungry since I came to this haven," Godwulf replied placidly. "God would provide. The next morning, Ywain arrived with meat.

That pussycat of his is quite a hunter, you know. We've plenty to spare again."

"Is Ywain still here?" Rhience asked.

"He left three days ago," the hermit said. "Do you prefer venison or boar for dinner?"

They stayed that night at the hermitage, then left the next morning, following Ywain's path to the north. Luneta thought for a while about the hermit Godwulf, then said, "Rhience?"

"Yes, lass?"

"You were a monk once, weren't you?"

"A novice only."

"But you've known a lot of religious men." Rhience nodded, and Luneta asked, "Are there others like Godwulf?"

Rhience began to laugh. "Nay. I might have stayed at the monastery if there were."

"So you think he's really a holy man? But he sounds so . . . almost simple-minded!"

Rhience nodded. "That he does. Sometimes I wish I had his simplicity, but I don't and doubt I ever will. Me, I couldn't have given away my last crumb of food and just expected something else to show up on my door in the morning. I would have thought about it first."

Luneta nodded emphatically. "That's just what I mean! All this talk about 'God sent Ywain to me' and

241

'God will provide'—doesn't it make you uncomfortable when someone speaks for God like that?"

"Not when it's Godwulf," Rhience said. "Oh, I know what you mean. I've heard dozens of religious people talking that way, but in their mouths it was always pompous nonsense. Godwulf's different." Rhience grinned at her. "And I can't even explain why, because I'm different, too. Now here's a path off to the left. We should take it."

"Why?"

"God told me so," he replied promptly. Luneta turned a scornful gaze at him, and he shrugged and added, "Also, there's a really big paw print in the soft dirt up there."

The path took them through quiet forests and over barren heaths. They rode all that day and all the next morning without seeing anyone, so it was a relief the next afternoon when they finally saw another person. Riding around a rocky outcropping, they came upon a cottage where a woman churned butter in the sunny yard. "Greetings, good lady," Rhience said, politely touching his forehead.

The woman scowled at them and said nothing.

"I wonder if you could help us," Rhience said doggedly. "We're looking for a knight who might have passed—"

"Why don't you get out of here?" the woman snapped. "We don't like your kind here."

Rhience and Luneta stared at each other, stunned. "Our kind?" Luneta asked.

"Your kind!"

"Why, thank you, my lady," Rhience said. "You're very kind, too. Now, as I was saying, we're looking for a knight. You can't miss him, because he has a lioness with—"

But the woman only turned sharply and stalked into her cottage, slamming the door behind her. A moment later, the shutters on the windows banged closed.

" 'You're very kind, too'?" Luneta said.

"I lied," Rhience said. "But look at that." He pointed to a patch of soft dirt at the edge of the cottage yard. There, clear as day, was the print of a lion's paw.

Twenty minutes later, they came to a woodcutter hauling a cart along the trail. Rhience waved to him and began to ask if he had seen a knight pass by, but barely had he opened his mouth when the woodcutter said, "If you aren't the ugliest fool I ever seen! How do you ever make someone laugh when any decent person looking at your face would just want to curl up and cry? As for that horrid wench you've got with you, you best keep her away from the kiddies at night or they'll never get to sleep, thinking of her uglies."

"I beg your pardon?" Rhience said, for once at a loss for words.

"She looks like she went chasin' after a standing cow and smacked her face into the cow's rear side. Hope the cow didn't turn around and look. Seein' a face like that'd turn milk sour."

Rhience and Luneta looked at each other blankly. "I say, Luneta, have you been chasing cows? This gentleman says—"

"Shut up, Rhience." Luneta turned to the woodcutter and said, "Look here, fellow. I don't know why you've taken such a dislike to us—"

"Because you look like something I'd go out of my way to keep from stepping in is why."

"—but you can say whatever you like so long as you also tell us if you've seen a knight with a lion pass this way."

"Will it make you go away if I do? I'll say any manner of lies to keep frights like you out of our land."

"Have you seen him, then?" asked Rhience.

The woodcutter shook his head vigorously, said, "Why don't you go away?" and then—as Rhience and Luneta stared in surprise—pointed furtively ahead up the road. "We don't like your type here," he added, and then made a long, rude noise at them.

"What in the world is going on here?" Luneta de-

244

manded as they rode on in the direction the woodcutter had pointed.

"I may be imagining things, but I don't think they like our type here," Rhience replied.

"But why? We've done them no harm. They've all seen Ywain, but they won't say a thing about him. Surely he can't have offended everyone in the country already."

"You wouldn't think so. Maybe it's Lass. You know, some people are just dog fanciers and don't care for cats."

"Especially cats that can eat their dogs," Luneta said. "But then what about that woodcutter? On the one hand, he tells us to go away, and then he sneaks out a hand and points us down this path."

"Yes, that does seem to call for an explanation. But I don't have one."

Neither did they come any closer to figuring things out over the next two hours. They met people regularly, and everyone they met was deliberatately rude and told them to get out of their country. Some of them, especially the children, seemed to enjoy being offensive and even illustrated their insults with hand gestures, but others seemed to be reluctantly repeating a memorized message. Finally, Rhience chose one of these latter people, a gray-haired farm wife whose good-natured countenance had dropped into a sulky scowl as soon as she'd seen them coming, and engaged her in conversation.

"Go away if you know what's good for you," the old farm wife said shortly.

"Ah, but that's what I've never done well," Rhience said mournfully. "Know what's good for me, I mean. Hard work, for instance. My father always said that it was good for me, but it always gave me sore muscles. Well, I ask you! What sort of sense does that make?"

The old woman tightened her lips and stared at the ground. "If it's sore muscles you're wanting to avoid, then just go away."

"It looks as though I'll have sore muscles whatever I do. You see, I've been riding all day, and more of that would give me sore muscles, too. Do you want to see which muscles would be sore?"

The woman choked back a laugh but resolutely stared at the ground.

"Another thing my father said," Rhience continued, "was that it would be good for me to travel and learn other customs. He was right, too: this country certainly has some peculiar customs."

"Rhience," Luneta said wearily, "let's go."

"Yes, go," the woman said. "We don't want people like you in this land, and Rhience is a stupid name, besides."

But Rhience wasn't listening. "Of course! Now I understand it, Luneta! This land simply has different customs than we're used to! In this country, you show

246

respect to people by scowling at them and telling them that they're ugly and that you don't like people like them! That's politeness in these parts!"

The old woman continued staring resolutely at the ground, but she raised one hand to cover her mouth.

Rhience continued, "Why, I'll wager that we've been offending everyone we met by speaking nicely to them and smiling! We should have been returning insult for insult, and instead we've been saying 'please' and 'thank you'! How insensitive of us!"

Luneta suppressed a grin. The old woman growled, "That's a silly idea, but it's no more than I'd expect from a clodpole like you."

"Oh, no, not at all," Rhience replied at once. "I'm sure that you're a much greater clodpole than I! And cross-eyed too!"

At last the woman looked up, her eyes wide with astonishment. Rhience nodded to Luneta. "Come, lass, where are your manners? Insult the woman!"

"I . . . I'm afraid I've not been brought up very well," Luneta said. "I can't think of a single horrid thing to say!"

Rhience sighed. "I shall have to help you, I suppose. Luneta, don't you think that this fine woman's face looks like a wart on a fishwife's bottom?"

"Yes, of course. I should have said so at once," Luneta said, fighting back giggles.

"And her eyes like pox scars? And her nose like a bleeding pustule crawling with worms?"

The old woman's shoulders began to shake, and her face contorted as she struggled against laughter. Rhience waited until she had just managed to regain control, and then he whispered, "Donkey breath, too."

The woman burst into laughter. "You ass!" she said, gasping. "You'll be the death of me, but I can't help laughing."

"Can you tell me why everyone's so surly, then?" Rhience asked.

The woman looked around quickly, then nodded. "We has to, you see. The lord of these lands has made it a law that all his vassals have to discourage every traveler who passes through. Any man who doesn't insult a stranger loses all his property, and any woman has to go sew with the prisoners. And Sir Carius and the Brothers have spies everywhere!"

"Why?" Luneta asked, but the woman only shook her head and again looked around her fearfully.

Rhience said, "Quickly, then, and you can get back to abusing us as you ought: Have you heard of a knight with a lion passing through here?"

The woman nodded quickly. "He went to the master's castle. It's that way, in the center of the village. He wouldn't go away, either."

"Thank you. You're a beastly woman."

The woman tried, not very successfully, to scowl, and said loudly, "And you're a nasty brute. Just the sort of people we don't want around here." With that, the woman winked, then stalked disdainfully away.

X

THE LAND OF DIRADVENT

An hour later, Luneta and Rhience came to the village the woman had told them about and rode toward the castle that rose from its center. As they passed through the town, villagers lined the streets, hissing and calling out insults at them. Some threw rotten food. "I wonder if they treated Ywain like this," Luneta said, hunching slightly as something unidentifiable but very soggy arched high above her head.

"Don't bother ducking," Rhience said softly. "Either these townspeople are the worst shots I've ever seen, or they're taking great pains to miss us. This is all for show. And no, I doubt they threw things at Ywain. Would you pelt a knight who had a lion at his side?"

Once they entered the castle, though, they received a very different reception. A slender servant in a lush velvet livery met them in the courtyard, favoring them with a deep, obsequious bow and bidding them welcome on his master's behalf. "My master begs your pardon for the churlish behavior of the villagers," the servant said smoothly. "He has warned them, but truly they are like children."

Luneta glanced once at Rhience, who only smiled sardonically. "It must be a sad trial to your master," he said. "I should be surprised if he ever has visitors, with such rude villagers at his gates."

The servant bowed again. "Indeed, it can be very lonely for my master, ruling such simple-minded people. But he loves his subjects and remains with them always."

"Admirable," murmured Rhience. "I'm sure that my lady here, Lady Luneta, should like to meet this noble landlord. What is his name?"

"Sir Carius, and he will be in raptures to meet the Lady Luneta," the servant said, his face a mask of empty politeness. Only his eyes seemed alive, as they flickered over Luneta's and Rhience's gear. "I see that you carry a sword, friend," the servant said to Rhience. "Is that usual for jesters?"

Rhience smiled, his face as bland as the servant's. "I carry it for show when I accompany Lady Luneta; I should hardly know what to do with it if she were to be in danger."

The servant nodded with satisfaction, then snapped

his fingers. At once two grooms appeared and took their horses' reins. Luneta and Rhience glanced at each other, then dismounted and watched their horses being led away. Rhience's sword was still on his saddle, and Luneta's magical supplies were still in her saddlebags. She felt suddenly vulnerable and moved closer to Rhience as the velvet valet bowed them through the great door into the keep.

They came into a vast entrance hall, evidently the heart of the castle. The walls were lined with doors, all closed and barred, and from the center of the hall rose a great stone staircase. The servant pointed at two chairs, and then, to Luneta's surprise, disappeared.

"I almost felt more welcome in the village," Rhience commented. "For all his smiles, this gentleman is hardly pleased to see us."

"Do you think Ywain is here?" Luneta asked.

"Let's look," Rhience replied, walking to the first of the closed doors, removing the bar, and pushing it open.

"I'll try upstairs," Luneta said, running lightly up the steps. At the top were more barred doors and, branching off to either side, dark corridors. Luneta checked first behind the doors but found only dusty, unused bed-chambers. Then she turned down the first corridor. In this hall, there were no doors, barred or otherwise, or windows. Luneta decided she would turn back once it got too dark to see, but just before the darkness became absolute, the passage ended at a very solid oaken door. Like every other door in this castle, it was barred, but this time when Luneta removed the bar and pushed, it didn't budge. This door was evidently barred on both sides. She was just about to return to Rhience when she heard a faint sound from the other side of the door. Luneta concentrated her inner ear at the door and listened: inside a woman was sobbing.

This was no solitary woman locked in her room, though. Something in the echoic quality of the sound indicated that the weeping woman was at the other end of a large room, and as Luneta listened, she heard another woman's voice, trying to comfort the crier. Then a man's voice broke in, gruffly telling them both to be quiet, and all sounds stopped. As Luneta looked uncertainly at the door, Rhience's voice came from the end of the hallway: "Luneta! I've found him!" Almost reluctantly, Luneta returned to the top of the stairs, where Rhience and Ywain awaited her.

"Luneta," Ywain said, with an anxious smile. "I must apologize to you. It was very rude for me to slip away so suddenly from Laudine's castle. Are you angry?"

Her mind still occupied with the crying woman, Luneta at first didn't understand what he was talking about. "Oh, that," she said at last. "Don't be silly. You were quite right. I *was* making plans for you and Laudine, and I shouldn't have been."

"Whether you know it or not," Rhience said wryly, "that's a magnificent concession for Luneta. To admit that she might not have known what was best for someone . . . an incredible display of humility."

"Shut up, Rhience," Luneta said automatically.

Ywain smiled and changed the subject. "Rhience says that you've come looking for me, but he didn't have time to tell me why."

Luneta briefly remembered Philomela's legal problems and the trial by combat, but she put them from her mind. Glancing again down the hallway behind her, she thought furiously. "Come back down to the entrance hall. Let's not let that servant know that we've been looking around."

"Why not?" Rhience asked.

"They're hiding something. Come on," Luneta said, hurrying down the steps.

"What's the matter?" Rhience asked when they were at the foot of the stairs.

"Where did you find Ywain?" Luneta asked.

"That doorway there leads to another room and then to another room beyond that. Ywain was in the third room."

"Actually," Ywain said, "I was kicking my heels in this hall until half an hour ago. Then that oppressive servant bustled me away."

Luneta nodded. "That must have been when they

saw us approaching through the town. They moved you because they didn't want us to meet."

"But why wouldn't they?" Rhience asked. He was watching Luneta's face closely.

"For the same reason all the peasants are supposed to discourage visitors," Luneta said.

"Oh, were they rude to you too?" Ywain asked. "Wasn't that horrible? I've never known such an ill-mannered populace. Why, if I hadn't had Lass with me, I think they might have even attacked, they were so beastly."

"They wouldn't have attacked," Rhience said.

"Where *is* Lass?" Luneta asked quickly.

"She's in a room near the stables, with my gear. The servant said that his master's daughter is afraid of large animals."

"Your weapons are there, too?" Luneta demanded.

"Yes, of course," Ywain said. His brow knitted. "Why?"

"Then we have no weapons at all," Luneta said.

"Do you think we'll need any?" Ywain asked. "I mean, the people outside were nasty, but it's been pleasant here in the castle. We may have been in some danger out there, but surely not here."

"There was no danger out there," Rhience said. Quickly he repeated to Ywain what the old women had told them. "If anyone's found being nice to a stranger, his lands are confiscated," Rhience concluded. "Or, if it's a woman, something else was to happen. Do you remember what, Luneta?"

"The woman said that she'd be forced to sew with the prisoners," Luneta said slowly.

"That's right," Rhience said. "I didn't quite understand that bit."

"Me neither, but I wish I'd asked her," Luneta said. She told Rhience and Ywain what she had heard through the door at the end of the corridor. "They've got some secret here that they don't want anyone finding out. There are women being held captive behind that door."

"Which explains why they discourage outsiders," Ywain said.

Luneta nodded. "And why they took our weapons from us and shut Lass up and tried to keep us apart."

Ywain frowned. "You don't think they mean to kill us? To keep some secret? But that servant was so polite."

"Once we're here, what would be the point of being rude?" Luneta replied. "Better to be nice, take our weapons away, and then get rid of us at their leisure."

"What should we do?" Rhience asked.

Ywain smiled suddenly, a hint of mischief in his eyes. "Well, if I'm about to be murdered, I'd like to know why. Let's go back to that door, Luneta."

Luneta led them back upstairs. Ywain's step was jaunty, and he whistled softly as he walked. Luneta realized again that danger only made her cousin cheerful, and she shook her head. At the door, Ywain felt all around the edges, then said, "Hinges on the inside, so it opens that way." He dropped to his knees and pressed his mouth to the crack beneath the door. "Knock on the door for me, will you, Rhience? Hard."

Rhience glanced at Luneta, shrugged, and then began banging on the door. At the first knock, Ywain began growling something indistinguishable in a gruff and impatient voice. Then he listened at the opening. "Do it again," he said.

Rhience knocked and Ywain gave his angry growl four times before Luneta heard hesitant footsteps coming near. Ywain leaped to his feet and said, "Stand back from the door." A moment later Luneta heard the unmistakable sound of a bar being drawn from its place, and the door moved.

Ywain threw his body against it, thrusting it wide open. Inside, Luneta had the vague sense of a huge torchlit room, but her eyes focused on the thin figure that was falling away from the door. Ywain leaped forward, then checked his attack. At his feet lay a terrified-looking woman.

"I'm so sorry," the woman whispered. "I'm so very,

very sorry. It was all my fault. I shouldn't have startled you like that!"

Ywain extended his hand to her. "*You* shouldn't have startled *me?*" he asked. "I should have thought it was the other way around. Do let me help you up, madam. I beg your pardon for knocking you down."

"Oh, no, you mustn't think of that," the woman said. She looked as if she were blushing. "I'm sure I brought it on myself." Looking away from Ywain's extended hand, she climbed to her feet without assistance.

"Permit me to introduce myself, madam," Ywain said, sweeping a courtly bow. "I am called the Knight of the Lion, and these are my friends Rhience and the Lady Luneta."

The woman bobbed a curtsy and looked at the dirty floor at their feet. "I'm very sorry that it took me so long," she gabbled self-consciously. "It is most unfortunate that the foreman should have stepped out just at this time, and of course we aren't used to new ladies coming in by that door, but I was afraid that the Brothers would be displeased with us if we kept them waiting, and truly you did sound very angry to me." The thin woman peeked up for a moment, then looked down. "Where are the other ladies?"

"There is only one lady with me," Ywain replied.

The woman looked at Luneta a gave a tremulous smile. "Welcome. You know, I didn't *think* it was already time for the regular thirty. You must be a special case. Let me show you around. I've been here the longest so I'm usually the one who does that."

Luneta was just about to ask the woman to explain what she meant when she heard Rhience say, "By all the gods!" and she looked up.

They were standing on a wooden landing at the top of a stairway, about midway up the wall of the largest room Luneta had ever seen outside a cathedral, and on the floor of the room were dozens of women sewing by torchlight. Three or four looked up at them, but most of the women simply hunched over their work.

"What is all this?" Luneta asked breathlessly.

"This is the workshop where you'll be working, of course," the thin woman replied, taking Luneta's hand and leading her downstairs. "You come at a good time. We've just had a place come open."

One of the women who had looked up spoke in a restrained but very clear voice. "Why don't you tell them why the place came open, Dorothea?"

"Sophia," the thin woman said sternly. "If I were you, I'd concentrate on my work. You're hardly healed from the last time you were found dawdling."

The woman called Sophia ignored the thin woman and looked at Luneta. "One of the workers died yesterday. Her name was Arivelle."

"Of course we're very sorry for poor Arivelle,"

Dorothea said, "but she was a very slow worker, and her unfortunate fate is a reminder to us all that if we simply do our best here, we can all live very happily."

"Very happily indeed," Sophia repeated, without expression.

"What is all this?" Luneta asked again, but this time addressing her question to Sophia. "Why are you all working here?"

"Don't you know?" Sophia asked. Luneta shook her head. "You mean that you haven't been brought here to work with us?"

"No," Luneta said. "We're travelers from outside this land who found our way to this castle and discovered this doorway."

Dorothea gasped and turned nearly white. "Oh, no! Please go away! If you're found here and the Brothers hear that I let an outsider into our community . . ." She trailed off, evidently unable either to imagine or to express the fate that would befall her.

"Where does that door lead?" demanded Sophia.

"Into the castle, up to the entrance hall," Luneta replied.

"No, Sophia! Don't even think it!" Dorothea said vehemently. "If you run away, the rest of us will be beaten! You know the rules."

"What if we *all* run away?" Sophia asked.

"They'll catch us!" Dorothea said despairingly. "The Brothers!"

"Are you prisoners here?" Luneta demanded.

Speaking simultaneously, Sophia said, "Yes," and Dorothea said, "No." Sophia gave Dorothea a weary look, then turned to Luneta. "Yes," she repeated. "We're all from the Isle of Wight. Ten years ago, the lord of this land, Sir Carius, fought a war against our king and defeated him, mostly because two monstrous fiends fought for Sir Carius, two brothers who are like demons of Hell. No one could stand before them, and our king surrendered. The terms of peace permitted our king to keep his throne, but every year he has to provide thirty women to serve Sir Carius here in Diradvent."

"Diradvent?" Ywain interrupted suddenly. "Is that the name of this land?"

"Yes," Sophia replied. "You've heard of us?"

"Everyone at court knows about Diradvent embroidery and clothing," Ywain said. "It is the finest in England and is much in demand." He looked around. "And this is where it is made?" he asked, horror in his voice.

Dorothea, who had been clutching her hands anxiously throughout this exchange, was suddenly distracted. "Oh, ladies! Did you hear that? Our embroidery is famous!"

Sophia ignored her, as did the other laboring women. "This is where it is made," she repeated softly. "We sew here ten hours at a time, then sleep for five hours, then start again."

"Fifteen hours is not a full day," Rhience pointed out. His voice was quiet.

"Day and night mean nothing here," Sophia replied. "I haven't seen the daylight since I came, three years ago."

Ywain was still gazing around in horror. "Your king sends thirty of his subjects, thirty women, to work in this hole, so that he can keep his throne?"

"That's right."

"Is a throne worth trading away your own soul?" Rhience whispered.

Ywain continued, "And he's done this for ten years? Three hundred women?" Sophia nodded. "I see less than a hundred here. Where are the rest?"

"These are all that live," Sophia replied simply. "We are fed poorly, and if we do not sew well, we are beaten."

Dorothea interrupted suddenly. "But you don't tell the whole story!" she snapped. "Why should we not sew our very best for the kind master who gives us food and shelter? And at least it is work that is suitable for us!"

"I see nothing suitable here," Ywain said.

"I only mean that sewing is what women are good at. We are asked to do only what we do well. And as for the food, women don't need as much as men. Only those women who have overly high opinions of themselves think that we're ill used." Here she looked pointedly at Sophia.

Luneta stared at Dorothea. "Do you defend your captors?" she asked.

"I am not a captive," Dorothea said proudly. "I am very comfortable with my lot here and do not ask for anything more."

"Don't think too harshly of Dorothea," Sophia said quickly, before Luneta could respond. "She's been here longer than any of us, the only survivor of the first group that came ten years ago. Whatever she says, she has survived."

"But I won't much longer if you're found!" Dorothea said urgently. "I opened that door only because I thought it might be the Brothers, but now you must leave!"

Ywain looked at Sophia. "Will you come with us?" he asked.

Sophia hesitated, but only for a moment. "Not unless everyone leaves with me," she said. "Dorothea was right. If one escapes, everyone will be beaten, and some here won't live through another beating. Can you get us all away?"

Rhience said, "We can't even guarantee we'll get away ourselves." Ywain started to speak, but Rhience said, "I know, Ywain. But the only thing to do is to leave for now. It sounds as if these Brothers are the key. Get rid of them, and we can come back."

Ywain nodded slowly. Luneta turned to Sophia. "You can trust this knight," she said. "He won't leave until you're free or he's dead." Then, as an afterthought, she added, "Neither will I." Then she and her friends went back up the stairs, barred the door behind them, and returned to the entrance hall together. No one spoke.

"Sir!" the velvet servant exclaimed as he came into the entrance hall and saw Ywain sitting with Rhience and Luneta. "I did not think to find you here!"

"Oh, no," Ywain replied blandly, "but I grew bored in that other room and found this lady and her friend. We've had a very pleasant visit while we waited for you to return."

The servant gave a forced smile. "I'm delighted to hear it," he said. "Indeed, I was just coming back to introduce you to each other, as would have been proper."

"That's so kind of you!" Luneta said brightly. "And will you now conduct us to your master? He seems such a fine man, to stay here ruling over his surly people!"

"Indeed," the servant said with a bow. "If the three of you will follow me."

He led them up the stairs and down the opposite hall-way from the one leading to the women. Unlike the other passage, this hall was well lit and lined with doors that stood open, revealing several opulently furnished salons and sitting rooms. Sir Carius seemed able to afford the very best. At the last door, the servant stopped. He spoke briefly to Ywain, making sure he had their names correct, then opened the door and said, "My lord and my lady, may I present to you the Knight of the Lion, Lady Luneta, and their companion, Rhience the Fool!"

Luneta followed Ywain into the room and, to her surprise, saw not only a kind-looking old man with fine white hair but a brightly smiling girl of about her own age. The girl saw Luneta, and her eyes sparkled with delight. "Oh, Father! Look! The Lady Luneta is just a girl like me!"

"Remember your manners, Floria," the white-haired man said indulgently.

"Oh, dear, my tongue has run away with me again," the girl said, blushing prettily. "I do beg your pardon, my lady, but we have so few visitors, and most of them are so old and *fusty* that I couldn't help being delighted to see someone near my own age!" Floria leaped to her feet to sweep a curtsy and then stopped as her eyes fell on Ywain's face. "Oh, my!" she said, suddenly wide-eyed and breathless.

Ywain bowed. "Lady Floria, is it?" he said, smiling. Glancing at him, Luneta realized that even through his beard, Ywain was quite good-looking.

"Oh, my!" Floria said again.

The white-haired man rose to his feet. "I hardly need say so, but we are also quite unused to having handsome young men to visit." Floria turned bright red but didn't take her eyes from Ywain's face. "I am Sir Carius, lord of these lands, and I am honored to greet you all."

Luneta could only gape at them. Was this gentle old man the one who had imprisoned three hundred women, killing more than half of them with cruel labor? She glanced at Rhience and found him looking at her, equal amazement in his eyes.

"We were just about to go to dinner," Sir Carius said. "I would be honored if you would join me. We are thin of company this evening, I'm afraid, and it will be a simple family gathering—just the five of us."

"We would be honored, Sir Carius," Ywain said. "But surely you were not expecting us and have not prepared for three more guests."

"I believe there will be enough," Sir Carius said placidly. Then he led them through a side door into the most extravagantly decorated dining hall Luneta had ever seen. Every wall was covered with brilliant tapestries, and the little bit of wall that showed between the hangings glowed with gilding. The long banquet table was covered with food, more than five people could eat in a week. The plates were of gold, and the goblets of purest crystal.

"Come sit beside me, Lady Luneta!" Floria called out. Luneta sat in the place that Floria had indicated and was immediately swept up in a flood of chatter.

"Floria!" her father said gently. "You forget yourself again. You will give our guests a very odd opinion of our manners here in Diradvent."

Rhience chose a place directly opposite Luneta and said, "Indeed, it is pleasant to meet someone so courteous here. I must confess that we saw little in the way of courtesy from your people."

Sir Carius nodded, a picture of benevolent tolerance. "We are a small land and have been beset by enemies. I'm afraid that it has made the people suspicious, and in their simple boorishness they treat outsiders ill. But"— he turned his attention back to his daughter—"the doltishness of our people is no excuse for us to talk our guests' ears off at dinner, my child."

Floria blushed, stammered an apology, then turned her attention to the dinner. For this Luneta could hardly blame her. Their meal was sumptuous beyond words. Luneta had thought that Laudine lived luxuriously, and she had reveled in the banquet at Camelot, but she had never even imagined such extravagance as she found here. Servants in silk and velvet hovered at their elbows, ready to refill every glass or whisk away every dish at a moment's notice. Luneta could not enjoy it, though. All this luxury, she realized, must have been paid for by the labor of those women down the dark hallway. Remembering them, Luneta could only be amazed by the casual indifference that Sir Carius and Floria showed to their opulent surroundings.

After dinner, Luneta was swept away by Floria to a private bedchamber where, evidently, Floria *would* be permitted to "talk her guest's ears off," which she did. For nearly three hours, Floria talked almost without stopping, while Luneta could only listen with incredulity to her cheerful, artless prattle. Luneta decided that the bubbling Floria could not possibly know about the prisoners whose labor allowed her to live in such style. If she did, she could hardly be so brightly cheerful. The only time that Floria stopped talking was when she discovered that Luneta, instead of being Ywain's lady, was his cousin. At that welcome news, her mouth dropped open and her eyes shone. "Do you think he liked me?" she asked suddenly, before bursting into embarrassed giggles.

Luneta blinked, swallowed, then managed a faint

smile. "I really couldn't say," she was able to reply. Floria launched into a rapturous appraisal of Ywain's beauty, and Luneta could only shake her head. They had determined earlier in the evening that only a few months separated them in age, but in some way that Luneta couldn't explain, Floria was years younger than she. At last a bell rang somewhere farther down the hall, and Floria broke off. "Oh," she said breathlessly. "That's Father ringing for bedtime prayers. I must go. Will I see you tomorrow? We have private mass in the chapel every morning at nine. You'll be there, won't you?" The bell rang again, and Floria gave a little squawk and rushed from Luneta's room.

Luneta listened at the door until Floria's footsteps had faded away, then waited another ten minutes. There was no sound. Apparently when Sir Carius called for prayers, he meant it. She crept from her room and began listening intently at every door she came to. She heard nothing until suddenly, from the room at the far end of the corridor, there were voices.

She stopped moving so as to listen more closely. A gruff, gutteral voice that she didn't know was saying, "They have to die, of course."

"Could it not wait for a few days?" came Sir Carius's voice, no longer quietly assured but faint and trembling. "At least let the girl live for a while. My daughter has no friends."

269

"Your daughter has more gold than Queen Guinevere," a third voice interjected. "Let that be enough for her. We can't let any of them live. Wendel says that at least one of them had been wandering about the castle, and we don't know what they might have found."

"But—"

"You'll do what you're told," said the first voice. "Tell them you're taking them to mass in the morning and lead them out to the courtyard. We'll handle it from there."

"Yes, sir," Sir Carius said, faint and weary-sounding.

These must be the Brothers, those demon men who had inspired such fear in Dorothea, Luneta thought. She heard their steps moving toward the chamber door and realized suddenly that she was in plain sight of anyone stepping from that room. Leaping forward to the next door, which providentially was unbarred, she opened it and slipped inside. Then she froze, seeing a fire burning in the hearth, but a moment later she relaxed: by the fire were Ywain and Rhience. Holding a warning finger to her lips, Luneta listened at the door until the Brothers had left Sir Carius's room and passed by. When at last their heavy footsteps had faded, she turned to her friends. "They're planning to kill us in the morning," she said.

"You heard them?" Rhience asked.

Luneta nodded. "Sir Carius will get us up for mass

tomorrow, lead us out to the courtyard, and these Brothers that everyone's so afraid of will be waiting."

"I'll need a weapon," Ywain said, his eyes bright. "My sword is in the little stone building just east of the stables."

"They'll have it locked," Rhience said.

"Maybe I can open it," Luneta said. "Let's go try, at least." Then she froze and put her fingers to her lips again. Someone was padding softly down the hall. She pointed at the door and the others nodded. Then, while they waited, they heard the gentle scrape of a wooden bar being dropped into place outside the door. They were barred in. Luneta looked around quickly, but there were no windows. The soft footsteps whispered away.

Rhience sighed. "And we only have two beds," he said. Neither spoke, and Rhience shrugged. "Never mind. I *like* sleeping in chairs."

After a brief conference, they came up with a plan, such as it was. As soon as they reached the courtyard the next morning, they would rush for the stone storage room and try to get Ywain's weapons. There was a chance that a sudden dash would take their assassins by surprise and give them some time. Having come to this decision, Ywain chose a club from the woodpile by the fire. It wasn't very long, but it was as thick as his wrist and seemed strong. Then, with a carefree smile, he turned in and was asleep immediately.

"He's enjoying this, isn't he?" Luneta asked.

Rhience nodded. "He'll do what he can to avoid fighting now, but when he can't escape it, he embraces the challenge. He's born to fight."

"*Insana,*" Luneta said.

"*Insanus,*" Rhience corrected in a stern voice. "One must use the masculine form of the adjective when speaking of a male lunatic. Now do it right."

"*Insani,*" Luneta said. "Masculine plural." Then she went to bed.

Sir Carius led them down a narrow stairway, apologizing as he walked ahead of them that Floria wasn't able to join them. "She's hardly ever ill," he was saying, "but she looked so pale this morning, I felt she should stay in bed."

More like you didn't want her to see us being murdered, Luneta thought briefly, but she was too busy listening ahead of them to dwell on Sir Carius's lies. At last, as they approached a door leading out to the courtyard, she heard what she was after, faint rustlings of clothing and shuffling of feet. She leaned close to Ywain and whispered, "They're on either side of that doorway."

"I'll just go ahead of you here," Sir Carius said, his voice shaking slightly, but Ywain reached out swiftly and grasped him by the collar. Taken completely by surprise, Sir Carius made no sound as Ywain dumped

272

him unceremoniously behind them and then with a powerful shove propelled Rhience and Luneta before him out the door and into the open courtyard.

The Brothers must have been waiting for Sir Carius to come out first, because they didn't strike. Rhience and Luneta sprawled face-first into the dusty yard, but from the corner of her eye Luneta saw that Ywain had already spun around like a cat and smashed his short cudgel against one of the Brothers' shins. An amazingly large shin. A howl of pain broke the silence, and then the other Brother brought a heavy axe down on the spot where Ywain had been a moment before.

Luneta became aware of Rhience shouting in her ear. "Quick, Luneta, to the storeroom!" he called, and Luneta turned away from the battle to race after him. He led her to a small stone structure, just where Ywain had said it would be, and they tugged at the door. It was locked.

"I'll go get my sword," Rhience shouted, racing into the stables, but Luneta barely heard him. Instead, she went to a small barred window to the left of the store-room door and peered in. For a long moment she could see nothing, but when her eyes adjusted to the gloom inside, she made out the shape of Ywain's sword against the far wall. The sounds of battle grew closer, but she resolutely ignored them. Reaching her hand through the bars, she uttered a sharp command, and Ywain's sword leaped from its scabbard and flew across to her waiting grasp. Drawing the blade through the window, she whirled around to see Ywain backing slowly away from two of the largest men that Luneta had ever seen. Both carried halberds that would have been too long for most men but that looked small in their massive paws. Their cruel faces grinned with anticipation as they raised their weapons to strike.

"Ywain!" Luneta screamed, throwing the sword to her cousin. The Brothers halted their advance for a second when she screamed, and Ywain snatched the sword deftly from the air and struck. He dived forward and to his right as his sword flashed, which placed one of the Brothers between him and the other. Both Brothers were frozen for a moment, as Ywain landed, rolled, and sprang back to his feet, and then Luneta realized that the first Brother was staring stupidly at the stump that had been his forearm. His hand, still clutching the halberd, lay in the dirt at his feet.

As one, the Brothers began screaming with berserk fury and threw themselves at Ywain, but he had the open courtyard behind him now and, being faster than his pursuers, was able to stay out of their reach. Rhience came panting up out of the stables. "My sword is gone," he said, "but I found your saddlebags. Is there something in here you could use?"

Luneta shook her head numbly. She had no weapons among her magical supplies. But at that moment a low growl from behind her cleared her head. "Lass!" she said. The lioness was locked in the storeroom. "Stand back!" Luneta shouted, rummaging in her bags. A moment later, she produced a clay flask filled with white powder. Dusting the storeroom door with the powder, she called in a firm voice, *"Attun nurah!"* and the door burst into white flames.

"Not bad," murmured Rhience's voice in her ear. "Can you do that with damp wood, too? Sometimes on the trail I have the deuce of a time—"

"Stand back, I said," she snapped. Waving her hand again, she called out, *"Tal shemayah!"* and the flames stopped abruptly. All that was left of the door was a smoking black hole ringed with a few charred fragments of wood. Then a long, tawny shape flew through the doorway and streaked across the courtyard toward Ywain and the Brothers.

The next few moments were a flurry of sound and motion. As Ywain told the story later, he had been penned into a corner and was about to be killed when Lass came to his rescue. Luneta didn't remember Ywain being so hard-pressed, but she always let Ywain tell the story his way. What was certain was that Lass struck one of the Brothers on the back, ripping with her claws and slashing with her great fangs, making that Brother bellow with surprise and rage and turn sharply around. Immediately, Ywain sliced off the head of the other Brother, and a few moments later, both Brothers lay dead in the courtyard.

Suddenly trembling and weak, Luneta sank to her knees, unable to tear her eyes from the monstrous bodies of the two horrible Brothers. "It's over, then?" she whispered.

"Not yet," Rhience said, gripping her shoulder reassuringly. "You stay here with Ywain and Lass. I'll be back in a few minutes." He strode across the courtyard to the front door that they had entered by the day before and disappeared inside. Ywain rumpled the lioness's ears and scratched her head, then the two of them walked back to Luneta.

"Are you hurt, cousin?" Ywain asked, seeing her kneeling in the dust. Luneta shook her head and smiled. Ywain grinned back at her. "Thanks for the sword—and for freeing Lass. It was looking a bit grim there." Taking Luneta's hand, Ywain raised her to her feet.

"No one else could have won such a battle," Luneta said.

"Of course not," Ywain replied. "No one else has a lion."

"Lioness," Luneta murmured.

The doors of the castle burst open and Sir Carius and Floria rushed out joyfully. Gazing with delight at the prone figures of the two Brothers, Sir Carius said, "The

Knight of the Lion! Such a battle! Sir, I am forever in your debt! Ever since those two demon spawn came to this land, eleven long years ago, they have held me in their power. They sent me to war against my wishes! They have kept me and my daughter veritable prisoners in our own castle! I dared not cross their will in anything! But you have delivered us! Sir Knight"—Sir Carius took a deep breath and lifted his chin—"In return for your bravery, I offer you the most precious gift I could ever give! I offer you my daughter's hand in marriage!"

Luneta blinked and looked at Floria, but the blushing girl was gazing limpidly up into Ywain's face and was clearly not at all averse to her father's plan.

"But I don't want to marry your daughter," Ywain said simply. Sir Carius and Floria looked stunned, and Ywain continued, "I ask a different gift instead."

"What is that, Sir Knight?" Sir Carius said, his voice far more restrained.

"Set your prisoners free," Ywain said.

For a long moment, no one spoke, and then Sir Carius replied in a mild voice, "Prisoners? I have no prisoners."

Ywain's tone grew harder. "The women who live as slaves in your castle, sewing the fine products of Diradvent."

Sir Carius smiled, but without enthusiasm. "Oh, the

workers! But they aren't prisoners! Why, those women are artists who have come to us to ply their skill! They are free to leave whenever they wish!"

"Sir Carius," Ywain said sternly, "they live behind barred doors in darkness, working as slaves. I gave you a chance to prove yourself a man of honor, and if you had agreed to let these poor women go, perhaps you could have claimed that you never meant such evil. Then you would have appeared a coward but not a villain. You refused, though."

"But all our land's prosperity comes from the women's wares! The well-being of all our people!" Sir Carius exclaimed. "Before the Brothers came, I was a poor baron, barely surviving off the rents of our land!"

"Nevertheless, you must set the women free," Ywain said.

"I won't!" Sir Carius declared.

"Never mind, Ywain," Luneta said, chuckling suddenly. She pointed at the main entrance of the castle, where Rhience had suddenly appeared. He had the slender servant who had met them the day before by the scruff of the neck and was dragging him along, while behind him strode the woman Sophia, followed by a flood of ragged and emaciated women. The women blinked and gazed about them as they stepped into the light, but they stayed behind Sophia and Rhience.

"Lady Sophia," Ywain said, as Rhience and Sophia drew near.

"I am no lady," Sophia replied. "I am a miller's daughter."

"Do not contradict me, Lady Sophia," Ywain said. "Welcome back to the world of the living."

Sophia shook her head slightly, but only said, "World of the living, indeed. Until now, we were like the dead, in a tomb. This is no less than a resurrection."

"Please, Father," Floria said suddenly, ignoring Ywain and Sophia. "Aren't the women going to sew for us anymore?"

Luneta looked uncomprehendingly at Floria. She had known all along about her father's slave labor.

"No, they are not," Ywain replied firmly.

"But, won't that change everything?" Floria asked, her eyes wide with sudden worry. "I mean, will we still have nice things?"

Luneta, Rhience, and Ywain stared at Floria. At last Ywain said, "Not the same ones, at any rate." Then, in a ringing voice, he declared, "I claim this castle by right of conquest! I have slain the true rulers of this land; now it is mine to do with as I will!" He raised his reddened sword in the air and called out, "Does anyone dispute my claim?"

Floria tugged on her father's sleeve, but Sir Carius stared at the ground and said nothing.

Ywain turned to Sophia. "Lady Sophia, yesterday you had a chance to leave your prison, but you stayed to protect others. This was the act of a great queen. I give this castle, and all its lands, buildings, and treasures, to you. Do with it as you deem best."

"No!" cried Sir Carius in a wrenching voice.

Sophia ignored him and nodded gravely at Ywain. "I accept," she said. Turning to the other women, she shouted, "You are free now! Whether you wish to go or stay, I will see to it that you are cared for!" A few ladies cheered, but most seemed too weak. They could only smile.

"And what about Sir Carius and his daughter, my lady?" Rhience asked.

Sophia considered them for a moment, then said, "You must leave this land. You may each take a horse and whatever you can pack in one bag, but do not return."

"You are too generous to them, my lady," Ywain said, his voice harsh. "Sir Carius is no less a murderer than the Brothers, even if he *was* just doing as he was told."

Sophia shook her head. "They are losing everything that they care for. It is enough."

Sir Carius stamped his foot and said, "This is not lawful!"

Ywain turned hard eyes on the old man. "Accept the grace that has been offered you. Go pack your bags or leave without them."

Slowly at first, then with sudden frenzy, Sir Carius turned and ran back into the castle, doubtless to fill a bag with gold and precious gems. Weeping with anger and frustration, Floria ran after him, screaming as she ran, "Why didn't you stop them? I don't *want* to leave the castle! Why didn't you *do* something?"

Rhience shook his head sadly. "Whatever they take away, they'll spend it in a month, and then they'll never let each other forget that one time they were rich. It would almost be kinder to kill them now." Then he shook the velvet servant, whom he still held by the collar. "And what about this miserable worm?"

Sophia hesitated, and Ywain said, "May I make a suggestion?" Sophia nodded, and Ywain rumpled Lass's ears. "My friend here is hungry. This fellow promised to feed her last night, but he did not. I would imagine that she could finish him off by evening."

The servant gave a yelp, wrenched himself free from Rhience's grasp, and sprinted toward the castle gate.

Sophia watched him run until he was out of sight, and then looked at Ywain and Rhience. "To say the truth, we're all hungry. Is there any food in this castle you've given me?"

Rhience chuckled. "Is there any food?" he repeated. "Just come with me to the kitchens and see."

XI

THE MIGHTIEST
BATTLE EVER

The next few days were busy for Luneta, Rhience, and Ywain. Having given Sir Carius's castle and lands to Sophia, Ywain couldn't simply ride away and leave her to get established on her own, so they all stayed and pitched in. To begin, they had to go through the whole castle and explain to its inhabitants the change in their circumstances. A few servants and guards left, but not many: nearly everyone was so pleased at the death of the cruel Brothers and the departure of the weak Sir Carius that they were inclined to accept any alternative without question. Once they had met Sophia, they accepted her for her own sake.

After that, the freed women were given the choice of returning to their old homes on the Isle of Wight or of staying in the castle with Sophia. Since the king of Wight had generally selected orphans and childless widows to send away, though, few had any reason to return to the king who had handed them into slavery, and all but a dozen or so decided to stay. Those who chose to return were given gifts out of Sir Carius's amassed wealth and sent home with an escort, and those who stayed were fed and clothed and given their own rooms. That was the next task: to open up all the closed and dusty bedchambers. There was a great housecleaning throughout the castle as servants and women aired and dusted the rooms and carpenters cut all the bars away from the doors. The day after this was done, though, a small delegation of the women brought a surprising request to Sophia, who was sitting with Luneta and Rhience in Sir Carius's old parlor. The women wanted to begin sewing again.

"Can you be serious?" Sophia asked with astonishment.

"Yes, my lady," said the leader of the delegation, a middle-aged woman named Anna. "It *is* what we're good at."

"But it's what you did as slaves! And, besides, not *all* the ladies were good at sewing. I know I wasn't."

"No, my lady," Anna replied. "But nearly all of us are. You see, the ones who weren't good at it were the ones who . . ." She hesitated.

"Who were beaten and died," Sophia said.

"That's right, my lady."

"Anna," Sophia said seriously, "I hope that you aren't offering this labor with some idea of paying for your keep. Because you don't have to pay for anything. Every farthing that I spend on your food and shelter has already come from your labor."

"I won't deny that that's a part of it," Anna said steadfastly. "We *would* like to do our bit to support the castle. But that's only part. You see, one of the sisters heard the Knight of the Lion say that he knew about our work, so we went to ask him about it. He says that the tapestries and embroideries of Diradvent are famous all over England. That's our work, that is. We're famous for what we can do, and it's a proud feeling." Sophia opened her mouth to argue, but Anna pressed on determinedly. "So we were wondering. There are two big sitting rooms on the second level here, connected by a big door, and those rooms have rich chairs to sit in and big fireplaces, and we wondered if you wouldn't mind giving us those rooms to sew in."

"Everything here is yours, Anna," Sophia said. "But are you sure?"

"My lady, when I think about spending the rest of my life sitting in a comfortable room by a fire, chatting freely with people I like, doing what I'm good at doing, and never having to worry about where my next meal

284

comes from, it feels more like heaven than anything I've ever dreamed of."

Sophia seemed struck by this and was silent. Rhience said quietly, "A wise holy man I know says that the secret of life is to enjoy your food, enjoy your work, and give thanks to God."

Sophia smiled. "The salons are yours," she said. Anna and the other ladies in the delegation beamed at each other and hurried away to lay claim to their new workrooms. Sophia turned to Luneta. "I would never have imagined this—a life spent sewing doesn't sound like any sort of heaven to me—but this may help me to solve another problem. Luneta, could you come with me?"

Luneta willingly followed Sophia, who led her down the dark corridor to the door where Luneta had first heard the sound of crying women.

"Why is this door still barred?" Luneta asked. "I thought all the bars were cut off."

Sophia sighed. "We tried, but she wouldn't let us."

"Who?"

"Dorothea. Come inside. I'll show you."

Sophia removed the bar and pushed the door open. For a moment Luneta saw nothing in the gloomy, cavernous room, but as her eyes adjusted to the dark she discerned a single torch burning against a far wall and, beneath it, a woman diligently sewing. Sophia led

Luneta down the stairs and across the empty room to the lone laborer. "Dorothea?" Sophia said gently.

"As you can see," Dorothea replied without looking up, "I'm very busy here."

"That's a magnificent dress," Sophia said. "No one can sew like you."

The compliment was calculated to please, Luneta knew, but for all that, it was no lie. The dress that Dorothea was embroidering would have been the envy of any lady at Camelot. Dorothea allowed herself to peek up at Sophia, then grunted noncommittally and returned to her work. "It's nearly done," she said. "So I hope you haven't come down here to waste my time again, trying to get me to leave my work."

"Not this time, Dorothea. In fact, I've come to ask if you would like to work with the other women."

Dorothea hesitated, then looked up at Sophia suspiciously. "Depends," she said. "Do they really want to work again? They seemed ready to drop everything the other day when that jester fellow opened the doors and said the Brothers were dead. Give laziness an inch, and it'll take an ell."

"Indeed, they want to work," Sophia said. "But not in this dark room."

"I've plenty of light," Dorothea said.

"They are setting up a new workroom in the castle above," Sophia continued. "It's a comfortable room

286

with great windows and fireplaces, and they will sit there and talk while they work."

"Harumph!" Dorothea snorted.

"They would love for you to work with them, and if I might say so, they could all learn from watching your skill."

"And who will make them work when they get lazy?" Dorothea demanded.

"No one will make them work at all," Sophia replied. "They will work because they want to."

"Who will be in charge? Who will set the hours? Who will make them pay attention to their work when they start gabbling?"

"No one, Dorothea," Sophia said. Her voice was sad.

"Not one of them will get as much done as I will," Dorothea snapped irritably. "Go away and bar the door behind you!"

Luneta stared at the old woman with horror. She tried to think of something to say that would help Sophia persuade the poor woman to leave her prison, but nothing occurred to her. Sophia stepped back beside Luneta and sighed softly. "Can you help?"

Luneta shook her head. "I can think of nothing else to say."

"I mean, is there anything else you can do? Something magical? I know that you have powers that the rest of us don't have."

287

"Oh, that's why you asked me to come," Luneta said slowly. Then she shook her head again. "But I can't. Not even the most powerful sorceress could help. One thing that none of us can do is change a person's will."

Sophia closed her eyes sadly. "Then we must leave her here in the darkness."

Luneta set her lips and said suddenly, "I can at least do something about that. Here, bring me that dead torch over there." Sophia brought the torch to her, and Luneta explained, "I can dust this with a special powder and light it. It will give much more light than that torch Dorothea is working by, and it won't burn out, either."

They set the torch in a sconce on the wall opposite the old woman's other torch. Luneta performed her charm, and the new firebrand leaped into brilliant light, illuminating the gorgeous dress that Dorothea was creating and casting sharp shadows around the room. But without a word, Dorothea turned her back on the new light, continuing to work in her own shadow, sewing only by the dim light of her old, flickering torch.

Neither Luneta nor Sophia spoke as they returned to the castle.

It was three days after the battle with the Brothers before Luneta and Rhience had time to explain to Ywain why they had come looking for him. They told him about Philomela's inheritance and about her sister's attempt to steal it by deceit—perhaps even by murder—and they explained why Philomela needed a champion to defend her rights in a trial by combat.

"It sounds like exactly the sort of thing I'd rather have nothing to do with," Ywain said frankly when they were done. "Don't think that I don't feel for this Philomela. It does sound as if her sister's done her wrong—well, having her stabbed in the back is a good sign of that—but I don't like the whole trial-by-combat business."

"I agree with you there," Rhience said. "And so does King Arthur. I hear that he's tried once or twice to put an end to the practice, but it must be hard to change an old tradition. Some barons feel very strongly about the custom, and the king's always stopped short of issuing an outright ban that wouldn't be obeyed anyway. At least he's changed the rules so that it isn't a fight to the death anymore."

"Any time you fight with real swords, someone can die," Ywain said gravely. "Who is the sister's champion?"

Luneta and Rhience looked at each other, then shook their heads. "We forgot to ask," Luneta admitted. "But Philomela said that her sister had chosen a good knight."

"There, you see? I don't want to be hurt, and I don't want to hurt a good knight. This should all be settled in some other way. Justice achieved by force is only partial justice."

289

"Isn't that a tad inconsistent of you, my friend?" Rhience asked. "After all, less than a week ago, you took a castle away from an old man by force."

"A castle he had used to enslave others," Ywain pointed out.

"No argument there," Rhience said. "What you did was right and just, but you still did it by force, and without force it wouldn't have happened."

Ywain thought about this, a heavy scowl on his face, but at last the scowl cleared, and he said simply, "Damn."

"Does that mean you'll help Philomela?" Luneta asked.

"When did you say this trial by combat is to be?" Ywain asked.

"The fourth of April," Luneta said. "What is today?"

"That's only five days away," Ywain said at once.

"So soon?" Rhience asked sharply. "Are you sure?"

"Yes," Ywain replied. "Today's the thirtieth of March. I never forget the date anymore, though Heaven only knows what good it will do me now. And where is the trial to take place?"

"Camelot," Luneta said.

Ywain shook his head. "I don't fancy going back to court, either. That was where I let my head get turned by fashion and fame and ruined my life. What will they all think when crazy Ywain returns?"

"Does that matter?" asked Rhience. Ywain didn't reply, and Rhience continued. "If you like, you could fight incognito. Just camp nearby until the day of the trial, then come in wearing your visor down, fight the battle, and leave."

Ywain nodded slowly, but added in a glum voice, "If I'm still alive after the battle."

"If it'll make you happy, I'll drag your corpse away myself. No one will see your dead face."

Ywain gave Rhience a sour look. "Thank you. You've always been a comfort to me."

"Then you'll do it?" Luneta asked.

Ywain nodded. "Ay," he said. "I'll do it, more for the two of you than for this Philomela, but I'll do it."

"Wonderful!" Luneta said. "Philomela's staying with Laudine, which is on the way to Camelot, so we can go by there and get her before heading on to the trial."

Ywain shook his head. "I'm not going to Laudine's castle. I'll go on to Camelot, and you go tell your Philomela I'll be there on the right day."

The three friends and their lioness companion left Diradvent the next morning. Sophia and all the freed women gathered outside in the courtyard to see them off. Every lady had to express thanks to all three of them—a few even ventured a tentative pat for Lass—and so it was almost an hour from the time they

291

mounted their horses to the time they actually rode out the gate. Rhience laughed and said, "Who would have thought that gratitude could be so tiring?"

"It was refreshing, though," Ywain commented. "Nobody offered to marry me."

But they weren't done. As soon as they went out the castle gates, they were surrounded by villagers, all wanting thank them and to apologize for their former rudeness. If it hadn't been for Lass, they might never have gotten away from the eager crowd, but since the townspeople gave the lioness a wide berth, the three riders were able at last to fall in behind Lass and ride out of town.

"Whew," Rhience said, wiping his brow as if exhausted. "If that's what comes of doing good, I've a mind to start doing evil instead."

"You?" Ywain asked scornfully.

"That's right," Rhience replied, brightening. "In my next career, I'll be a recreant knight."

"You'd be terrible at it," Ywain said bluntly.

Rhience looked affronted. "I don't see why you have to be insulting. If I tried very, very hard, I could—"

"He's right, you know," Luneta said. "You laugh too much."

"And, worst of all, you laugh at yourself," Ywain added. "I assure you that no self-respecting recreant knight would ever do that."

Rhience looked crestfallen. "First the church, now this!" he moaned. "Every promising future is blighted by my fatal habit of laughing. If only I weren't so ridiculous!"

Luneta smiled but reflected inwardly that she didn't think Rhience ridiculous at all.

Ywain parted from them late the next day, just over the hill from Laudine's castle, and Luneta and Rhience took their news to Philomela and Laudine. Philomela received it with delight, and when they told about Ywain's victory over the Brothers, she was ecstatic. "Then I'm saved!" she said with a sigh. "I will have a home to return to after all!"

Laudine said quietly, "No matter what happens, you have a home. Even if you lose your claim, you have a home here whenever you need it." Philomela, overwhelmed, thanked her hostess with great warmth. Watching the two of them, Luneta realized that in the brief time that Philomela had been with Laudine, the two women had formed a friendship much closer than the one Luneta and Laudine had formed in six months. Luneta saw now that there had always been a barrier between her and her hostess, and in honesty she had to admit that the wall had been largely of her own making. Luneta could not help thinking that Laudine was in many ways weak and silly, so even while they were doing magic together, she had always felt distant from her

293

hostess. Luneta wasn't envious of Philomela's close friendship with Laudine, but seeing the depth of the two friends' affection did make Luneta realize something important: it was time for her to leave Laudine's castle.

Laudine looked up suddenly. "But where is the Knight of the Lion?"

"He says to tell the Lady Philomela that he will be at Camelot on the fourth, without fail," Rhience replied.

Laudine looked stern for a moment. "Do you trust him, Rhience? I have known knights who made such promises before."

"I do trust him, my lady," Rhience replied. "You are thinking of a young and thoughtless knight whom we both remember well, but I promise you that the Knight of the Lion is very different from that knight."

"Let us hope so," Laudine said. She turned to Philomela and said, "I wish I could go with you, my dear. It would be so good to be able to travel."

"But it would be beyond everything if you came!" Philomela exclaimed. "Why can you not?"

"It's this wretched Storm Stone. Even though I have guards posted around it, someone could still disturb it, and the magic says clearly that so long as the storms can be summoned, the ruler of this land must be here in the castle. It feels like a prison sometimes."

Philomela looked mournful for a moment, then lifted her chin and said firmly, "Then I shall have to visit you often. Indeed, with your permission, I will come back as soon as the Knight of the Lion has confirmed my claim. You'll want to hear all about it anyway, because it should be a grand contest, and I'm sure all the fashionable lords and ladies of England will come to see it. Think of it! The famous Knight of the Lion against the great Sir Gawain!"

"Sir Gawain!" Luneta exclaimed with a gasp.

"Didn't I tell you? That's who my sister's champion is."

"I am shocked, utterly shocked," Rhience said. "Aghast, no less. I would never have imagined that a gently born young lady like you would have even known such words, let alone utter them! And all strung together like that, too!"

"Shut up, Rhience," Luneta said, panting.

They were in Luneta's new bedchamber—Laudine having given Luneta's old room to Philomela when Luneta had left the week before—and were at last able to discuss privately Philomela's revelation. Indeed, Luneta had been pacing the room and discussing it animatedly for several minutes, but she had finally run out of vocabulary.

"As you wish, lass," Rhience said mildly.

"Oh, Rhience, what are we going to do?" Luneta wailed. "If only we'd asked ahead of time who the sister's champion was! But now we've practically forced Ywain into a promise to fight his own cousin! Isn't there any way for him to back out?"

"I can't think of one," Rhience admitted. "They've both given their word."

"Isn't the duty to your own family a prior commitment? Can't we argue that the ties of blood are more important than a promise?"

"You can try," Rhience said dryly, "but you won't get any support from me." Luneta glanced at him, surprised, and Rhience said, "Remember that you're speaking to a man who has worn a fool's costume and refrained from fighting all these many months because I gave my word."

Luneta nodded, then looked curiously at Rhience. "That's true, isn't it? In all the adventures you've been in, you've never taken up arms against any man, have you?"

Rhience shook his head, then grinned. "No, I haven't, but don't take me wrong: if I'd had no other choice, I'd have fought, all right. The truth is that there was always something I could be doing that was more useful than fighting—like when I set you free from the stake and gave you the ring. If I'd tried to fight then, I'd have been killed and you'd have been burned before Ywain got there. As it turned out, no matter what the situation, I could always find a way to be more helpful without a sword than I would have been with one."

Luneta considered this. "Maybe. But the reason that you looked for something to do besides fighting was because of your promise to a dead man, right?"

Serious again, Rhience nodded. "Yes. And Ywain and Sir Gawain will care about their promises, too. Ywain broke his word once; you can be sure he won't do it again."

Luneta sank into a chair. "What if one of them kills the other?"

"It shouldn't come to that, lass," Rhience said. "Remember that these trials are no longer to the death."

"How do they end, then?"

"When one of them yields to the other," Rhience said slowly. He sighed. "Oh, blast," he muttered. "That's not very likely either, is it?"

"We've got to do something," Luneta said. "Maybe King Arthur can stop it. We must talk to him as soon as we get to Camelot."

"Er, Luneta?" Rhience said suddenly. "I've been meaning to tell you this for the past few days, but it's never seemed the right time."

"Tell me what?"

"I'm not going with you to Camelot," Rhience said.

"You're not?" Luneta exclaimed, dismayed. "But why?"

"I have to go home to Sussex for something," Rhience said. "I'll be leaving in the morning, in fact."

"But I might need you to help me stop the fight!" Luneta said.

"I don't think it can be done, actually," Rhience said, "but if you manage, it will be with the king's help, not mine."

Luneta argued for another hour, but Rhience was adamant. He would not agree to go with her, nor would he tell her what his pressing errand at home was. All he would say was that if he made good time, he might be able to join her at Camelot by the day of the fight itself. And with that Luneta had to be content.

The journey to Camelot with Philomela and a few of Laudine's guards riding as escorts might have delighted Luneta only a year before. Philomela was a pleasant, good-natured, and fashionable companion—just the sort of friend that Luneta, confined to the family estates in Orkney, used to dream of having. But far from enjoying a friend of her own age, Luneta found herself irritated by everything that Philomela did or said. Either she rode too slowly or she talked too much or she had nothing interesting to say. Luneta kept comparing this journey to her travels with Ywain and Rhience, journeys that she remembered as times of free and easy wandering.

They arrived at Camelot shortly after noon the day before the trial, and Luneta was never so pleased to end a journey. Although she knew that neither Ywain nor

Rhience would be there, just to be sure, she identified herself to the guard at the front gate and asked if either had arrived yet. No, the guard had heard nothing of either of them. Irrationally disappointed, Luneta turned her attention to the task before her and said, "Very well. Is Sir Gawain at court?"

This the guard was able to answer. "Yes, my lady. Sir Gawain is all set to fight in a trial by combat two days from now. He's at court, you can be sure."

Luneta found him in his rooms, drowsing lazily in an armchair while his squire, Terence, polished his armor. Luneta strode into the room without knocking and plunged directly into the matter. "Good afternoon, Uncle Gawain. Glad to see you're well, and all that. Is it true that you're promised to fight in a trial by combat next week for some property-crazy wench named Philomena?" Gawain sat up quickly, blinked a few times, then opened his mouth to answer, but Luneta pressed on. "Never mind answering that. I already know that you're pledged to the fight. Can you get out of it?"

Gawain blinked again and stared at her, and at last his squire came to his rescue. "Lady Luneta," Terence said, bowing gracefully. "How delightful to see you again. Have you been at court long?"

"Less than an hour. Don't waste time. Can you get out of the fight?"

"Do you always stroll into men's chambers without

knocking? What if I hadn't been dressed?" Gawain demanded.

"I wouldn't care if you were wearing a pink ball gown if you'd only pay attention and answer my question," Luneta said, exasperated. "Can you get—?"

"Good Gog!" Gawain said. "You may *look* different, but when it comes to your tone of voice and attitude, you're the mirror image of—"

"My mother?" Luneta said. Gawain nodded. Luneta rolled her eyes. "A year ago I would have turned you into a frog for saying that—except, of course, that a year ago I couldn't have done so if I'd wanted—but today I just don't have the time."

His voice shaking with laughter, Terence said, "I gather that if you *did* have time today, you would be able to change my master into a frog?"

Luneta hesitated. "I *think* so," she said. "I mean, I know how, but I've never actually done it, so I'm not sure how it would turn out. Sometimes the first try goes amiss."

Terence nodded gravely. "Then it is probably best that you not try. I gather that you've been with your Aunt Morgan."

"Great-aunt, yes. Can we get back to the matter at hand? What about this stupid trial by combat? *Can you get out of it?*"

"I wish I could," Gawain said with a sigh.

"Oh?" Luneta asked. "What do you mean?"

With a guilty glance at his squire, Gawain said, "This Philomena *sounded* so pathetic, telling us all about how her wicked sister was trying to steal her lands. My heart went out to her. Then I heard that she'd also been around the court getting everyone else to promise not to be her sister's champion, which is hardly playing fair. Finally, I met the sister when she came to appeal to Arthur, and—whatever the rights of the case are—the sister's certainly not as wicked as she was painted."

"Hmm," Luneta said, shaking her head. "But you'd already promised to help Philomena."

"You see, I made this promise once to always help maidens in need," Gawain explained. "The only thing is, it's not always clear how best to do that. I have a strong suspicion that I've been used here."

Terence rolled his eyes and said softly, "Do you think?"

Gawain ignored his squire and said to Luneta, "I'm hoping that nothing will come of it, after all. The younger sister was sent out to find a champion nearly three weeks ago, and nothing's been heard of her since. Maybe she won't show up."

"She almost didn't," Luneta said. "About two weeks

301

ago I found her lying in a ditch. She had been stabbed in the back."

Terence looked up sharply, and Gawain's face grew grim. "But she's alive?" Gawain demanded.

"She's fine," Luneta said.

Terence's face broke into a bright smile. "With your help, I gather?"

"That's right."

"Then you chose the third vial," Terence said.

"Yes," Luneta said. "Like my mother."

"What are you two talking about?" Gawain demanded.

"I'll explain it to you someday, maybe," Terence said, his eyes still resting approvingly on Luneta's face.

"Dash it, Terence! I *hate* being treated like a five-year-old! I gather that it has to do with some magical Seelie Court business that you seem to think I wouldn't understand, but I'll have you know that I—"

Terence broke in on his master, asking Luneta, "And I gather that you've brought the younger sister to Camelot with you?"

Luneta nodded.

"With a champion?" Terence continued.

Luneta nodded.

The three were silent for a moment, then Gawain said resignedly, "Blast. Who is it?"

"He's called the Knight of the Lion," Luneta said.

"That fellow who's been killing giants and saving whole towns off in the midlands?" Gawain asked.

"That's right, except that it wasn't really a giant."

"It hardly ever is," Gawain said. "But he still sounds formidable. They're already making up songs about him. Do you know him?"

Luneta nodded. "So do you," she said. "It's Ywain."

For a long minute no one spoke. Then Gawain lowered his chin to his chest and said, "Double blast."

"I don't understand," Terence said after another moment. "Why would Ywain agree to fight Gawain?"

"He didn't know who Philomena's champion was," Luneta said. "Still doesn't, in fact. None of us knew." Then Luneta swallowed and lifted her chin. "And because I didn't know, I talked him into it."

"You did?" Terence asked mildly.

"That's right," Luneta said bitterly. "You'd be astonished at how much misery I can cause by talking people into doing things. Is there anything we can do? Can you go to the king and say that the duty to family is more important than the vow you've taken?"

"No," Gawain said simply.

"Can Arthur outlaw all trials by combat?"

"He'd love to have an excuse to do that," Gawain replied. "But even if he did, it wouldn't change this one. He can't take back a trial he's already sanctioned."

"Can you . . . can you not fight very hard?" Luneta

asked helplessly. Gawain didn't even bother answering, and after a moment Luneta said, "No, you can't do that. For one thing, Ywain won't be holding back. You'll fight until one of you collapses."

"Which will take hours," Terence said.

For several minutes they sat in silence, pondering the problem. Luneta was thinking about what Terence had said, that the fight would take hours. At last, Gawain shrugged and sighed and said, "Maybe nothing very bad will come of this. After all, the trials by combat aren't to the death anymore."

"That's what Rhience said to Ywain," Luneta replied. "But Ywain said only that any time you fight with real swords, someone can die."

"What was that?" Terence asked suddenly.

Luneta repeated what Ywain had said, and Terence nodded slowly. "Yes," he said, "that's very true."

Luneta didn't give up. That evening Gawain was able to get her a private audience with King Arthur and his chief counselor, Sir Kai. A year before, she had been tongue-tied in the presence of her great relative and sovereign, but this time she was too concerned about Ywain and Gawain, and she poured out her story to the king. He listened gravely, but then only said, "I don't know of a thing I can do, my dear."

304

"The problem," Luneta said, "is that neither Ywain nor Gawain will do less than his best."

"That's why they are the men that they are," King Arthur said, nodding.

"But don't you see, if that's the case, then it hasn't done a bit of good for you to say that these trials should not be fights to the death, because neither one of them will yield to the other!" Luneta said, allowing frustration to creep into her voice.

"I am aware of the futility of my command," the king replied. "It was all I could think of at the time. Have you any further ideas?"

Luneta hesitated, feeling the king's gentle irony, then said, "Actually, there *is* one more thing you could do."

The king's brows rose, but he replied evenly, "I am open to any suggestion."

Luneta pressed on doggedly. "I was thinking about this last night after talking to Gawain and Terence. You can't stop them from fighting or from fighting their hardest, but do you think you could put a time limit on the combat?"

King Arthur blinked and looked sharply at Sir Kai, then back at Luneta. "A time limit?" he repeated.

Sir Kai began to laugh softly. "You *did* ask for suggestions, Arthur. Don't be too surprised when you get one—and a damned good one at that."

The king's face softened. He gave a boyish smile and began to speak slowly. "A time limit. The battle shall be limited to one hour. If neither knight has yielded by then, the matter shall be decided by the court. It's so obvious. Lady Luneta, I thank you. It shall be done just as you say."

Luneta was relieved, but only partially. "What happens if one of them accidentally kills the other before the first hour is up?" she asked.

The king's smile disappeared. "I can do nothing about that," he said sadly.

Pleased but not yet satisfied, Luneta walked back to the room that she had been assigned by Sir Kai. It wasn't very large, but word had gotten out to the nobility of England that there was to be a trial by combat, which was almost as good as a tournament, and rooms were scarce. As she made her way through the castle halls, Luneta passed several gatherings of courtiers and ladies, and they were all speculating excitedly on the forthcoming contest between Sir Gawain and the famous Knight of the Lion. No one seemed to know that the knight was Ywain, which was good, but it hardly mattered. The notion of a knight who had a lion had taken strong possession of the court's imagination, and all were agog to see this wonderful new thing. It was being spoken of throughout the court as "The Mightiest Battle Ever," and no one seemed to care a straw that one of these great knights might be killed. Luneta wondered if Rhience had arrived yet.

Luneta pushed open the door to her private bed-chamber and noticed that a small fire was burning on the hearth. A man's voice said, "Hello, lass."

Her heart leaped, but the voice wasn't Rhience's. Blinking into the gloom, Luneta made out two figures seated by a small fire. Then she gasped.

"Father! Mother!" she said.

"Hope you don't mind us invading your room," her father said, rising to his feet. "But there weren't any other spots to be had."

"Of course not," Luneta said automatically. She was looking at her mother.

"Hello, Luneta," her mother said. "You look well."

"You too," Luneta said. "It's good to see you."

"And me too?" asked her father.

Luneta laughed softly. "Yes, of course, Father. It's good to see you, too."

"Good Lord!" Luneta's mother said suddenly. "Luneta, look at me!"

Luneta did, stepping forward into the light of the fire. She smiled, knowing exactly what her mother was looking at. She was looking at her mother the same way. Why had she never noticed it before? The deep and piercing eyes of an enchantress. "Why didn't you ever tell me, Mother?" Luneta asked.

"Will you tell your daughter, if you have one?" her mother replied simply.

Luneta considered this, then shook her head. "Of course not."

"Was it Morgan?"

"Yes."

Her mother said slowly, "Well, you aren't a radiant beauty."

"Why, thank you very much, Mother," Luneta said, dipping an ironic curtsy.

"You know very well what I'm talking about," her mother said tartly.

"I'm glad that *she* does, anyway," Luneta's father murmured.

"If you had chosen the second cordial, you'd be stunning right now, maybe more beautiful even than Morgan, since you're so pretty to start with. So you didn't pick that one."

"I chose the third vial, Mother. Like you."

Luneta's father sank slowly back into his chair. "Oh, no," he said simply, covering his eyes with his hand. "No, no, no. Please don't tell me that—"

Luneta's mother said briskly, "I told you two years ago that it was possible, Gary. I wasn't sure, but sometimes I thought I could see the look in her."

"Just what I need," Luneta's father said glumly. "Another witch in the house!"

308

"Enchantress," Luneta and her mother said in unison. Their eyes met, and then they began to laugh. Luneta held out her arms, and they embraced.

At last they drew apart, and Luneta said, "But what are you two doing here? Don't tell me you've come to see this dreadful trial by combat."

"You mean 'The Mightiest Battle Ever'?" Luneta's father asked. "No, we knew nothing about it until we heard a town crier announcing it yesterday some fifty miles up the road. Is it true? Did Gawain really consent to fight in this thing? Has he lost his mind?"

"He thought he was helping a damsel in distress," Luneta explained.

"Silly sod," her father remarked. "Nothing more dangerous than a damsel in distress—except perhaps a damsel who isn't in distress. I shall have to think about that."

"Don't wear yourself out, Gary," Luneta's mother said. "And this Knight of the Lion, do you know anything about him? Is he as powerful as they say?"

"Very nearly, I imagine," Luneta said. "It's Ywain."

"'Struth?" demanded Luneta's father. "Little Ywain?"

"How in Heaven did all this come about?" Luneta's mother asked, aghast.

Luneta felt tears come to her eyes, and she brushed them away angrily. "It was my fault," she said.

"Would you like to explain?" her mother asked.

309

"From the beginning, please," added her father. "I'll build up the fire."

Three hours and two armloads of wood later, Luneta finished her story, and she and her parents sat around her fire, staring at the coals.

At last Luneta's mother said, "So you used the maturity charm on apple blossoms and got them to produce apples?"

"Yes."

"But that's amazing. Even some of the most advanced enchantresses can't do that. I know that I certainly could never make the maturity charm work."

"Perhaps the two of you could talk shop some other time," Luneta's father said.

"If I could, I would have used it on your father long ago," Luneta's mother said.

Luneta's father chuckled. "*Touché*. But all I meant was that we need to think what we can do about this trial. Could we effect a reconciliation between the two sisters, do you think?"

"After the elder had a knife stuck in the younger's back?" Luneta's mother asked.

"Can't hurt to try," her father said. "Especially since I can't think what else to do."

At these words, a new voice said, "Ah, I've come just in time."

Luneta and her parents started and whirled around, to see Terence standing just inside Luneta's door. "Deuce it, Terence!" Luneta's father expostulated. "You'll kill someone that way someday! How did you get inside without any of us hearing you?"

"I came in the door, of course," Terence replied, stepping forward. He held two swords in scabbards, which he tossed onto Luneta's bed as he approached.

"For anyone else, the hinges would have squeaked," Luneta's father muttered.

Terence smiled but turned his eyes to Luneta. "I just wanted to let you know that I've taken a step of my own to help matters—at least, I hope it will serve."

"What's that?" Luneta demanded.

"You said the other night that any time people fight with real swords, someone can be killed. That set me to thinking. First of all, I realized that Gawain should not use his own sword in the battle." Terence glanced at Luneta and added, "His sword is faery-made, you see. Quite an advantage for him. Then I began to wonder if this could be used another way. So I've just been to visit a blacksmith friend, and he's worked pretty well non-stop for the past two days to put these together." Terence gestured at the swords.

"They aren't real swords?" Luneta said, light slowly dawning.

"Oh, they're real enough," Terence said. "I feel sure

that there's a rule somewhere against using wooden swords. But these are different. The blades aren't made of steel, but of untreated iron."

"I see," Luneta's father said. "And iron will break more easily than steel."

"As you say," Terence said.

"I can't say I think much of this plan," Luneta's father pointed out. "What happens if one person's sword breaks and the other person's doesn't?"

"True," Terence said gravely. "But it was all I could think of." And with that, he turned and departed as silently as he had come.

"Well, of all the daft-headed notions!" Luneta's father said disgustedly. "I've never known Terence to be so absurd!"

"And he's gone off and left the swords here, too," Luneta's mother said. "Very unlike him."

"Mother!" Luneta said, joy suddenly leaping up in her breast. "Oh, Mother! It's perfect!"

"What are you talking about, Luneta? What's perfect?"

"They're iron! Don't you see? Untreated iron!"

XII

THE LIONESS AND
HER KNIGHT

The hard part would be getting the right sword to Ywain. Gawain was easy: they simply gave his sword to Terence, who promised to see that Gawain used it. But not only did Ywain have no squire, but he wasn't even coming to the court until just before the combat. Luneta simply had to wait.

As time for the trial approached, Luneta took the sword to the front gates, where several dozen other courtiers were casually loitering, clearly waiting to gawk at the famous Knight of the Lion. At last a guard on the castle wall called out, "Lone knight approaching!" which was followed by a babble of other shouts—"It's him! It's him! I see the lion! Where's his mane?" Luneta chose a spot a few yards back from the gate, behind the crowd, and waited. Just as she had expected, when Ywain and Lass grew close, those onlookers who were in the center of the crowd had second thoughts about being in a lion's path and pressed frantically away from the middle, opening a path right to where Luneta waited. Ywain, in full armor and with his visor over his face, rode through this gap and stopped in front of her.

"Good morning, Sir Knight," Luneta said. Ywain nodded a silent greeting. Luneta guessed that he was trying not to speak so that no one would recognize his voice. Then Lass, who had been padding quietly beside Ywain and ignoring the crowd, paced majestically forward to Luneta and sniffed at her. The crowd backed away farther, and several of the courtiers uttered muffled oaths. "And good morning to you, too," Luneta said. Lass appeared to be satisfied and sat down.

Ywain dismounted and stepped up to Luneta. In a low voice he said, "I don't suppose you've found a way to stop this trial, have you?"

"No," Luneta said. "But the king has made a new law. If neither of you has yielded after an hour, then the case goes to him for his decision." Ywain nodded appreciatively, and Luneta added, softening her own voice, "And when you fight, will you do me the favor of using this sword?"

"Why?"

"Because I ask? Gawain has already agreed."

314

"Gawain?"

"Oh, yes, you don't know, do you? He's the one you're fighting."

Ywain was silent for a moment. At last he said, "Luneta, if you hadn't saved my life so many times, I feel sure that I would strangle you now."

"I know," Luneta said. "I'm sorry. You were right to want nothing to do with this, and I was wrong to talk you into it. But I'm doing my best to fix things. Trust me?"

Luneta half expected Ywain to refuse—she wasn't at all sure that, in his position, *she* would trust her—but Ywain didn't hesitate. "Give me the sword. Where's this silly fight to be?"

"I'll take you there," Luneta said.

The combat was to take place in an inner courtyard, behind the main keep of the castle. This courtyard had been roped off since the night before, but by the time of the battle the people were so tightly packed around the sides that one could barely get through. Every castle window that overlooked this court was clogged with the faces of spectators, and as Ywain, Luneta, and Lass approached, a buzz of excitement ran through the packed people. If they hadn't had Lass with them, they might not have gotten to the field at all, but the lioness worked her usual magic on the crowd, and they scraped through without much trouble.

At the edge of the field, Ywain stopped and looked

around. Opposite them was the royal pavilion, where King Arthur sat with Queen Guinevere and a few of his knights. Luneta saw Philomela there, along with another lady whom she didn't know—doubtless Philomela's older sister Philomena. Gawain waited calmly in front of the pavilion. The king stood. "Welcome, Sir Knight," he said in a ringing voice. "Our court has heard much of your deeds, and we have longed to meet you."

Ywain bowed deeply in reply. After the barest pause, the king continued, now addressing all the crowd. "As you know, we are here for a trial by combat. These two knights, each defending one of the sisters of Blackthorn, will weigh arms against each other, the winner being held to have vindicated the cause of his sponsor. If, however"—the king's voice became even stronger—"neither has defeated the other after the space of one hour, then I declare the trial by combat to be concluded, and the cause will be decided by me and my counselors! Are there any who object to these terms?"

Both the sisters of Blackthorn looked surprised at the one-hour rule, but neither spoke. The king waited a moment, then lifted his arm and said, "Let the contest begin."

At that point, a problem arose. Ywain strode toward the center of the courtyard but was followed immediately by Lass. Ywain stopped. "No, Lass," he whispered to the lioness. "Go on back to Luneta." But Lass had seen Gawain stepping forward with drawn sword and had grown tense, her tail beginning to whip sharply about. Clearly she had no intention of letting Ywain face this threatening knight alone. Ywain looked helplessly back at Luneta.

"Come here, Lass," Luneta called. The lioness paid no attention, and as Gawain approached she lowered into a crouch, ready to pounce.

"I'll be all right, Lass, go on back, now," Ywain said, but the lioness ignored him as well. Gawain stopped advancing, and he and Ywain looked uncertainly at each other.

"Cats don't mind all that well, do they?" Gawain asked, amusement in his voice.

"I'll have to take her somewhere and shut her in, I suppose," Ywain replied.

But just then a new voice called out, from right beside Luneta, "Lass, girl! Come here!"

The lioness's ears pricked up, and she turned. Luneta looked up to see a tall young man in a sober black outfit standing beside her. It wasn't until he called again that she recognized Rhience, no longer wearing his fool's motley. Lass turned and loped back toward Rhience, picking up speed as she came. When she was near enough, she sprang lightly up, placing her paws on Rhience's shoulders and nearly knocking him over. The people in the crowd nearby shrieked and surged away. "Hallo, old girl," Rhience said to the lioness. She pressed her head against his chest and rubbed her cheek against him.

Luneta could only stare. In simple black clothes, Rhience looked like a different man, and for some reason she found herself overcome with shyness. Rhience grinned at her dumbfounded face and said, "I must be very handsome in these clothes. I've never had a female throw herself in my arms before."

Luneta's shyness disappeared at once. "Don't get used to it," she said.

"That's better, lass," Rhience said. Then he rubbed the lioness's ears. "No, not you, girl. The other lioness." Lifting his face toward the courtyard, Rhience called out, "Go ahead, Sir Knight! I'll hang on to your lady friend!"

Ywain waved his arm in greeting and acknowledgment, then turned to Gawain. Luneta focused her inner ear on the two knights and made out Gawain saying softly, "Sorry about this, cousin. I didn't know it would be you."

"Nor I you, Gawain."

"I know. Well, we might as well begin. May the best knights not win."

The two took their positions and lifted their swords to the sky briefly. Then Gawain slashed at Ywain, who parried the blow with his sword. The crowd burst into a roar at the blow, but the roar faded at once, and the two knights stepped back from each other, both looking at their blades.

"Do you know, my dear," Rhience said calmly, "that that looked very odd in this light? It almost seemed as if their swords bent when they struck each other, then straightened out all by themselves."

"How is that possible?" Luneta asked demurely. "Both of those swords are made of iron."

The combatants came together again. This time it was Ywain who struck and Gawain who parried, but there was no mistaking what happened. When the swords met, they both bent nearly in half at the impact, then popped back to their former position, as if they were willow branches. Ywain struck again, harder this time, and his sword nearly wrapped itself all the way around Gawain's sword before it snapped straight again. Again the two knights backed away and examined their blades.

"It occurs to me, Luneta," Rhience said, speaking very softly, "that there might be a magic spell of some sort that could do that to a sword."

Luneta frowned thoughtfully. "I *have* heard of a magical lotion that would make iron bend in that way," she admitted.

"I see," Rhience replied. "I don't suppose that those swords have been in the hands of an enchantress, have they?"

"That hardly seems possible," Luneta said, wide-eyed. "My mother and I took care of those swords ourselves until time for the combat."

"Your mother?" Rhience asked, giving her a surprised look.

"Yes, both of my parents are here. They arrived yesterday. You should meet them. I think you'll like them."

"I have every intention of doing so," Rhience replied.

The battle in the courtyard was quickly becoming a farce. Gawain and Ywain were trying their best to hack at each other, but their swords would not cooperate. Even when one of them managed to score a hit on the other's armor or helm, the sword simply conformed itself to the shape of the armor, then bounced back. Gawain began to laugh, and a minute later Ywain joined him.

"Do we really have to keep this up for an hour?" Gawain managed to gasp.

"Giving up, eh?" Ywain replied between chuckles.

"You impugn my honor, sir," declared Gawain, and at once he swung his sword at Ywain's ankle. When it hit, the sword wrapped itself around Ywain's leg, and Gawain pulled it sharply back. Ywain's left foot flew up, and he fell flat on his back. The crowd roared with delight, but when Gawain rushed forward, Ywain rolled over and managed to wrap his own sword around Gawain's thigh, making him stumble and fall. The knights leaped to their feet, both of them now swinging their swords like cudgels instead of blades, trying to hit the other with the flat of their swords instead of the edges. Neither made any further effort to parry the other's blows with their swords but instead protected themselves with their free hands while striking return blows with their swords. After all, Luneta thought with satisfaction, it was clear that those pliable weapons were not going to inflict any damage.

Gawain managed to wrap his sword around Ywain's forearm, but Ywain pulled back faster than Gawain did, and Gawain staggered forward, off-balance, and, with some help from Ywain's right foot, sprawled on his face. "Take that, churl!" Ywain said grandly. Luneta realized that he was no longer trying to hide his voice, but was talking loudly enough for all to hear. Gawain rolled over and dived into Ywain's legs, bringing both of them down in a heap.

"Stop this! Stop this at once!" shrieked a furious female voice from the king's pavilion.

"I take it that's Philomena, the evil sister?" Rhience asked Luneta.

"I think so. She doesn't seem best pleased, does she?"

"Your majesty! This is no battle! Stop it and give them new swords!" Philomena screamed.

King Arthur rose deliberately to his feet. "My lady," he said. "You and your sister have demanded of this court that we hold a trial by combat. Now, as I understand these trials, the idea is that God will give victory to the one who is in the right. You are placing your cause before God and waiting for his answer, are you not?"

The king waited for a moment, allowing both of the sisters to nod.

"Well, then," King Arthur said. "How do you know that this is not God's reply?" Returning to his seat, he smiled at Gawain and Ywain. "Continue, please. You have three-quarters of an hour left." The knights looked at each other, then back at the king. "No, I'm serious," King Arthur said. "Go ahead and fight. I haven't enjoyed anything so much in years."

By the time the full hour was done, all the courtiers and ladies of Camelot, with the exception of Philomena, were weak with laughter. Even Gawain and Ywain had to stop periodically to hold their sides and shake their heads with irrepressible mirth. During one of these lulls, Rhience commented to Luneta, "It's a dashed good thing that I've given up being a fool. I could never top this performance. A fine thing when noble knights trespass on the business of honest jesters!"

"About that," Luneta said. "Why *did* you put off the fool's clothes?"

"My year was up," Rhience replied. "Three days ago, actually, on the first of this month. Remember? The Fool's New Year?"

"I'd forgotten," Luneta admitted.

"I had, too, until Ywain told us the date on the thirtieth of March. That's why I had to leave you. I wanted to go home, get my own clothes, and resume my old self before I conducted you back to your home, as I'd promised."

"Was *that* what your important errand was? But I didn't care what clothes you wore!"

"I wanted to be myself when I met your parents," Rhience said. "And, since they're already here, it's a dashed good thing I changed when I did, isn't it? Look sharp, lass. The king's standing up."

Sure enough, King Arthur had risen and stepped forward. "The hour has come!" he called out. At once Gawain and Ywain threw down their swords and, bubbling with mutual laughter, embraced each other. The king grinned at them, then lifted his voice again. "I think we can all agree that this match has ended without a winner! So the case of the sisters of Blackthorn now falls to my decision." He turned to the two sisters and said, "As I understand the matter, Lady Philomena claims that her father died without a will, and so all his estate falls to her, as the firstborn. Lady Philomela, however, claims that her father had indeed made a will, dividing the property in half. This will was not found, however. Are these the facts of the case?"

Both of the sisters nodded. King Arthur lifted his chin and declared grandly, "The case would be impossible to decide," he said, "unless by the grace of God that original will *were found!*" With that he held one hand back to Sir Kai, who stood behind him. Sir Kai drew a roll of parchment from his cloak and placed it in the king's hands. King Arthur lifted the parchment triumphantly over his head.

Philomena screamed angrily, "That can't be my father's will!"

King Arthur lowered the parchment, and said, "No, it isn't, my dear. I believe it's a stable inventory or something tedious like that. But I do have a question, child. How could you be so certain that this is not the missing will—unless you had yourself destroyed it?"

Philomena blanched and was silent. King Arthur's face grew stern, and he turned to Philomela. "Lady Philomela, I declare your claim vindicated. But I will leave the final resolution to you. You say that your father left his property equally to the two of you, and if that is what you wish, you may take your half now, sharing that property for all time with your sister. However, because Lady Philomena sought to steal your half, she has forfeited her own rights. If you want to have the entire property for yourself, it is yours. I declare it."

Philomena's eyes grew wide, and she looked about to faint. Then Philomela said, "But I don't want to turn my sister out of her home."

"Even though she would have done just that to you?" the king asked.

Philomela ignored the king's question and frowned in deep thought. Finally, with an expression of wonder on her face, she said, "And I don't want to share the property with her, either. You see, Your Highness, I don't like her."

King Arthur pursed his lips and nodded. "A dilemma indeed. What do you decide?"

Philomela's face cleared. "I hereby renounce all rights to my inheritance. Mena, you can have it."

A murmur of astonishment came from the crowd. King Arthur said, "I confess, Lady Philomela, that I hadn't considered that option. If I may ask, where will you go?"

"I will go to live with a dear friend who has told me that I could stay with her forever. My home was never happy, sire, and I was never happy in it. Mena can have it with my blessing."

Luneta shook her head and said to Rhience, "She's going back to Laudine's, of course."

"Good thing nobody got killed over this," Rhience commented wryly. "Since we ended up just where we started."

"Not quite," Luneta said, beginning to smile. "It's different for Philomela. If she had had her rightful property taken away from her, she would have resented it the rest of her life. But now she's given it up freely."

"That's very true," Rhience said. "The thing that we do of our own choice is quite different from the thing that someone else forces us—or manipulates us—into doing." Then he chuckled. "And it will be different for poor Philomena, too."

"*Poor* Philomena?" Luneta repeated. "But she got everything."

"Yes, but only because her sister let her have it. She'll never be able to enjoy it, because she'll never forget that her little sister tossed it to her like a bone."

Luneta began to laugh with Rhience and glanced at the royal pavilion. From the sickly expression on Philomena's face, Luneta could see that this realization was slowly sinking in, that somehow she had gotten everything she wanted and lost it at the same time. Luneta looked back at Rhience and remembered what he had asked her one time—"What do *you* want?"—and for the first time, she knew.

* * *

A knock came from the door to Gawain's chambers, where they were holding what Gawain referred to as a "nonvictory celebration." Luneta looked up hopefully, but it was only Ywain. He came in and greeted them all.

"Where's your lion?" Luneta's father asked.

"Lioness," Luneta said automatically.

"In my rooms," Ywain replied. "She was tired, and besides, sometimes she, ah, inhibits conversation."

Luneta realized that Ywain was bareheaded and shaved and said, "You're not incognito anymore?"

"No," Ywain said. "That was all foolish pride. I decided to let the court know that the Knight of the Lion was really just me, mad Ywain."

Another rap came from the door, and Rhience entered. Luneta smiled a greeting at him, then stood. "Father, Mother," she said. "This is Rhience, the fool I told you about, who rode with us in all our travels."

Luneta's father nodded pleasantly, but said, "Pleased to meet you, but I must apologize for my daughter's introduction. You don't *look* like a fool."

Rhience grinned back at him. "Ah, but surely you've noticed, sir. The biggest fools never look like it."

Gawain frowned. "I'm not sure, but I think we could all take offense at that. You would say that if we don't *appear* to be fools, then we probably are."

Terence, bringing a cup of wine to Rhience, glanced

casually at his master and said, "I see no reason for *you* to be offended by that, milord. Only those of us who don't look like fools should be concerned."

"Indeed, I meant no disrespect," Rhience said, after the general laughter had died. "I spoke only of myself. I learned more wisdom in my fool's motley than I ever did before I put it on."

"And now that you've put it off," Luneta's father asked, "what now?"

"Well," Rhience said reflectively, "I've tried the church, and that didn't work for me, and I'd as soon not be a fool any longer. I did think about becoming a recreant knight—"

"A what?" Luneta's mother asked.

"A recreant knight. You know, kidnapping damsels in stress and all that."

"You mean damsels in *distress*, don't you?" Ywain said.

"Well, not at first," Rhience replied. "Once I got better at it, maybe. I thought I'd start small."

Luneta's father's shoulders began to shake. "But it seems to me that for the past year you and Luneta and Ywain have been busily putting recreant knights out of business."

"Well, there, you see?" Rhience said. "There ought to be some openings just now."

"I thought we'd settled this back on the trail," Ywain

said. "You'd be a terrible recreant knight. Worst ever. And besides, recreant knights always end up fighting people like Gawain and me."

Rhience frowned. "Couldn't I be a cowardly recreant knight? I could just run away, couldn't I?"

"No," Luneta said. "You couldn't." Rhience glanced at her, and she added, "At least *I've* never seen you do it."

Their eyes held for a moment. Then Rhience shrugged. "Nothing for it, then. I'll go back to my father's estate and manage the lands that I'll inherit one day." He added reflectively, "And about time, too. I've been away from home only a couple of years, but when I was back this week, it near made me cry to see what things have come to. Father hasn't put a penny back into that land since I left."

Luneta's father's interest sharpened. "Short-term leases?" he asked.

Rhience nodded glumly. "That and a steward who's grown too old for his job."

Gawain interrupted quickly. "Before the two of you begin talking land husbandry and putting the rest of us off to sleep, I want to ask a question. Is anyone here interested in escorting Lady Philomela back to her friend's home? Arthur wants to send a knight or two along to make sure she arrives safely."

"Where is she going?" Ywain asked.

"Lady Laudine's castle, of course," Luneta said. For

a moment, Ywain's face grew empty, and Luneta's heart ached for him. He still loved her. To draw attention away from his pain, Luneta spoke rapidly. "Didn't you know? She and Laudine have struck up a true friendship. Philomela already sees herself as Laudine's chief companion and confidante, which I never was. It's a good arrangement for them both, I think—especially since the magic of the Storm Stone requires that the lord of the castle has to stay there all the time."

"The Storm Stone," Ywain muttered angrily. "I've grown to hate that thing."

Luneta's father spoke suddenly. "I've been thinking about that Storm Stone, actually, ever since Luneta told us about it the other day. As I understand it, it's the center of a magical spell that requires the lord of the castle to stay in one place and to fight anyone who pours water on it. Am I correct?"

Luneta and Ywain nodded.

"I suppose someone has already tried to just smash the blame thing?" Luneta's father asked.

Ywain looked at Luneta, who looked at Rhience, who looked at Ywain. After a long silence, Ywain said, "I'll take Philomela back to Laudine." He smiled at Rhience and Luneta. "You coming?"

It was a pleasant, chattering group that left the next morning to escort Philomela back to Laudine. In addition to Ywain, Rhience, and Luneta, Luneta's parents had decided to come along, and Luneta had never had a more pleasant journey. She rode with Rhience much of the way, but she also spent hours with her mother, talking about the properties of the various herbs that they passed. At those times, Rhience rode with Luneta's father, and Luneta left them alone. One could never tell when those two would begin comparing notes on the best way to drain a swamp or something oppressively boring like that. The only thing that marred her enjoyment of the ride and the company was the occasional glimpse that she had of Ywain's private pain. Every so often he would grow grimly quiet, and as they neared Laudine's castle, these moments of bleak silence grew more frequent.

Once they came to the Storm Stone, Ywain's silence grew so fierce that Luneta could almost feel it as a thickening of the air. He said not a word when they came to the clearing, or when he pointed his sword at Laudine's guards and sent them scurrying away, or when he took out the great iron maul he had brought with him and smashed the stone basin to rubble. All the others waited on their horses, respecting and sharing Ywain's silence. No one offered to help; all knew that this was Ywain's task. When he was done, he scooped all the remnants of the smashed stone into a canvas bag, tied it closed, and then straightened up.

"Shall we go on in?" he asked calmly.

"Sure you didn't leave anything?" Rhience asked.

"I'm sure," Ywain said. He mounted his horse, then put on his helm and closed the visor. He turned to Lady Philomela. "My lady, may I ask a favor from you?"

"Of course, Sir Ywain."

"I hate to ask you to do this, but I need you to conceal something from Lady Laudine. While we are there, I ask you to speak of me only as the Knight of the Lion, and not by my name. Once I am gone, then you may tell her what you wish." Lady Philomela agreed, though clearly she did not understand the request.

A few minutes later, the guards at the gate were announcing their arrival, and Laudine was hurrying across the courtyard to welcome them. For several minutes all was confusion and delight as Laudine first greeted Philomela, then Luneta's mother, then Luneta and Rhience. After that, Philomela had to describe to Laudine how she had turned down her inheritance, preferring to come and live with her dearest friend Laudine, which led Laudine to embark on another whirl of excitement, embracing Philomela ecstatically and telling her how pleased she was and how everything had turned out better than she could ever have hoped.

Through all of this, Ywain sat immobile on his horse, his face hidden behind his visor. At last, Philomela

332

turned and said, "And Laudine, this is . . . but you've already met the Knight of the Lion, haven't you?"

Laudine rushed forward and gripped Ywain's gauntleted hand. "Indeed, I thank you again, Sir Knight, this time for defending my friend. Please, will you come inside—oh, goodness, I'm all a-flutter today, aren't I? Receiving you out here in the courtyard like a hoyden! Please, come in! You've been traveling and are in need of refreshment! Rufus!"

Laudine's ever-competent steward appeared at the main door to the castle keep, bowed slightly, and said, "My lady. I have taken the liberty of having refreshments sent to the green salon, if you would like to take your guests there. The hostlers will see to their horses."

"Thank you, Rufus," Laudine said. She turned back to the traveling party and said, "Er, and this lion?"

Ywain didn't answer. Even from the side, Luneta could sense the hungry force of his gaze on Laudine. At last Rhience said, "If you don't mind, I believe the lioness should come with us. She won't hurt anyone."

"Er . . . of course," Laudine replied uncertainly, and then they all dismounted and followed their hostess into the castle to the green salon. Ywain brought the canvas bag containing the smashed fragments of the Storm Stone.

Once they were in the salon, everyone sat but Ywain,

who walked up to Laudine and stood before her. "Sir Knight?" she said inquiringly.

Ywain dropped the sack before her, then spoke softly, using a raspy whisper. "It is yours, my lady."

"This sack?" Ywain nodded. Laudine untied the string and looked inside. "Gravel?"

"It is your Storm Stone," Ywain whispered hoarsely. For a long moment, Laudine only stared. Luneta watched as the realization of what this meant slowly began to dawn on her. "Then the curse is broken?" she asked.

"Broken or just circumvented," Rhience said, stepping between Luneta and Ywain. "And by the simplest and most obvious of all means, too. The Knight of the Lion smashed the stone a little bit ago."

"You did this for me?" Laudine asked Ywain.

He nodded. "I had heard how this stone imprisoned you. Now you are free."

"So I can leave the castle whenever I wish?" Laudine said.

Ywain nodded again. "And marry whomever you wish." Laudine's face grew still, and she stared blankly at the floor. Ywain took an audible breath, then said heavily, "You see, I know that you once felt you had to marry someone who would defend the stone. Now you can marry whenever and whomever you want—or not marry at all."

Laudine's eyes stayed on the floor. She nodded once, slowly. "I think . . . I think that I shall never marry," she said at last.

Luneta looked at Laudine's bleak and rigid face, then at Ywain's stiff, armored figure. They loved each other. Nothing could be more obvious, except that they were going to let their chance slip.

"I can hardly repay you, O Knight," Laudine said, forcing herself to smile, with fairly ghastly results. "But may I give you any token of my gratitude?"

Ywain shook his head in solemn silence. Luneta looked between them once more, then took a breath and whispered to Rhience, "Sorry. I wasn't going to interfere, because I know I always make things worse, but things can't be worse than this." She stepped forward and spoke clearly. "Actually, there is one thing you might be able to do for the Knight of the Lion. I mean, Lioness."

Ywain shook his helm at her vehemently, but Laudine looked up. "Whatever is in my power, I shall be glad to do. A horse? Gold?"

"Only your influence as a woman," Luneta said. "I must explain to you that the Knight of the Lion is in love with a beautiful lady, but he has been separated from her." Laudine looked sympathetic and started to speak, but Luneta pressed on. "The break between him and the lady is his own fault, as he'll be the first to admit. He betrayed her trust. He did it out of foolishness, not from ill intent, but it makes no difference. Now he is too ashamed even to ask for her forgiveness."

Laudine looked seriously at Ywain. "But how can your lady forgive you if you do not ask?"

Ywain hesitated, and Luneta said, "Would you, as a woman, help him? Will you take his cause and plead for him?"

Laudine nodded decisively. "I will. I promise you this, O Knight, that if it is in my power to procure your forgiveness, I will do so. Who is the lady?"

Slowly, Ywain sank to his knees before Laudine. Then he reached up and, with trembling fingers, removed his helm. "Her name is Lady Laudine," Ywain said. "Can you forgive me?"

Laudine's eyes grew round and bright. "I have been waiting to do so for an eternity."

After that, everything was kissing and murmuring apologies and tender nothings to each other. It was appalling stuff, for the most part, and Luneta had to turn away and concentrate hard so as not to hear any of it with her inner ear. As soon as they could break in, she and the others made their excuses and left the lovers alone, even taking Lass with them. Out in the hallway, Luneta sighed with relief. "Whew!" she said. "I can see it's going to be excessively dull around here for a while."

"Oh?" Luneta's mother asked. "Do you find love so uninteresting?"

"Don't you?" Luneta said.

Luneta's father took Luneta's arm. "You put your mother in an awkward position," he said. "Even supposing that she agrees with you, she can hardly say so in front of me. It would hurt my feelings."

"Oh, you know I don't mean that," Luneta protested. "I meant all that snuggling and kissing that *young* lovers do."

Her father's lips quivered, but he managed to control his countenance as he replied, "I see. Whereas the sort of love that decrepit specimens like your mother and I might have is less disgusting to you." Luneta started to answer indignantly, but he waved away her protests and led them out of the hall and into another room. "It doesn't matter, really, my dear. Because I agree with you—we should leave Ywain and Laudine as soon as we are able. But I was wondering, where would you like to go?"

Luneta hesitated. Knowing what she wanted and saying it aloud were two different matters.

"Because," her father continued, "I thought I might invite your friend Rhience to come back to Orkney with us to see the estate, and it would be nice if you'd come along to help us entertain him."

A warm feeling filled Luneta's breast, but the

pleasant sense came abruptly to an end when Rhience said, "Very kind of you, Sir Gaheris, but I'm not sure that I can accept."

"Oh?" Luneta's father asked, surprised. "You've other plans?"

Rhience nodded. He looked apologetically at Luneta and said, "You see, I've a secret that I haven't told anyone in all the past months when I've been cavorting about in my fool's clothing."

"Something terrible, I imagine," Luneta's mother said placidly, sitting in an armchair.

"Indeed, I almost think it is, Lady Lynet," Rhience said. "At least in light of some recently expressed opinions. You see, my lady, I—like my friend Ywain—am in love."

Luneta's heart shrank and withered, and for a moment she felt dizzy. "Really?" she asked brightly. "But you never said anything about this lady at all."

"Fancy that," Luneta's mother murmured.

"No, I didn't," Rhience said. "I thought it might cause some awkwardness as we rode."

"Of course," Luneta said. "It would have been cruel to speak of love in front of Ywain."

"Just so," Rhience said soberly.

Feeling the need to keep talking so that her own despair wouldn't show, Luneta said, "And who is this lucky lady? Does she know of your love?"

"I don't think so," Rhience replied.

"Well, does she love you?"

"I've never seen any sign of it."

A faint hope rose in Luneta's breast: maybe this un-known lady, whom she already hated, would turn Rhience down. But she forced herself to continue speaking calmly. "Well, haven't you learned anything from Ywain? If you love this woman, you should tell her so."

"Ah, but that's where my problem comes in. Terrible shy around ladies, I am. So I was wondering . . . ," he trailed off hesitantly.

"Yes?" Luneta asked.

"I thought maybe I could get you to put in a good word for me. You see, you did such a good job just now getting Ywain and Laudine together—in fact, you've done it twice."

"I thought you disapproved of my interfering in other people's lives," Luneta said quickly.

"But I love this lady so much," Rhience said. "I don't know what I'd do if she turned me down. No, I won't think of it. The idea's too horrible."

Luneta swallowed. This was Rhience, and if she could do something to make him happy, then she would. "All right," she said in a small voice. She looked at the floor between them, and with an effort said, "I'll do whatever I can for you."

Then, to her surprise, Rhience took her hand. Startled, she looked up. Rhience's eyes were glowing as he looked into hers. "Do you promise?" he said softly.

The world began to whirl, and Luneta nodded, suddenly understanding but unable to speak for joy. The silence was broken by her father. "Lynet, my love, I believe it's time we went to the other room."

"Don't be ridiculous, Gary. It's just now getting interesting."

"All the same, I think we are in the way here and should go away," Luneta's father said firmly.

Her mother sighed. "But I wanted to see my hoity-toity daughter snuggling and kissing and all that boring stuff," she complained as she rose to her feet. "Oh, well—I'm sure I'll have other opportunities."

Then Rhience kissed Luneta, who found it not at all dull. When they parted, she looked up into Rhience's face. "I love you," she whispered.

"Excuse me," came the voice of Luneta's father from the door. "We're just leaving, I promise, but I was wondering, would you like me to take the lioness out with me?"

"Which one?" Rhience said, his eyes still on Luneta but his lips curving into a gentle smile.

"The four-legged one, of course," Luneta's father replied. "The other one's far too dangerous."

Author's Note

The great writers of the ancient world didn't go in for love stories much. The epics of Homer and Virgil are really just elaborate adventure stories for boys, and their female characters are like the women in modern action movies, mostly disposable. This literary attitude didn't start to change until around the eleventh century, when the minstrels of southern France began to compose stories in which women had a more important role. These singers still told of brave warriors duking it out, just as Homer did, but these new heroes—now, knights in armor—were fighting for their adored ladies, and the stories ended not just with victory, but with requited love.

I don't mean to say that these love stories were exactly like the ones that we're familiar with today,

341

though. For one thing, the lovers hardly ever got married. In fact, usually the lady was already married to someone else. But to the French minstrels, this wasn't a problem. You see, in the eleventh century, marriage didn't have anything to do with love anyway. Marriage was an economic agreement between families, usually arranged by people who didn't have to live with either of the principal characters. People got married in order to form alliances between families and to have offspring. Love? That would just complicate things. This is why the great love affairs of Arthurian literature are between Lancelot and Guinevere and Tristram and Iseult, not one of whom was married to his or her beloved.

The greatest writer from this tradition—although he was rather more than just a minstrel—was the court poet Chrétien de Troyes, and in several of his works he celebrates the typical extramarital love affairs of his time. In his greatest poem, though, he does something surprising and new. In this marvelous poem, called *The Knight of the Lion*, Chrétien brings together two people whose love actually leads to marriage. The tale of Ywain and Laudine's complex love affair, including mistakes and misunderstandings and finally forgiveness and reconciliation, is centuries ahead of its time.

In my own retelling of this tale, I've used as much of Chrétien's original as I could. Of course, by telling the story through the experience of Luneta, I've changed some of the focus, but I didn't invent my heroine: Chrétien also tells of a smart, willful lady working behind the scenes to bring Ywain and Laudine together—twice. I did add the character of Rhience the Fool and change Ywain's lion to a lioness, but most of what is left came in some form from the wonderful original story.

You ought to read it someday.

—Gerald Morris

DISCOVER THE TALES OF KING ARTHUR AND THE KNIGHTS OF THE ROUND TABLE!